Sometimes it's not about winning…

One bad tackle. That's all it took to put wide receiver Jake Russell in a cast for the rest of the NFL season. From being a high school all-star to getting drafted by the Austin Mustangs, football has been Jake's life for as long as he can remember. It's what defines him—because he has a secret he never shares. But now that he's laid up in bed with a nurse displaying a lot of distracting bedside manners, he's discovering life on the sidelines might have its perks…

One last paycheck. That's all Erin Bass has left to her name when the resort she works at shuts down. Desperate, she agrees to be a caregiver to hardass jock Jake Russell, who also happens to be a memorable one-night stand. Before long, caring leads to daring new ways to catch up in bed, especially with Jake still in a cast. But with football on the sidelines, this time the game is serious…

Books by Desiree Holt

Finding Julia

Game On Series
Forward Pass
Line of Scrimmage

Published by Kensington Publishing Corporation

Line of Scrimmage

A Game on Romance

Desiree Holt

LYRICAL PRESS
Kensington Publishing Corp.
www.kensingtonbooks.com

Lyrical Press books are published by
Kensington Publishing Corp. 119 West 40th Street New York, NY 10018

All Kensington titles, imprints, and distributed lines are available at special quantity discounts for bulk purchases for sales promotion, premiums, fund-raising, and educational or institutional use.

Special book excerpts or customized printings can also be created to fit specific needs. For details, write or phone the office of the Kensington Special Sales Manager:
Kensington Publishing Corp.
119 West 40th Street
New York, NY 10018
Attn. Special Sales Department. Phone: 1-800-221-2647.

Kensington and the K logo Reg. U.S. Pat. & TM Off.
Lyrical Press and the L logo are trademarks of Kensington Publishing Corp.

First Electronic Edition: December 2015
eISBN-13: 978-1-61650-731-2
eISBN-10: 1-61650-731-4

First Print Edition: December 2015
ISBN-13: 978-1-61650-732-9
ISBN-10: 1-61650-732-2

Printed in the United States of America

As always, to my late beloved David who thought I could do it all.

Acknowledgements

First of all, I have to acknowledge Frank and Lynn Barrett who wrote How to Watch a Football Game and made a football junkie out of me. Then there is the staff of the Michigan Daily who many years ago accepted me on the sports staff and started my crazy addictions. Of course to my family, who supports me one hundred percent and helps with all the stuff I don't have time to do when I'm writing. A little extra to my son Steven who lets me talk football with him endlessly. Thank you, everyone.

Author's Foreword

People ask me all the time why I write and I tell them it's because I'm a storyteller. I always have at least ten stories whirling in my brain trying to get out. But I also write for my readers, who make the writing worthwhile. Your emails and Facebook posts make me smile every day and inspire me. My family has asked me for ages why I didn't write stories about football, since I am such an obsessed nut Every football weekend I am glued to the television and woe to the person who dares to interrupt me. So at their urging I decided it was time to put my passion to work and created a series of stories whose heroes are former or current football players. And because I live in Texas, where football trumps every other religion, where Friday Night Lights is more than a television program, I stated with the heroes of a small Texas town football team, fast forward fifteen years. Writing this book has been such enjoyment for me. I hope I convey my passion to all of you who read my books and have become part of my extended family. This is for you.

Chapter 1

Erin Bass came awake slowly, tried to shift her position in the bed, and discovered an arm banding around her waist. A *male* arm. A very muscular male arm, with soft hair tickling the underside of her breasts, held her against a very masculine body that she was startled to realize was sporting a very firm morning woody. She closed her eyes, counted to ten, and opened them again, hoping it had all been a bad dream. That the party last night, and everything afterward, would just disappear.

"I know you're awake." His raspy, rough voice sent shivers rippling through her.

He knew she was awake? But she'd been so very still, not daring to breathe or make a sound.

"Erin?"

The deep voice was tinged with humor and all too familiar. Apparently she was in bed with Jake Russell. Football hero. Ladies' man. The gridiron hero the people fawned over. And her friend Ivy's brother. It also seemed she'd gone there very willingly and participated in the night's activities with great enthusiasm, if the pleasant aches in her body were any indication.

Oh, wait. Pleasant was too weak a word for it.

She certainly had no trouble remembering the touch of his hands or the slick feel of his tongue on her clit. The warmth of his lips as they pulled on her nipples, the leanness of his fingers as they stroked her to completion. Or thick feel of his cock inside her as he pushed her to one orgasm after another.

When had she last had sex like that? Ever? The chemistry between them was off the charts, hotter than anything she'd ever experienced. On the one hand, she wanted to lock the doors and shut out the world until they managed to wear themselves out, if that was even possible. Jake seemed to have a remarkably short recovery time.

On the other, she wanted to pull the covers over her head and pretend the whole thing hadn't happened. She had broken her own hard and fast rule. If she stepped outside the lines to have a one-night stand, she'd have been better off hooking up with a stranger—with *anyone*—other than sexy, full-of-himself Jake Russell. At least then it wouldn't matter so much when the guy gave her the expected good-bye speech.

How in God's name had she managed this, anyway? She liked to think she was a lot smarter than that. Really had her shit together.

Oh, yeah. The damn party. The one she hadn't wanted to go to. The one Ivy had insisted on dragging her to. With her brother Jake.

Her friend's words played over again in her head.

"It's a reunion party with a lot of Jake's teammates from the Granite Falls Coyotes. The big state championship team. It's the first time they've all been together in ages." She'd winked. "And I can finally introduce you to Jake."

Erin remembered protesting. "Ivy, listen. I don't really want to go to a party with football jocks." And she hadn't wanted to. Bad memories cropped up when she heard the words football player. "And I don't want to get involved with Jake. It can only end badly and affect our friendship."

"Oh, come on," Ivy had urged. "You're making too much of it. It's a last night out for those in the NFL. Training camp starts Monday, then preseason, then the regular season. Besides, it will take your mind off your problem for a while."

Her *problem*. Unemployment. She had a good excuse for one lapse in judgment. Her life was about to implode. If she didn't resolve something soon, she'd have to go home to Dallas with her tail between her legs—something no woman at the age of thirty wanted to do—and she'd wanted to get away from the disaster for just a few hours.

So she'd let Ivy bully her into going to the party, where she'd felt as if she were swimming in a pool overloaded with testosterone.

They weren't there for five minutes before Ivy dragged Jake over to say hello and *bam*! In that instant a lightning bolt struck, her body went liquid, and her hormones began an unending happy dance. Try as she might she hadn't been able to shut them down. The man had glued himself to her side, and every touch, every glance only stoked the flames between them higher. She'd been tipsy on white wine and an overload of sexual anticipation, blotting out the uncertainty of her future.

She'd forgotten all about the dangers of football jocks. Forgotten all about reminding herself football players were on her forbidden list and that included players from the Mustangs, the darlings of Austin.

And she'd stupidly let Jake take her home and—

So much for all her firm resolutions.

They'd barely been inside her apartment before they were tearing each other's clothes off. He was so hot and sexy, consuming her with his presence, igniting a wildness in her she hadn't even known she possessed. For one very brief moment, sanity had tried to intrude and she'd considered stopping the action. Then she'd thought, *What the hell?* Her life was rapidly being flushed down the drain, so didn't she deserve just one little treat?

Now here she was. Still in bed. *Her* bed. With Jake Russell.

Great. Just great.

"Erin?" His mouth was close to her ear, his breath like a soft breeze against her skin.

Maybe if she didn't answer him he'd go back to sleep and she could sneak out of the apartment and leave. Oh, wait. They were at her place. *He* had to be the one to head out the door. She had to get him out of here now, right this minute, and pretend it had never, ever happened.

She looked around through barely opened eyes. Sunlight slanted into the room through partially closed blinds, spotlighting clothes dropped to the floor in haste. The comforter might be covering her but it looked as if it had been quickly yanked into position. The air around her was scented with a combination of sex and a spicy male cologne.

She'd been so sure last night could be one and done, that she could have wild monkey sex with Jake Russell and easily walk away from it. But pulling herself away from that hot male body was easier said than done. Just being next to him, skin to skin, ignited a need she hadn't even known she possessed.

She gave herself a mental smack on the forehead.

Well, Erin, you've gone and done it again. You'd better get yourself out of this right this minute.

"I can almost hear your brain going a million miles an hour." He paused a minute. "You okay?"

Okay? Okay? She was naked in bed with Jake Freakin' Russell. No, she wasn't okay. How in the hell had she let this happen? He was off limits. Forbidden. Verboten. And any other language she could think of. He was Ivy's brother, for the love of God. And known by reputation to be so allergic to relationships he broke out in a rash if anyone even said the word out loud.

Been there, done that, had a closet filled with the T-shirts.

"I'm fine." Did she just growl that? "Why wouldn't I be?"

"Fine indeed." He smoothed her hair back from her face. "You were damn fine last night. Better than fine."

She didn't know quite what to say to that so she just ignored it. She lay there, still as a statue cocooned in his arms while she tried to figure out how to ease herself out of bed. Or at least how to respond to that comment, but then Jake took that out of her hands.

"Listen, last night was unexpected, but—"

She tensed. Here it came. Of course. "But what?"

He kissed her bare shoulder. "But it turned out just great, didn't it?"

"Great. Yeah. Okay." No, no, no. Great but dangerous.

"Unexpected," he repeated. "And actually maybe better than great." More shoulder kisses. "So, I'm thinking," he went on, "I mean we should probably talk about it."

Erin's stomach knotted. Talk about it. Right. What was there to say? Was he afraid she'd attach herself to him like a barnacle? Did he think she wanted some kind of commitment from him after one night? She should have known. This whole damn thing was her fault for letting him take her home, kiss her, invite himself inside.

Where they'd done a hell of a lot more than kissing.

Now it was time to pay the piper. He wanted to talk? Fine. But she'd be the one doing the talking. No one gave Erin Bass *The Speech*. At least not anymore. She'd just take the lead on it here and surprise Mr. Macho.

It was hard to gather her thoughts, however, when one warm hand cupped her breast, his thumb and forefinger tweaking her nipple. His lips trailed soft kisses along her shoulder and his warm breath caressed her ear. Just like that, her body woke up and said, *Give me more.* Her pulse set up a steady tattoo in all her erogenous zones.

No, no, no.

"I don't do anything without coffee," she told him, trying to ease herself away from him. But before she slipped out from beneath the covers, she remembered she'd have to make the coffee because they were in her place and no way was she getting out of this bed while Jake Russell could get another eyeful of her exposed body.

What do you think he did last night, idiot? Kept his eyes closed?

"On second thought, maybe I'll skip the coffee." She inched herself upward, clutching the sheet as high as she could. "If you could maybe put on some clothes, though, I won't look while you do it."

He chuckled, a sound so unexpectedly sexy she had to squeeze her legs together against the throbbing his voice ignited.

Stop! Stop it now! This is a huge mistake, Erin! Fix it!

"How about if I just get dressed," he offered. "And run out for some coffee with maybe a pastry or two." He started to toss the covers back.

"No. Don't move." She squeezed her eyes shut and slapped her hands over her face.

Jake laughed again. "Make up your mind." Then she felt the bed shift as he stood up. "It's okay," he told her a minute later. "All the important parts are covered, although last night you couldn't seem to get enough of seeing them." He paused. "Or touching them."

She opened one eye partway and discovered he had told the truth. Not that this was much better. He'd pulled on his boxer briefs, but they did little to disguise the outline of his thick and obviously swollen cock. His streaky blond mane was sexily rumpled, and the darker hair on his chest called attention to broad shoulders and hard muscle, reminding her of nothing less than a proud lion. His arms and legs looked just as powerful, just as hard, just as defined. Of course they should be. Wasn't he the Mustangs' number one running back?

Some said he was getting close to the end of his career, but looking at him now, Erin would have to argue with them. He was still in excellent shape, with flat abs, sculpted muscles, and long powerful legs. It took a lot of restraint to keep from drooling.

"Think you've looked long enough?' There was a hint of laughter in his voice and mischief danced in the chocolate brown of his eyes.

Unfortunately, none of it distracted her from the sight of his morning woody. She felt her face flame when she saw him studying her carefully, a big shit-eating grin on his face.

"I didn't—I'm sorry, I—Oh, hell. Turn around so I can put something on," she ordered. "Be a gentleman for once."

"For once?" His eyebrows lifted. "I think I'm insulted. I always try to behave like a gentleman."

"Fine. Then close your eyes, or turn around, or both."

When he turned his back on her, she scrambled off the bed and reached for the nearest piece of clothing, which just happened to be the shirt Jake wore the night before. Well, too bad. No way was she having this conversation while she was in her current state of undress. It was hard to be indignant when you were stark naked.

Even though the shirt covered her almost to her knees, she still hopped back in bed to pull the bedclothes up to her waist. No skin, she told herself. Running her fingers through the tangled mass of her hair that always refused to behave, she pushed it back and tucked it behind her ears. She dearly wanted to wash her face, brush her teeth, and make herself presentable, but she didn't want to take the time. It was important to get out in front of this and have it over with quickly. She was determined that she'd have the upper hand here, so she folded her hands on her lap and wet her lips.

"Can I look yet?" His voice still had its morning huskiness.

"Yes. I'm ready," she told him in a prim voice, smoothing out the covers.

He grinned when he saw her. "You look like you're about to give a lecture to a misbehaving class."

"Not at all. You said we had to talk and I agree. Absolutely. Talking is important." She frowned. "But could you, um, put the rest of your clothes on?"

"Since you're wearing my shirt, that's impossible at the moment, but I'll do the best I can." He yanked on his pants and zipped them up, shoved his feet in his shoes, and stuck his socks in his pockets. "This work for you?"

"Fine, fine, fine. Sit down. Please." She waved a hand in the air. "No, not there," she snapped when he moved to sit on the bed, and pointed to the small chair next to her dresser. "Over there."

She nearly laughed watching him try to fit his large frame into the small slipper chair, but she was determined to be serious. He finally squeezed his very fine butt in, rested his elbows on his knees, and turned his chocolate velvet eyes on her.

"So, Erin—" he began.

"Wait." No, no, no. She was taking the lead in this. She cleared her throat and let out a slow breath.

"You said we needed to talk," she pointed out, "and I completely agree." Yes, she'd definitely get the upper hand here.

He cocked an eyebrow, as if surprised she agreed with him. "You do?"

"Yes. I know exactly what's on your mind, and I am in complete agreement. This whole thing—last night—was a big mistake. For both of us."

Jake's eyebrows rose so high they almost hit his hairline. "What?"

"We both got a little carried away," she went on. "The party was fun, but I—we—probably had a little too much to drink." And wasn't that an understatement. "We had a good time, but honestly, Jake, we can't do this again."

He sat there with his mouth hanging open, a stunned look on his face.

"Well, really, that was what you planned to say, right? When we had our 'talk'?" She formed air quotes around the word talk. "And you'd be absolutely right. We needed to get it out there. 'Last night was great but we need to put it out of our minds.' Did I get that right?"

He studied her for a long moment. "What if that wasn't what I was going to say at all?"

Erin pinched her eyebrows together. "What? You weren't?" A funny little wiggle shimmied through her system. Then she forced a smile. "Come on. We both know this wouldn't work. I just wanted to save you the pain of giving me the 'It was nice but this can't go anywhere' speech."

He shook his head. "As a matter of fact, no. That wasn't what I planned at all."

"Oh, come on." She picked at the fabric of the sheet. "You have plenty of other fish to fry. You'll never notice the loss, right? Besides, your sister is my friend and how would that work, exactly?"

"It might work just fine," he disagreed. The dumbfounded look on his face was replaced now by one of growing irritation. "I don't get in Ivy's business, and she doesn't get in mine."

"Besides," she went on as if he hadn't said a word, "football season starts in a week, you have a packed schedule and I'm sure a cheerleader at every stadium. I wouldn't want you to feel obligated or anything. I mean, just because I'm friends with Ivy."

"So which is it?" he demanded. "We can't see each other because you're my sister's friend or you think I'd string you along *because* you're her friend? Make up your mind."

"I have made it up." She used her best lady-like tone.

He pushed himself out of the small chair. "As a matter of fact, I was going to suggest we take this slow but see where it goes. Hooking up turned out great for both of us, so maybe there's something there to explore. And yes, I have a busy fall. It's all football from August to February. Yes, I have other obligations, but I can work around those, that is if you were reasonable about them—"

"Reasonable?" she broke in. "Did you just say reasonable?"

He raked his fingers through his hair. "Okay, bad choice of words. But damn, Erin, last night was great. I thought we could—"

Could what? she wanted to ask. Roll in the hay for a few weeks when he could find time and then he'd leave her holding the bag? Not gonna happen. Maybe under different circumstances, but her life was falling apart. She couldn't risk heartbreak along with everything else.

"You know it wouldn't last. At least this way we can part friends." She forced a smile. "Right?"

"Friends?" Each word sounded as if he'd bitten it off. "Friends don't act this way with each other."

"What way?" She frowned. "I'm not an idiot here. I know all about hotshot football players and their so-called social lives."

"And apparently don't have a very high opinion of us. Where did you get it, from the gossip rags?"

No. From her brothers. Worse than that, from past experience. "Come on. I'm giving you a free pass here. Anyway, I have a lot going on in my life right now, too much to be a notch on someone's bedpost, so let's just say it was great and let it go at that."

"You know nothing about me. Nothing at all." He gave her a penetrating look. "I'm not who you think I am, but I guess you're not interested in finding out."

"I don't need to," she insisted. "Besides, what are you so mad about? I should think you'd be happy I said this for you. Isn't that what guys like you want?"

"Guys like me?" Every muscle in his face tightened. "What, do we come with a stamp on our foreheads that says 'macho asshole'?"

"No." She blew out a breath. "But I wish you would. It would make it easier on all of us."

"Listen, Erin," he began.

She held up a hand. "Just say thank you, take your stuff, and go. There. I've made it easy for you."

He stared at her, unbelieving, and something flared in his eyes. For a moment, she thought it was hurt, but that couldn't be right. Then the anger flashed again.

"You want to toss me out on my ass? Fine. I can take a hint. But don't expect me to be all warm and fuzzy the next time I see you with my sister. In fact, don't expect me to acknowledge you at all."

He looked around the room, then back at Erin, as if just remembering she was wearing his shirt.

"You can keep the damn shirt." He raked his fingers through his gorgeously mussed hair. "Keep it as a souvenir. Besides, it's probably the only thing that will get close to you with your attitude."

"*My* attitude?" She stared at him. "There's nothing wrong with my attitude. You're just mad because I got to the point before you did."

Golden flecks like tiny flames sparked in his eyes and a muscle twitched in his jaw. Why was he so upset? She'd given him his easy out. He should be grateful to her. It couldn't be possible she'd hurt his feelings.

"You know," he said, his words slow and measured. "Ivy's talked about you so much I thought now *there's* a woman I could get to know. Spend some time with. She'd probably be cool with my schedule during the season. Last night it felt like fate had played right into our hands. I just didn't realize you had such a stick up your ass." He shook his head.

"A stick up my ass?" She rose to her knees, outraged. "Isn't that the pot calling the kettle black?"

"Not the same thing." He gave her a long, hard look. "We could have had something good going here, Erin. I guess now we'll never know."

Then he was gone. Out of her bedroom, out of her house, out of her life.

Good riddance.

But when she lay back down in bed, trying to cool her mad down, she couldn't help rubbing the soft fabric of his shirt against her or inhaling the clean male scent that clung to it. Wondering if, like everything else lately, she'd made a huge mistake.

Chapter 2

Jake stood on the sidelines, taking in the sight of all the pregame activity. The first game of the regular season always got his blood really pumping, and he couldn't wait to get out there. All the players had completed their warm-ups, people on the sidelines with special passes were laughing and high fiving as they waited for kickoff, and music blared over the loudspeaker. Cheerleaders from both teams were doing their thing with loud cheers and high kicks. As the Mustangs squad finished their current cheer, the blonde at the end of the line glanced at him and winked.

Great. Hadn't he made it plain enough over the years, as politely as possible, that he wasn't interested in that kind of connection?

He knew several of his teammates were into hooking up with the cheerleaders, but that wasn't his thing. For one thing, he didn't believe in mixing pleasure with his business. From what he'd seen over the years, it usually ended badly. For another, he had always been pretty selective in his dating. There was too much in his past that he had no intention of sharing with anyone. Except... For a brief moment, the image of Erin, naked, flashed into his head, bringing with it a fierce hunger combined, as always, with a surge of hurt and anger. He'd found himself so strongly attracted to her at that party, the chemistry so intense, that he just couldn't help himself. The night they'd spent together was still imprinted on his brain, every erotic moment of it.

Anger and irritation bubbled up inside him every time that night flashed back across his mental video screen. The way she'd tossed him out made him grind his teeth in frustration because he had no idea why. He'd sure been mistaken about her if the connection they'd made was only one-sided and meant so little to her. *No, it wasn't,* the voice in his head always told him. He wanted to hunt her down, knock on her door, and make her spell it out for him, except then he'd probably have stalker written all over his forehead. And it wasn't his style.

Deep down, when the memories slammed into him, he was still convinced they had the start of something good. Obviously she didn't think so. Okay. The hell with her. He could take a hint, especially one that obvious. Good thing he hadn't decided to share his deepest, most intimate secrets with her.

Thank God training camp had started the following Monday and then they were into a full routine. He was more than ready to throw himself into this season and make it his entire focal point. Football defined him. Gave him respect and acknowledgment. Who would he be without that? No damn woman was going to mess that up.

"All set, Jake?"

He turned to see the running backs coach had come up beside him.

"You bet. The Austin Mustangs are gonna take it all this year."

"Good, good." He looked at Jake. "We all think this is going to be your best year, Russell. The biggest yet."

"Hope so. I guess I don't have too many left in me."

And wasn't that just the pits. Aging out of a game that was brutal in its physical demands was not an easy thing to do. What would he do when that happened?

"Let's get through this one before we worry about the next." The coach tapped his arm. "I know you'll do it for us out there today, facing our longtime rivals."

"You can count on me," he assured the man.

The announcer caught his attention, introducing the color guard. Four abreast in full military uniform, they marched to the center of the field and came to a precise measured stop. Next came the local celebrity vocalist and the singing of the "Star Spangled Banner." Jake never failed to be impressed and moved by the thrill of the moment with every fan standing tall, every player and coach doing the same on the sidelines. The song ended and sixty thousand fans roared in expectation as the referees handled the coin toss.

Jake fastened his helmet and jogged out onto the field with his teammates. All around him fans chanted, "Jake! Jake! Jake!" He knew they all wanted their so-called golden boy with the magic legs to pull off another long running play.

Austin had the ball first. The teams took their places at the line of scrimmage, the center snapped the ball, and the game was on. Jake was hyped and in the zone. On the third play from scrimmage the quarterback handed off to him, the offensive line opened a hole, and the crowd got the long touchdown run it was screaming for. He scored and everyone went wild.

One minute before half time, with the score tied at twenty-one, the quarterback took the snap from center, dropped back, and handed off to Jake again. The crowd was on its feet, yelling and screaming, as he avoided tackles and let the fullbacks and tight ends block for him.

"Jake! Jake! Jake!" The chant filled the air.

He was nearly past the entire defense, digging for those extra few yards to a clear stretch of field in front of him, when one of the defensive backs came flying at him and tackled him. Hard. And he was flat on his back, his leg twisted sideways and pinned beneath him, the enormous tackle still on top of him. The crack was so loud he was sure everyone in the stadium heard it.

For a moment, he was numb, the way he often was when he was tackled, before the sensation of bruising hit. He had no sensation anywhere in his body, as if every nerve from his neck on down had been severed. He didn't even feel his chest move as he tried to draw a breath.

I'm fine. Fine, fine, fine. Just had the breath knocked out of me. In a minute I'll get up, and we'll line up for the next play. I just hope I didn't miss the fucking ball.

Then, in the next second, the numbness fled and that was when it all turned to shit. The most excruciating pain he'd ever experienced slammed through him. He felt as if someone had shoved a hot poker into his leg, the burn racing like wildfire through his body. The nerves that a moment ago might have been frozen now flared hot, like a million fire ants crawling all over him.

And Jake was suddenly aware that the entire stadium had fallen silent.

He sensed someone beside him and forced his eyes open to see the left guard who had tackled him. The man had concern and fear etched into his face, an expression that sent fear ratcheting through Jake. He tried to get up and was swamped with such intense nausea he nearly vomited all over himself.

"Don't move, Jake," the guy said.

But I have to get up.

Panic gripped him like an icy claw.

Get up, get up, get up. Don't be a pussy.

He struggled to rise, to push himself up from the ground, but pain screamed in every cell and he nearly passed out. Why was someone telling him not to move? Of course he had to move. He had to get up for the next play. But he couldn't make his body obey.

He tried to move again, but now the quarterback had come to crouch down beside him and he put his hand on Jake's shoulder.

"Don't move, buddy. They're on their way out to you."

With the fresh wave of pain, Jake knew he couldn't move if his life depended on it. He knew it was bad. Really bad. He was afraid to look or ask. The first thing he thought of, even in his pain, was Joe Theismann. A severely broken leg had ended Joe's career when he was at his peak and he never played again. The thought made Jake even sicker. Without football, who was he?

Football is who I am. Without it I'm just nobody. Worthless. Even less than that. It was a lesson he'd learned in his childhood and he'd never forgotten it.

Then Coach Raymond was kneeling beside him, the trainer was there, the team doctor, and Jake didn't know who else. All he knew was now the pain was so bad he thought he might pass out from it. He saw one of the assistants speaking into a radio.

"We'll get you fixed right up, Jake," Coach Raymond said in a calm voice. "We'll take real good care of you."

An ambulance rolled out of the tunnel, and two paramedics nudged everyone else aside. "It's gonna hurt when we move you," one of them told him, "so we'll give you something for the pain. Okay?"

Okay? Yes. Please, God. And do it now.

He felt the stick of the needle in his arm, but the medication had barely begun to hit his system before they were doing something with his leg. He clenched his jaw so tightly he thought he might break it, as fierce agony scorched every nerve ending.

"It's okay, Jake," Coach Raymond said. "They've got it in an inflated cast so they can move you. In a second, they'll be putting you into the ambulance. Dr. Moline will meet you at the hospital."

Jake could only nod. He hurt so badly he had lost the ability to speak.

He felt the bumping of the wheels on the concrete of the tunnel as the ambulance rolled out of the stadium. Every jolt sent a fresh wave of pain through him. Then, finally, the pain became too much, and he blissfully, thankfully, passed out.

* * * *

"H-How is he?" Ivy's voice was barely a whisper. She was sure her heart stopped when she saw Jake lying on the field, the rush of people to assist him, and the ambulance roll out.

"He's awake," the Mustang's General Manager, Jim DiMarco, told her, "which is always a good sign, although he's in a lot of pain. The damage is to his leg and we don't know yet how bad it is."

"Is-is it a Joe Theismann injury?" she asked in a hesitant voice. Every football fan knew the disaster Theismann's broken leg was. If that happened to Jake it would completely destroy him.

"We don't know yet. Come on with me." He waved her into the elevator, killed the Stop button, and pushed the one marked Lobby. "I've got a ride waiting. Give me your keys and I'll have someone bring your car to the hospital."

Ivy felt sick to her stomach. Football was Jake's life. Since the two of them had moved to Granite Falls with their mom to get a fresh start, it was the only thing that had mattered to him. The thing he used to validate himself. No one knew their dreadful family history or how her brother had set himself up as the protector of her and their mother. No matter how many times she told him what an incredible person he was, how he'd been her rock and protector from the time she was a little girl, he never believed her. Nothing mattered to him except football. It gave him the first sense of self-worth he'd ever known, and he clung to it like a life preserver.

What would happen to him if he lost all that?

She hadn't been much for praying for a very long time. As a child, it hadn't helped, and she'd long ago gotten out of the habit. But now, as they rode silently through the streets of Austin, she prayed hard, afraid to even think about the worst-case scenario.

She was so lost in thought she didn't realize they'd reached the hospital until the car came to a stop. DiMarco was speaking softly on his cell phone but he disconnected when she climbed out.

"I'll take you right up to where he is," he told her. "They've already x-rayed him, and the orthopedic surgeon will meet us in emergency."

Ivy wasn't sure if she was impressed by the number of Mustangs people at the hospital or worried about what it might mean. Jake was a valuable commodity to them, so of course they'd pull out all the stops. That's all it was, right?

Two men in Mustangs polo shirts and khakis stood outside one of the rooms in Emergency. Ivy tried not to read anything into their solemn expressions, but the fear she'd been swallowing back surged through her again.

Jake lay on a hospital bed, his face nearly as white as the sheets draped over his lower body. One leg was exposed, wrapped in an inflatable cast.

His left arm extended out from his body, strapped to a board with an IV shunt in his vein. His eyes were closed and lines of pain etched his face.

"Miss Russell?" A tall, thin man in scrubs and a white jacket stepped toward her. "Dr. Moline. I'm the orthopedist called in for your brother."

"Hello." She shook his hand. "How is Jake?"

Moline's face gave nothing away as he answered her. "He's okay for now. I gave him something for the pain so he's not in a lot of discomfort."

She gripped her hands together so tightly she nearly shut off the blood supply. "How bad is it?"

"I won't lie to you. It's not good. We need to get him up to surgery right away."

"I don't know what on earth Jake will do if he can't play again," Ivy said. "Football is his life." Much more so than any of these people knew.

He had spent so much of his life taking care of her. Now she had to be strong for him. If he was done with football, he'd need someone to pick up the pieces and help him rebuild his life.

"Let's not buy trouble until we have to," DiMarco said.

"You don't understand." She twisted her hands together again. *No one* understood and she couldn't tell them. Jake would die if she told anyone their family history.

Time seemed to stretch endlessly. By nine o'clock that night, Jake was in his hospital room, and Ivy had spoken to the surgeon again. Nothing had changed. The news was still bad. Severe complicated break, exactly like the one Joe Theismann suffered, but each person healed differently, they held out great hope here, yada yada yada.

By the time she walked in the door of her condo she felt as if she'd been awake for a year. She couldn't erase from her mind the picture of Jake lying in the examining room. Right now, she wanted a good stiff drink to settle her nerves. She'd get what sleep she could because tomorrow he'd need her. When he was awake enough to understand what happened, he'd go off the rails.

* * * *

Jake tried to open his eyes, but it seemed someone had placed lead weights on his eyelids. It took herculean strength just to raise them an infinitesimal amount. When he did, nausea surged through him, and he was afraid he'd vomit all over himself. He tried to sit up but something seemed to be holding him down. Maybe some *things*. He didn't seem to be able to lift his left wrist too well, but worse than that, his right leg was immobilized.

He tried to draw a full breath and was smacked with the odor of antiseptic. From somewhere next to him he heard the steady *beep, beep, beep,* of some kind of machine.

What the fuck?

With superhuman effort he forced his eyes open a little more and looked around. He was in a hospital room, in a bed, his leg in a cast and hooked up to some contraption. Pain covered him like a second skin.

So it hadn't been a dream. The scene on the football field was real. Too fucking real. He knew all about the danger of injuries in football and the sometimes devastating results. But... Maybe this wasn't as bad as he thought. Maybe they were just being extra cautious with whatever they were doing so he could get back on his feet quicker.

Okay, hospital room. Nurses. Call button. He fumbled with his right hand and discovered the unit clipped to the bed. He pressed his thumb hard on the red button. In what seemed like minutes, but was probably only seconds, a nurse in baby blue scrubs appeared beside him.

"You're awake." She smiled at him. "Good."

"Not so good," he said thickly. "I have to—" He slapped his hand over his mouth.

"I've got it covered," the nurse said in a calm voice.

The next thing he knew she had propped his head with one hand and with the other held a small metal barf tray. He was glad she was that observant and that fast, because in the next minute he was heaving his guts. It was both embarrassing and debilitating. When his stomach was empty, the nurse helped him rinse his mouth before she gently wiped his face and eased his head back to the pillow.

Jake squinted at her, trying harder to focus.

"I'm Regina," she told him in her soothing voice. "I'll be one of your nurses." She gave him a tiny smile. "We had to flip to see who got to take care of Jake Russell."

"Not much left of Jake Russell at the moment," he said wearily. And how much was left he still had no idea.

"There's a gentleman waiting to see you," she told him. "Let me just take your vitals and I'll let him in."

"Wait." He held up his uninjured hand. He wasn't sure if he wanted to see anyone at this particular moment. "Who is it?"

"He said his name is Scott. He said he's a good friend."

Scott Manchin was more than just a friend. He was Jake's agent who had overseen his career from the day of the NFL draft. If he was here, things couldn't be too good. Scott had clients playing today all over the country; he wasn't scheduled for a Mustangs game and a sit-down with Jake for a couple of weeks yet.

"Can I tell him it's okay to come in?" Regina asked. "He's been waiting a long time."

"Yeah, sure." Whatever. Better to get the bad news over with. He tried to shift, and groaned as pain stabbed through him. "What's with my leg?"

"It was broken and you've had surgery. Dr. Moline wanted it in traction for the first few days. I know it hurts. Let me get you some pain medication."

Broken, broken, broken.

The word bounced around in his brain like a ping pong ball. Broken was not good. Broken meant no football. Broken meant there was nothing left of Jake Russell. Broken meant he was back to being that worthless kid. The adjective drummed into him over and over and over.

The nurse finished taking his vital signs and hurried from the room. Jake closed his eyes, and when he opened them again Scott was standing beside his bed, trying to look calm despite the lines of worry creasing his forehead.

"Hey, buddy," he said to Jake.

"You can skip the pleasantries," Jake growled. "Just go straight to the death sentence."

Scott gave what Jake thought was supposed to be a reassuring grin. "Nothing is ever as bad as it seems. You know that."

"I know that I got hurt and I'm fucked, so let me have it."

At that moment, Regina came back, wheeling in a small machine of some kind on a metal stand. With her other hand she held a syringe.

"Is that my happy juice?" Jake asked. "Because right now I'm not happy."

"This is a morphine pump. I'm going to show you how it works, how you can press this button for pain meds when you need them. But I'll give you a shot first so we can take the edge off right now. I'm sure you must be hurting like crazy."

Jake waited while the nurse took care of business. When she was gone, he turned back to Scott.

"Okay. You're on. What's the diagnosis?" Jake grimaced as he shifted in bed. "You didn't drop everything to fly into Austin because I got a little nick or bump. And give it to me straight. No sugar coating."

"Okay. You have a complicated multiple fracture in your leg. The docs pretty much had to put it back together again."

Fear rose up in Jake's throat. "That means I'm done for the season, right?"

"Maybe." But Scott said the word hesitantly.

"Worse than that?" Jake could hardly get the words out. "Is this a Joe Theismann break?"

"Let's not apply terminology. We'll let the doctors do that."

Fuck. The man was evading the issue. If possible, Jake felt even sicker. Football was his savior. The sport was what made him who he was. Made people look up to him and respect him. If he lost that, he lost everything.

"Don't lie to me."

Scott sighed. "They won't make any determination right now beyond getting you through recovery and rehab. If all goes well, you'll be back on the field next season."

"If all goes well?" Rage at his situation coursed through him. "I'm not sure I want to know what that means. But this season is over for me, right?"

"You'll be getting the best care," the agent guaranteed him. "We want to get you back on your feet as soon as we can."

"That's dodging the issue," Jake pointed out, his words beginning to slur from the medication.

Scott took his right hand and squeezed it.

"We'll worry about that issue later. Right now just concentrate on healing."

Yeah, right. Healing. Who cared if a worthless no-good healed or not?

"You are so much more than football, Jake. You need to believe that."

He could hear his mother's voice in his head, but it didn't help now any more than it had when she first said it.

Scott was barely out of the room before Regina was back.

"I want to make sure you'll be as comfortable as possible," she told him. "That morphine's going to hit you full force any minute."

Even as she spoke the words, he felt himself fading. At least for a few hours he wouldn't have to face the terrible reality his life had become.

Chapter 3

"I see they've taken the leg out of traction."

Jake looked up as his sister walked into his hospital room and frowned. "Yeah, big deal. And by the way, nice of you to show up today."

Ivy stopped just shy of the bed and glared at him. "Are you for real? I was here every damn day for the first two weeks. Took off work so I could do it and handle things for you. And I've been here every other day since then, listening to you bitch, answering your questions, talking you off the ledge. You've got some nerve, Jacob Marlowe Russell."

He managed to pull out a tiny smile. "The full name, huh? You must be really mad at me."

"Trust me. It's hard sometimes not to be. I understand the nurses just want to throw you raw meat before they come in to check you and give you meds."

"You try having your whole life jerked out from under you and destroyed and see how happy you'd be."

The grim lines on her face softened as she moved closer to the bed. "I know this is hard on you. And yes, I'd probably be in the same snit you are if I was in that bed. But Jake, all you do when you get angry is make yourself sick. You need to think healing thoughts right now."

Jake grimaced. He needed a hell of a lot more than healing thoughts to get him out of this fix. He couldn't gripe about the way the Mustangs were treating him. DiMarco had been in to see him several times along with Coach Raymond. Trip Faulkner, the quarterback, had been in every day after practice along with some of the other players. And Larry O'Donnell, the offensive lineman who'd missed tackling the defender who'd taken him to the ground, had practically cried all over the bed.

But Jake could hardly talk to them. None of them could possibly understand how devastating this was to him. After all, they were still out there, admired and respected. While he was just…just…a lump of nothing.

Scott had stayed in town for nearly a week, a record for the man with all he had going. But, to give him credit, he'd been at the hospital every day checking on Jake and his condition. And feeding him equal doses of optimism and practicality. If anyone knew what the devastating possibilities of an injury like this were, it was Scott, and he was a realist. It was his job to look out for Jake's future if indeed his playing days were over, although that was the last thing Jake wanted to discuss right now.

He appreciated all of it, but it still didn't change things. One bad break—pun intended—and he was out for the season. He just hoped whoever they socked into the lineup in his place wasn't such a standout that he, Jake, ended up playing backup when he returned. For one brief moment, he felt a tiny sliver of guilt for wishing the team bad luck. Then he forced the thought away. He was more honorable than that. At least he liked to think so. He knew his playing career was nudging the finish line, but he truly believed he had at least two excellent years left to give the Mustangs. He didn't want this injury to cheat him out of them.

Football is who I am. It kept echoing in his brain. *It's all I am.*

He heaved a sigh. His life was in the toilet and being pleasant was a real chore. Still, he shouldn't keep taking this out on his sister. She'd been more than great, taking time off from work, spending it here listening to him bitch, soothing him when the frustration became too intense.

"Sorry, Ivy. I know I'm being a pain in the ass, but try putting yourself in my place." He took her hand and squeezed it. Sometimes he wondered how he'd ever have made it this far without her. "Half a game and my season is over."

"I do understand," she told him, "and I'm really trying to cut you some slack."

"I know, I know," he said. "I don't know what I'd do without you. You're all I've got to get me through this, you know."

"And isn't that a sad commentary on your life. That the only person you can lean on is your sister."

"I don't—"

"Too bad you shy away from relationships." She sighed. "Right now you could use the attention of someone special."

Like a bolt of lightning striking from the sky an image of Erin Bass flashed across his brain. She was pretty damn special.

What the hell had gone on in her life that she had such a bitter, jaded opinion of football players? She'd never given him the chance to tell her who he really was. What kind of person he was. He'd never really wanted to do that with another woman before. Too much garbage from his past always got in the way.

Only she'd dumped him like yesterday's trash, and that still burned him. He hadn't been able to erase the memories, and that made him even angrier.

Why the hell was he thinking of her, anyway? She was in the past and she'd stay there. Had to. Period.

"I don't need anyone." He raked his fingers through his hair. "I didn't expect my life to change so drastically, and no woman's going to fix that. Trust me." He dug up a semblance of a smile. "Anyway, I'll try to behave. For you."

"Ha! That'll be the day." But she gave him an answering smile before she pulled a chair up to the bed. "So. I hear they're letting you out of here Sunday."

"Yeah. That ought to be a barrel of laughs." And just like that depression crept over him. "I still haven't figured out how I'm going to get around with crutches while sporting a cast on my left hand." Hadn't that thought just given him nightmares.

"No crutches at first," she told him. "I spoke with Dr. Moline this morning. They're going to send you home with one of those foldout walkers. That way you can grip with your right hand and—"

"And hop like some deformed creature because they won't give me a walking cast," he growled. "I'll be lucky if I don't fall down and this time break my damn neck."

"No, they won't give you a walking cast yet. It's too soon. Dr. Moline and Coach Raymond said they explained all of this to you, in great detail. Did you listen to them?"

"Yeah, yeah, yeah." He scraped his hand over his jaw. "But they aren't the ones stuck in this situation while the season goes on without them. They don't have to figure out how to get through the next couple of months. Or even the rest of their lives. They aren't—" He flapped his uninjured hand in the air.

"No, they aren't," she agreed. "But you might as well deal with it because bitching isn't going to change things." Her features softened. "No one argues this is a very bad situation. But getting better and healing is going to be in large part up to you."

"Okay, sure." He grunted. "I'm in great shape to take care of myself."

"Well." She scooted her chair a little closer. "As a matter of fact, funny you should say that. It's exactly what I came here to discuss with you today."

He frowned. "Oh! You have some ideas? Like getting the hospital to keep me a while longer?"

"Forget it. You no longer require hospital care."

"Well, that sucks." Then a thought popped into his head. "Hey. I could stay with you for a while. Or you could come to my house. Right?"

Ivy shook her head. "Bad idea. Besides the fact I might end up killing you, I work for a living and don't have the time to do what needs to be done for you."

"Thanks a lot, sis." He glared at her.

"Anyway, you'll be better off in your own place. You can hide away from everyone until you get over this little hump and get back on your feet." She grinned. "Literally."

"Little hump? Fuck." The cast on his wrist was making him itch like a motherfucker, and he tried to scratch beneath it. One month, Moline had said, to give the torn ligaments a chance to heal. "Okay, maybe you're right. I don't need to socialize and put up with anyone's pity. I don't feel very social, anyway. I can just drop out of everything until I get the casts off and I'm back on the field."

Ivy gave him a look of worry. "Jake, you have to be prepared for the fact that—"

He sliced a hand though the air. "Don't say it. I'm going to get back, start conditioning again, and be good as new for next season. I already told coach and everyone. So shut up about that."

"Okay, okay, okay. I'm just—never mind. Let's take care of this problem first." Ivy took out her cell phone and brought up the notepad. "I did get the names of some excellent caregivers from Dr. Moline. I have a whole list here—"

"Caregivers?" He shook his head. "A stranger living in my house? A drill sergeant in scrubs? No thanks. No agency creeps." A sudden wave of sadness gripped him. "Besides, it would remind me too much of Mom."

He didn't think he'd ever forget those last couple of years when their mother was dying and the parade of nurses and attendants through the house. He was just glad he'd had the bucks by then to get her the best. But he knew having someone from an agency around would creep him out. Besides, somehow in his mind, hiring a caretaker or caregiver or whatever the fuck Ivy wanted to call that person was an admission of the severity of his situation. He knew it didn't make sense but he couldn't help it.

Ivy sighed. "Jake, get used to the fact that you can't live alone until you're back on both feet. Literally. I mean, for sure someone needs to take care of you," she added. "You certainly can't cook for yourself, or clean, among other things."

"I have a maid who comes in regularly. I can add more days. And I have every takeout place on speed dial." He was getting more depressed by the minute. He had no idea what kind of person he could tolerate in his home for the indefinite future.

"Your laundry needs to be done. You—"

"The maid does my laundry, too," he pointed out.

"Jake." Ivy shook her head. "This is serious. It's more than that. Why are you being such an ass about this? Face facts. When you get home, you'll be pretty incapacitated, at least until you get that cast off your wrist. Getting around won't be as easy as you think."

"You're just a ball of cheer, aren't you?" he complained. Goddamn that linebacker who fell on him the wrong way. If he had a gun, he might shoot the guy.

"I'm trying to be practical here." She lifted up his hand and squeezed it. "I just want to help you get through this, Jakie. You're my brother and I love you."

"Please don't call me that stupid name." He frowned. "Someone might hear you."

"Okay." She giggled. "Jakie." She wiped the smile from her face. "I'm trying to do the best for you, okay?"

He knew that. He just couldn't help letting his bitterness come through. He saw his life lying in tatters and shreds around him. And having a stranger living in his house, seeing how incapacitated he was, didn't sit well with him, even though he knew he couldn't avoid it. He guessed he thought if he refused, then miraculously the situation would go away.

"So have you got any other ideas about a babysitter for me?"

She nodded. "I agree with you an agency worker probably wouldn't fit the bill, but I promised I'd bring it up. DiMarco was very firm we get someone who can handle more things for you than just personal care. Someone to deal with things like the media when it starts sniffing you out. Groupies who might try to show up at your house. Then there's your e-mail and snail mail. Stuff like that."

"Again I point out that you'd be perfect for this."

"Har, har, har. Don't change the subject. I want to get this fixed so I can feel comfortable going to work knowing you're in a good situation."

He hadn't really meant to be so flippant with her. Ivy had a plum job with a marketing firm, and he actually knew what a great job she did. In fact, the owner of the Mustangs had spoken to him not too long ago about his opinion of bringing her on to the team staff. He'd wondered if it would be awkward for either of them. But before anything could be worked out the disaster had happened.

"Okay, okay, okay," he grumbled. Shit, could things get any worse for him? "I get the message. So let's hear what else you came up with."

"I had some thoughts on this." Ivy had what he called her inscrutable look on her face. Usually it meant trouble for someone else. He was afraid this time it meant trouble for him. He just hoped to hell he was wrong.

"What's going on in your head?" he asked. "Should I be afraid?"

"No." She shook her head. "You should be impressed. What if I could find someone who just fit the bill? Could handle everything we discussed and do it very efficiently. Cook for you. Shop for you. Haul your ass back and forth to the doctor and physical therapy. Answer your phone. Deal with your mail. Keep the female vultures away from you. Sort of executive assistant with a few extra duties thrown in. Someone who would make herself invisible except when you need her. And was smart and easy on the eyes to boot. What would you say?"

Jake stared at her. Somehow this sounded too good to be true. "I'd say you're crazy. No one like that exists. Or if she did, she probably wouldn't work for me."

"But what if she did?" Ivy persisted. "What would you say? And would you pay her commensurately?"

"Hell, I know these people don't come cheap. What do you want me to say? Sky's the limit? You've got it." An unpleasant thought rolled through him and he narrowed his eyes. "She wouldn't be someone trying to get her mitts on me, would she?"

"You know I'd never do that to you. Trust me." Ivy laughed. "If I can even persuade her to take this job, that's the last thing she'd want. You can take that to the bank."

"Yeah? So what's this paragon's name?"

"Her name?" Ivy stared at him blankly.

"Yeah. Her name. She has one, right? Especially if she's so fucking perfect."

"Oh, um, Anne. Her name is Anne Hardy."

Why did she have such a problem remembering the name? What the hell was his sister doing?

"What's going on here, Ivy? Are you up to some kind of trick? Because I gotta tell you, I'm not up to dealing with it right now."

"No, no, no," she said, hastily. "No tricks."

Still, the feeling of unease wouldn't go away.

"Does she have references?" he demanded. He wasn't going to have some dip shit idiot female in his house. Or worse yet, a candidate for guard at a women's prison.

Ivy giggled. "Yes. Me. And that should be good enough for you."

"All right." He sighed. He had a feeling this wasn't going to go as well as his sister thought, but he'd give it a shot. What other choices did he have that wouldn't involve a test of his sanity?

"She's not helping me shower." He knew he sounded like a petulant kid, but he didn't want some damn woman washing his junk, not when it wasn't foreplay. He punched the covers in exasperation. "I foresee all kinds of problems here, my sweet sister."

"Like what?" she asked, and looked at her notes again. "I already took care of that. Home Health Care is sending someone once a day to help you shower—a man—and please don't bite his head off."

"Goddamn it." None of this sat well with him. Every single thing just underscored the extent of his situation and the possibility of the worst possible outcome.

"I know you can manage to get to the bathroom," she went on, "because I've seen you do it here since they removed the traction. It may not be beautiful but it works."

"Maybe I *will* fall and break my damn neck." He couldn't keep the bitterness and resentment out of his voice. This just wasn't fair. "At least I'd be out of my misery."

"I'm not even going to try and reason with you when you're like this," she told him. "No one understands more than I do, but I have to believe things will be okay."

"Yeah." He wanted to scream and throw things. "At least one of us does. How will I get home on Sunday, and when will Miss Perfect show up."

Ivy scrolled through her notes on her phone before typing rapidly. "I'll be here Sunday morning to take you home." She looked up at him. "We'll use a wheelchair to get you into the house, and then you'll have it if you need it."

"I'm not riding in a fucking wheelchair." He could feel the irritation rising in his gorge, choking him.

"You'll do what I say if you want them to let you out of this place. And trust me, you'll be damn grateful for it." She lifted her gaze to his. "I'll spend the night and get you set. I'll have Anne arrive Monday morning before you get up and before I have to leave."

She rose from the chair and stood so close to the bed her face was inches from his. "Listen. I know this has turned your life upside down. We all know it. The team is paying for the best of everything to help you heal. I'm getting someone in the house for you. But no one can fix your head except you." She grabbed his chin and forced him to look her in the eye. "Get it?"

Oh, he got it. He just didn't like it. "I hear you."

"Good. Now." She reached for the small box she'd brought with her. "How about one of those spiced muffins you like?"

He hated to tell her but the best muffins in the world weren't going to fix what was wrong with him. He just had a sick feeling his life was about to fall apart even more than it had.

* * * *

Erin stared at her friend as if she hadn't heard right.

"You want me to *babysit* some guy? Is that what you're asking me? Did I hear right?"

Ivy shook her head. "No. Not babysit. Use your skills to help someone who is incapacitated and needs assistance for the moment."

Erin scrubbed her face, wiping away fatigue as if that had made her hear wrong. After all, she had hardly arrived back in her apartment before Ivy showed up. Her suitcases weren't even unpacked yet. Two weeks on a luxury yacht playing personal trainer to a dozen rich women was a lot more stressful than it sounded. Her brain was probably asleep.

"I'm not sure that's what I'm hearing, so maybe you'd better tell me again."

Ivy took a sip of the tea Erin had fixed. "I'm just glad you're back. I was afraid I'd be out of luck. Honey, this is a win/win situation for everyone."

"Yeah?" Erin quirked an eyebrow. "How do you figure that?"

"You need a job and I need someone with your skills in training people's bodies. See? Win/win."

Erin took a swallow of her tea. She could certainly use a job. The two weeks at sea had paid well, but her reserve funds were low and not much stood between her and shit-out-of-luck. Who knew her job situation would be suddenly turned on its ear? Or that no place in the entire Greater Austin area was hiring a trainer either for a spa or a fitness center? Not even a plain old gym. How was that even possible? Her luck just sucked.

She'd gotten a great severance package, and she'd been able to pick up jobs here and there, filling in for people going on vacation. But that buggy ride was about to come to a halt.

Her rent was due, she was nearly out of money, and she was facing the task of having to relocate. Everything just sucked. The offer to spend two weeks at sea with a bunch of women who wanted to exercise and tone every day had been a lifeline. It also got her out of Austin where it seemed every living person was talking about the opening of football season, the Mustangs, and the gridiron god, Jake Russell.

Sometimes, in the deepest dark of night, when she lay in bed, wondering how her life had taken such a sharp turn for the worse, images of that night together floated through her brain, tantalizing and torturing her. She'd been right to stop it before it got started. She just knew it. The pain she carried from the past was a constant reminder of that. But oh, lordy, how her traitorous body yearned for him. If he were here now, she knew she'd be tempted to throw caution to the winds. Then she'd just regret the hell out of it afterward. For a moment, she was tempted to ask about him, but she clamped down on her mouth. That way was trouble.

"Come on," Ivy coaxed. "We can help each other. You need a job and I have a situation."

Uh-oh.

"Ivy, your *situations* mean trouble nine times out of ten."

"No, no, no," her friend said in a hurried tone. "This is really, really legit. Like I said, I have a client who's in need of your services."

"A client? From the marketing firm? Doing what? You don't have any clients that require your services full time, as far as I know."

"This is special. He needs someone who can provide personal services. It would be a live-in job for at least a couple of months."

"A couple of months? Live in?" Erin stared at her. "What the hell kind of job is it, anyway? And does whoever this is know that *personal services* doesn't extend to the bedroom?"

Now Ivy laughed. "Don't worry. That's not in the job description."

"Okay, so give me the details." She held up a hand. "I haven't said I'd take it yet. I'm not a nursemaid or babysitter, remember?"

Ivy nodded, sipped her tea, and leaned back in the couch. Her bland expression and relaxed posture should have been a warning to Erin that she was being softened up. But all she could think of was the bills coming and needing a place to live.

"The agency has a client who had a surfboarding accident," she told Erin. "He broke his leg."

Erin made a rolling motion with her hand. "And?"

"And he's coming home from the hospital Sunday. A friend of his and I are taking care of that, but then he needs help."

By the time Ivy had finished describing the injuries, the restrictions, and some of what the job would entail, Erin had to admit she was at least halfway intrigued.

"I'm not sure I'm fully qualified, though," she told her friend.

"Phooey." Ivy flicked her fingers in a dismissive gesture. "You have all the skills. You're a certified trainer so you can deal with his limitations and help him with his therapy when he gets started on it. I know you've temped at offices before enough to be able to handle that kind of stuff. And remember, too, I've tasted your cooking. He'll think he's died and gone to heaven."

If she had all these wonderful qualities, how come she was still single and nearly unemployed?

She studied her friend. "Who is this guy, anyway? What's he like? Maybe he's a jackass and I'll walk out the first day."

Ivy waved her hand in the air. "You'll be fine. He's understandably a little irritated about his, um, situation, but you can handle that."

"Yeah? How little is a little irritated?"

"You'll be fine," Ivy repeated.

Erin tried not to notice her friend had deftly avoided a direct answer. "What's the pay?" she asked.

Ivy named a figure that made Erin's eyes pop wide. "No kidding?"

"No kidding." Ivy nodded her head for emphasis.

Erin let everything roll around in her mind for a minute. "You're going to an awful damn lot of trouble for someone who's just a client of the agency," she pointed out.

"My boss asked me to do this as a personal favor for him. The guy is a close friend of his, and I've worked with him on several projects over the years."

"Doesn't your boss have a wife or a girlfriend or someone he could ask?" Erin wanted to know.

Ivy shook her head. "No, and I'm probably closer to him than anyone at the agency. Besides, he knows I have a lot of contacts and I said I'd help." Ivy sat there with a pleading expression on her face. "It would really score me a lot of points at work if I can make this happen. And your particular skills as a trainer would be good to help him with his exercises." She winked. "My boss got really excited about that."

Erin's eyes widened. "You *told* him about me?"

Ivy shrugged. "Just a little, so he'd know I had someone perfect in mind."

"But you had no idea if I'd say yes."

"Honey, this man needs help and you need a job. Don't tell me that's not a good fit."

"So tell me a little about him, besides the fact he's a *close* friend of your boss." When she didn't say anything, Erin lifted an eyebrow. "Should I be settling in for a long story? Does he have dark secrets or something?"

"No, no, no. It's really very simple. He's, uh, thirty-two, and—"

"Ivy, I don't care how old he is unless he's over seventy. I'm not looking for a hookup, okay? Just the basics."

"That *is* part of the basics." Ivy grinned. "He's good looking, too."

"Ivy," Erin warned.

Ivy gave her a sly look. "Can't blame a gal for thinking maybe—" She held up a hand. "I'll be good. I promise." She blew out a puff of air. "He's in a very high profile position. He's very much in demand in his line of work, so being incapacitated has really put a crimp in his life."

"Poor baby." Erin couldn't keep the sarcasm out of her voice. "What's the name of this Mr. Perfect?"

"Of course. He's…Russ Jacobs." Ivy cleared her throat. "Moving right along. He's in a cast and on crutches. He can't drive or otherwise get around very well."

"And his requirements are what, again?"

"Grocery shopping, cooking, answering phone calls and mail, checking his e-mail. He does some philanthropic work, so he'll get calls about that. He gets visitors so someone will need to manage those. Keep them to a minimum. Also he needs to make sure he uses his undamaged muscles. Just simple exercises. I figured with all your experience as a trainer you'd be perfect for this. And it will keep you in chocolate bars until you land another gig."

"And why can't he answer the phone himself?"

"Right now he's not in much of a mood to talk to people, so someone needs to be his buffer."

Erin couldn't help being curious. "Why doesn't he have someone from his business or corporation help him out? How come he asked your boss to help him?"

"I told you, they're very close friends. And he's a very private person. He doesn't want people he works with to see him incapacitated."

"Jeez, Ivy." Erin carried her mug into the kitchen and popped another cup of tea in the single serving coffee machine. "People get hurt or have surgery all the time. What's so friggin' special about this guy he wants to hide away?"

"He doesn't deal well with adversity. Anyway," she rushed on, "if you just ignore his grumpiness, you'll be fine. You may have to take him a couple of places—"

"Take him?" Erin interrupted. "A couple of places? Like where?"

"I don't know. I'm just throwing it out there. In case."

"Yeah, some throwing. Who takes care of his personal needs? Like showering with his cast and all." She twisted her lips. "Not me, that's for sure."

"Someone will be coming in on a daily basis, usually in the morning, to help him with needs like that. However, he's a very strong-willed person and he's ticked off that he is in this position to begin with."

Erin wrinkled her forehead. "Why do I have the feeling there's something here you're not telling me?"

Ivy widened her gaze. "Me? You wound me. Look. It could be a creampuff gig if you ignore his occasional temper tantrum. The pay is damn good, and you can still use your downtime to keep looking for another position." She paused. "So will you do it?"

"When did you say he's coming home?" Erin asked.

"Sunday. I said I'd babysit him that night, but you'll need to get there very early Monday morning. Like I said, he'll probably be a little grouchy, considering the circumstances, but things will even out. And if you have his coffee and juice ready, he might not be such a bear."

"And I have to stay there, right?"

"Well, duh." Ivy threw up her hands. "Of course."

"How long did you say this job was for?" she asked.

"Oh, just a few weeks." Ivy shrugged. "Once he's on a walking cast we can make other arrangements."

Erin chewed her bottom lip, thinking. She saw so many pitfalls to this whole thing. Living in a stranger's house. Putting up with what might be adult temper tantrums. Being housekeeper, secretary, and maid, not to mention pseudo physical therapist. Still, she certainly could use the money.

"And you know him well enough to vouch for him?"

"Like I said, we've worked together on a number of projects. Besides, I wouldn't toss you into a setup like this with just anyone. Honest."

"And how much did you say I'm getting paid?" She was still shocked at the salary Ivy repeated to her. "I know there's a catch here somewhere, but I'm just not seeing it."

"This guy can afford it," Ivy assured her. "He makes a disgusting amount of money. So? What do you think?"

Erin thought about it for a long moment, then blew out a long breath. "Okay. I'll do it. You can tell him yes."

"Ohmigod!" Ivy squealed with glee and threw her arms around Erin. "Thank you, thank you, thank you."

"But if it turns out to be a disaster, I'm taking a hike."

Chapter 4

As Erin pulled up the long driveway, she noticed Ivy's car parked at the curve by the front door. She punched the door opener Ivy had given her and drove into the garage. Two of the spaces were occupied by a silver gray SUV and a black sports car, so she pulled into the only empty one, the one closest to the entrance of the house, and got out.

"Oh, good, you're here." Ivy stood in the doorway, a bright smile on her face, obviously ready to make her getaway.

"I said I'd be here, right?" After opening her trunk, Erin pulled out the two suitcases she'd packed as well as her laptop case. She had no idea how this would work or how long she'd actually end up staying, so she'd tried to prepare for all eventualities. "Where do I put these?"

"I'll show you to your room." Her friend's voice was pitched very low. "Just follow me. And give me one of those suitcases." She grabbed one from where Erin had set it down.

"Why are we whispering?"

Ivy smiled. "Don't want to wake the sleeping dragon any sooner than we have to. Come on."

"Am I dressed okay for this?" She asked the question anxiously. She had worn slacks and a casual but neat top and comfortable flats. The clothes in her suitcases were more of the same. She figured she'd covered all the bases for her job as nursemaid/waitress/personal assistant, or whatever it actually turned out to be.

"You're fine. Just fine. Come on."

From the huge foyer, Erin could see a living room and dining room straight ahead. She caught a tiny glimpse of the kitchen as well. Two hallways branched off from there. The house spoke of tasteful wealth, with its hardwood floors, soaring ceilings, and carefully selected furniture and art. Whoever this guy was, he obviously had good taste and the pocketbook to enjoy it.

"Your client's master suite is to the right," Ivy explained and pointed.

The door was just slightly ajar, but Erin couldn't see much of anything. She gave her friend a long look. "I'm still not sure about this, you know."

"You'll be fine." Ivy gave her a smile. "This will be a piece of cake." She started down the other hallway. "Guest rooms are down here. This will at least give you some privacy."

The room she led Erin to was decorated in shades of green and ivory. With its queen bed and its polished wood furniture, it could have served for either a man or a woman. Idly Erin wondered if her new boss—or whatever she was supposed to call him—had women sleep over in a room other than his. And who they might be.

But Ivy was urging her along.

"Just set your stuff down in here. You can put it away later."

"Isn't this a little far from this guy's room?" Erin was beginning to develop an uncertain feeling about this again. "What if he needs me in the middle of the night or something? Can he get out of bed himself?"

"He has a walker that he can use to move in a small area."

Erin wrinkled her forehead. "No crutches?"

"No. He has a wrist injury that make crutches not feasible."

Okay, not good. Why hadn't Ivy told her this before? "So he's okay at night by himself?" she persisted.

"We set up a temporary intercom system just between the two rooms while he's incapacitated. There's a unit on his nightstand and one on yours that are hooked into the house system."

"Oh, great." Erin made a rude noise. "So he can buzz me any time he wants, right?"

"Yes, but that won't happen. He gave me his word he wouldn't be a demanding patient."

"Yeah, right. I'll bet he said anything he could just to get you to hire someone for him."

Sympathy washed across Ivy's face. "He's doing his best, Erin. Truly."

Erin looked at her friend with curiosity. "If this guy is so important to you, how come I've never heard about him before?"

"You don't know everything about me, sweetie," Ivy teased. "He and I go back a long way." She handed Erin a large envelope. "Instructions for his care. Nothing fancy," she added hastily. "Just the stuff we talked about, his meds, and that his leg needs to be kept elevated. I e-mailed you about everything else—visitors, phone calls, his mail, stuff like that." Her eyes strayed to the watch on her wrist "So are we good here?"

"You told me someone comes in daily to help him shower and shave, right?" Erin wanted to make doubly sure of that.

"Yes, there is. I told you." Ivy looked at her watch again. "In fact, home care should be here in about two hours. If we're lucky, he'll sleep until then."

Erin chewed her bottom lip. "If we're lucky. Okay. And if we're not?"

"He can do basic things for himself," Ivy explained. "He's just—well, I told you, he's pretty unhappy about the situation. And moving is very awkward for him."

"And you want to throw me in the cage with this particular bear? I thought you were my friend."

"I am," Ivy told her in a confident tone. "I got you a high dollar job, didn't I? Listen, the maid comes in twice a week. I filled the refrigerator and freezer with stuff for both of you for now, but you'll need to shop. He'll give you money for that. He eats practically anything so he's easy to please."

"Good, because I—"

"And don't forget," Ivy interrupted, "you'll have to be on the lookout for unwanted guests and get rid of them."

"Unwanted guests?" Erin repeated. "Don't his friends have enough respect for him to leave him alone if that's what he wants?"

Ivy lifted one shoulder and let it drop. "There are always people who don't respect boundaries, especially with someone who has a lot of money."

"Maybe I missed the part where I'm supposed to be a bodyguard, too. Should we go over that again?"

"No, no, it will be fine."

"Ivy?" Erin followed her to the foyer. "What do I do first?" Erin stood there, hands outspread, palms up.

"Hit the coffee machine. You'll need it and so will your patient. Oh, and here." She pulled a file card from her pocket. "The combination to the alarm system." She showed Erin the panel on the wall by the front door. "There's one by the door from the garage, too. You have twenty seconds to shut it off before it starts screeching."

"Wait, wait, wait!" Erin held up a hand.

"There's a monitor in the kitchen for the security cameras." Ivy rushed ahead as if Erin hadn't even spoken. "Come on, I'll show you."

"Does the alarm system cover the whole lot? Everything outside. What—"

"No, unfortunately. Apparently, he only wanted to make sure if someone broke in through any of the doors the alarm would go off. Maybe you can convince him he needs to up the system."

Erin paid careful attention as Ivy rushed through the instructions. Why was the woman in such a hurry? So what if she was a few minutes late for work? It wasn't as if she was an hourly employee on the clock.

"Okay. We good?" her friend asked.

"Um, I guess, but—"

Ivy glanced at her watch again. "Oh, look at the time. I need to get going." She opened the front door and blew a kiss at Erin. "I'll check in with you later."

Then she was gone, leaving Erin standing in the foyer in a puddle of uncertainty with the feeling that she'd made a big mistake.

Oh, well. At least she could get through today. She hoped.

The kitchen was a gourmet's delight. On one of the granite countertops, she found a shiny one-cup brewer that looked like the largest one made. Next to it was a carousel of single serving cups. In the cupboard directly above it, she found coffee mugs, took two of them down, and brewed a cup for herself.

One step down from the kitchen was a large family room with an enormous flat screen television on one wall. Of course. Men and their toys. She carried her coffee over to the big picture window that looked out to a well-landscaped back yard. Whoever this guy was, he did indeed have plenty of money. No expense had been spared with anything. Would he be like many of the assholes she'd met at the hotels where she worked, who thought his money entitled him to treat everyone like shit? Or would she be lucky and he'd at least be a decent guy?

Well, at least she had a nice place to stay and a steady income for a while, providing she could stand the man. She still had no real idea what this job would entail, and Ivy had been less than forthcoming, a sure sign this was a bad mistake. But she was already committed and at least she'd stay for one day.

She stood at the window for a long time, thinking about her situation, sipping her coffee. She really hoped this worked out, because the salary would put her in a good place until she got another job. Maybe she could even start her own business as a personal trainer. She was about to make another cup of coffee for herself and sit down to review the information Ivy had given her when she heard a crash from the direction of the master bedroom. She nearly dropped her mug.

"Ivy?" The shout reverberated through the house.

Oh, hell. What a way to start the day.

She put her cup on the counter and hurried down the hall.

"Ivy?" The roar came again.

"Ivy has left already," Erin said, pushing open the door to the master suite. "But I'm here. I'm—"

She stopped, shock freezing her in place.

"Jake?"

"Erin?"

Erin was sure her heart would stop beating. There, sitting on the edge of the bed in all his nearly naked glory, was Jake Russell. Her hot, hot one-night stand. The man she had literally pushed out of her life before he could do the same to her.

Oh. My. God.

Jake's jaw dropped. "What the fuck?"

Erin finally unstuck her tongue from the roof of her mouth. "My words exactly. Holy crap!" She pointed a finger at him. "You're not Russ Jacobs."

He glared at her. "And you're not Anne Hardy."

They stared at each other for a long moment, and Erin realized now what people meant by a deafening silence.

"No wonder Ivy used false names." She could hardly contain her anger. "She set this whole thing up for God knows whatever reason."

"I'm going to kill her," Jake said at last, clenching his one good fist. "I will absolutely fucking kill her."

"Not if I get to her first," Erin snapped. "I thought she was my friend."

In a flash, everything from her night with Jake zipped through her mind, including the angry words they'd exchanged the next morning. Okay, so she'd prompted those words, but history had given her a damn good reason to do so. She knew all about football players, from high school jocks to the overpaid pros, including the one who'd ripped her heart out, stomped on it, and then run over it for good measure.

The thought of Trace McKay called up way too much pain. Deliberately she banished any trace of him from her mind. She'd spent too much time letting him live there after the big disaster. Now she tended to look at all football players through the same lens. The fact that Jake was Ivy's brother didn't mean his scruples were any different than any of the other jocks she knew. She'd done what she had to, protecting herself...and her heart. She'd just been looking out for her welfare. Since then, she'd managed to stay out of his way.

Damn Ivy! She'd maneuvered this whole thing in her cute little way. Erin could not stay here. Not even for one more minute. This was an impossible situation.

"What are—what do you—" Her brain wouldn't form sentences. "What are you doing in bed?" Now there was a stupid question. Ivy had told her he was injured. She just hadn't expected—what? What had she expected?

"What the hell does it look like? I fucking broke my leg."

"But what—but how—" God, she was turning into a blithering idiot. She couldn't reconcile the big, formidable athlete with this man wearing a cast on his leg and his wrist. "I thought you were playing football?" Oh, there was a brilliant statement.

"In case you aren't aware of it, they don't let you on the field with a full leg cast." His tone was laced with bitterness.

"Of course, of course," she said quickly. And still she stared, somehow unable to take it in.

"Well?" Jake's angry voice broke into her thoughts. "Are you going to stand there all day or can you come and help me? As long as you're still here, how about making yourself useful?"

"Help you?" She frowned. "Make myself useful? Doing what, for God's sake?" The situation was getting worse by the minute. "I have to leave. I can't stay here with you. This can't possibly work."

"You can't leave now," he snapped. "I need to get up."

Without thinking, Erin moved closer and her eyes widened. She hadn't realized just how much damage had been done to his leg. The cast covered the area to well over his knee. Another little detail Ivy had left out.

He wore only the gym shorts he'd slept in, leaving the rest of his mouthwatering body naked. The slatted blinds on his windows were partially opened, letting shafts of sunlight into the room. It highlighted his rumpled hair and the golden scruff decorating his strong jawline.

Jake's voice was morning gruff. "When you're through gawking, do you think you could help me to the bathroom?"

Her jaw dropped. "Help you? To the bathroom?"

"Yes, damn it, unless you want me to embarrass myself. Oh, wait, maybe that's your plan, right? And can you please stop repeating everything I say?"

Erin would have liked to jab at him more, but it was obvious he was in great discomfort. She really wanted to grab her things from her room and hightail it out of there, but her conscience wouldn't let her do that. Sighing inwardly, she moved farther into the bedroom.

"Can you walk at all?"

How on earth was she going to do this? Damn Ivy for getting her into this, anyway. Then she noticed a walker lying on the floor. She guessed he'd tried to set it up to help him out of bed, but it had fallen over and banged against the nightstand. Obviously the cause of the sound she'd heard.

"Yes." He nodded at the contraption. "With a little bit of help. But it's very awkward because of the cast on my left wrist. That's why I don't have crutches. At least not yet." He glared at her. "Believe me, asking you to do this is not my first choice."

Erin swallowed the immediate reply that sprang to her lips and righted the walker. "Okay. Let's try to do this."

Jake pulled the walker over in front of him, flipped it open, and used it to pull himself upright. He had a lot of trouble balancing himself, so Erin took pity on him and put his arm over her shoulders, wrapping her arm around his waist.

Zing!

Electric tingles shot through her system and an unwelcome flutter set up in her pussy. Holy crap! Not good, not good, not good.

"Hey! We just gonna stand here?"

Until Jake spoke, she hadn't realized that the electric contact had made her stop in her tracks.

"Sorry. Just getting a better balance here."

Taking a deep breath, she steeled herself against the contact with his warm skin and navigated him the rest of the way. It wasn't pretty, especially since he couldn't put any weight on his broken leg and had to hop, but somehow they made it to the bathroom. Erin wasn't sure who was more uncomfortable, her or Jake.

At the bathroom door, she stepped back and frowned at him. "You don't need me to come in with you, do you?" She was sure that wasn't included in her list of duties, although with Ivy pulling this stunt she supposed anything was possible.

"Fuck, no," he growled. "I can't do much for myself but I can still do this." Cursing under his breath, he edged himself into the bathroom and slammed the door.

Okay, Erin, deep breath.

She knew football season had opened the day after she left on her trip. It was impossible to live in Austin and not be aware of it as every television and radio station pumped it and newspapers shouted it. At the time, she'd been grateful she'd have two weeks away from that insanity. And now—

Erin took a moment to look around the room. This, too, was well done, in pale orange, tan, and ivory, with solid furniture. Masculine without being overbearing. She wondered idly whose taste this was—Jake's, Ivy's, or some anonymous decorator. Or maybe not so anonymous. Maybe one of his many playmates, of which she was sure he had many.

What did she care, anyway? That zippy little tingle she'd felt when their bodies connected was probably just some kind of static in the air. Right? She'd prove it to herself when she helped him back to bed. Because no way could she allow herself to be attracted to this man.

While she waited, she might as well do something useful. She turned back to the bed, smoothing the sheets and plumping the pillows, even as she cursed Ivy under her breath for getting her a job as a damned maid. She had just finished folding back the covers when she heard the sound of the toilet flushing, then water running. She didn't figure he was doing much more than brushing his teeth. The home care person Ivy had arranged for—at least she'd said she had—would take care of his shower and shave, thank the Lord. The door flew open and there was Jake, gripping the walker with one hand. His forehead was creased with a scowl as he stood there, glaring at her.

"Well?" he snarled. "Are you through staring?"

She sighed and swallowed her immediate retort. "Sorry. I'm very happy to assist you back to bed."

"Ha!" He spat the word out and ungraciously accepted her assistance. "I'll just fucking bet."

"Listen, sport." She had to bite back what she really wanted to say. "This wasn't my idea any more than it was yours, so can you clean up the language and at least act halfway decent?"

"You're right. It wasn't my idea, either," he told her, resentment sparking from him like electrical current. "So can I just ask you to help me back to bed, and then you can go on your merry way?"

Erin knew that wasn't going to happen, at least not in the next couple of hours. Not until she got hold of Ivy, read her the riot act, and had her get someone else to take her place. So she just walked over to where he waited and moved into place beside him. The damn tingle zapped her again, but she clenched her teeth against it and helped him back to the bed with the same awkward, halting progress as before. He was obviously in distress, so she took pity on him and helped him get his legs up onto the mattress and tucked the sheet over him. She couldn't ignore the fact that his face was white with pain, and there were deep grooves bracketing his mouth.

Yet even with all that, when her hands touched his bare skin, she saw something like hunger flare in his eyes. Their gazes locked and for a moment time stood absolutely still. She broke away first, looking for a distraction. Glancing at his nightstand, she spotted an array of pharmacy prescription containers and a bottle of water that had probably been there all night.

"Let me replace this drink with a cold one," she told him, determined at least for the time she was here, to do what she was supposed to. "I know some of those pills are for pain. You look like you could use a couple of them."

When he didn't object, she hurried into the kitchen and grabbed fresh water from the fridge. Taking a few extra seconds, she filled a mug and carried both of them back to the bedroom.

"Here." She twisted off the cap on the water and handed him the bottle, then picked up the prescription containers. The directions on the label said one or two caplets as needed and he sure looked like he could use two right now. She shook them out into her palm and held them out to him, surprised when he only took one.

"One will do. I need to wean myself off these as soon as I can. I've seen too many guys get addicted to them."

"You should take them if you're in pain," she pointed out.

"They won't help me heal or rehab," he snapped, "and that's what I need to focus on. In fact, why don't you just take these out of here?" He practically threw the little bottle at her. "Stick them in the bathroom. I can do without them."

"Are you sure?"

"I said I don't need them."

"But—"

"They only gave them to me in case of an emergency," he told her, a muscle twitching in his cheek. "Getting to the bathroom and back was worse than I expected, but now I'll be prepared for it. There's some acetaminophen in the bathroom. I'll take that from now on."

Erin just shrugged, silently took the bottle, and stuck it in her pocket. She waited while he swallowed the pill, then pointed to the mug. "I didn't know how you take it so I just guessed at black."

"Good. Fine. That's how I take it, but anything will do. I'd hate to put you out any." His voice was tight. "Just leave it there. I'll get it in a minute." Then, as if making a supreme effort to call up some vestige of courtesy, he ground out, "Thanks."

He lay back against the pillows and closed his eyes. Erin wasn't sure exactly what to do, so she busied herself reading the prescription labels, the name and the dosage. Antibiotics to prevent infection, pills for pain and sleep if needed, although she got the feeling Jake wouldn't take the last one, either. She made a mental note to double check what was written on the sheet Ivy had handed her.

The sheet. The instructions. Elevate his leg.

Well, hell. That meant she'd have to touch him. Bend over him. Telling herself it was just a job and she really needed the money, she dragged some of his many extra pillows—how many did he need to sleep with, anyway?—and worked them as gently as possible under the cast from ankle to thigh. She was acutely aware of Jake watching her, even though she couldn't see his face. She felt as if two hot pokers were boring into her and when she straightened up and looked at him, sure enough, his gaze was fixed on her.

"You're supposed to keep it elevated," she said, aware she was just stating the obvious.

"I got the memo." He closed his eyes, obviously waiting for the pain meds to kick in.

Erin got the bottle of acetaminophen and stuck it on his nightstand. Then she stood there, analyzing this impossible situation and cursing Ivy under her breath. She hated to leave him until the meds kicked in, in case she needed to do something else, although she didn't know what. Finally, after what seemed an interminable amount of time, he opened his eyes and looked at her.

"You're still here."

"Well, I didn't evaporate." She shoved her hands into the pockets of her slacks. "This is probably not the best time to bring this up again, but I can't stay here. You have to know that. The situation is just impossible. I don't know what Ivy was thinking."

He let his gaze roam over her from head to toe, faint heat blooming in his eyes despite his obvious pain. Erin shivered under the impact of his stare and closed her hands into fists, digging her fingernails into her palms. Shit, shit, shit. That unwanted thread of sexual attraction was still pulling her toward him, no matter how bad he was for her. Her nipples tightened, her pulse ratcheted up, and between her thighs the throb in her pussy ramped up in force. Yes, she definitely had to get out of here.

"Jake?" she prompted. "Did you hear me?"

"I heard you." He scowled. "So you're gonna run scared the first time I tell you to scram? You're really planning to leave me here like this? Helpless?"

"What's the matter with you?" she demanded, her anger boiling over. "First you tell me to go away, and then you get mad because I said fine. You know as well as I do this is an impossible situation. Damn it." She clenched her fists tighter. "Your home care person will be here in two hours. I'll stay until I get hold of Ivy and get her back here. She's just going to have to make other arrangements. I'll tell her that and make sure she understands."

"Yes, tell her." He scrubbed a hand over his face. "What the fuck was she thinking, anyway? Do you think I want a woman taking care of me who practically threw me out of her place? Or maybe you just can't put your personal feelings aside to do the job you were hired for."

"I was *hired* to take care of Russ Jacobs." She did her best to keep her tone even. "That's not you, so I'm out of here. Ivy can just get you someone else."

She turned to walk out of the room, fighting to keep herself under control.

"Chicken," he called after her.

Erin stopped. *Chicken?*

"What did you just say?"

"I called you chicken," he repeated. "Cluck! Cluck! Cluck!"

She turned around, anger seething through her. "I am a lot of things, but chicken is not one of them. How dare you?"

"How dare I?" He made a sound that was part laugh, part grunt of pain. "What else would you call a woman who's so afraid of a relationship she pushes the other person away before it even gets started?"

"Pushes away? Relationship? Are you referring to the little sexual fandango we engaged it?"

"Wow! Sexual fandango? Fancy words for someone who's a chicken."

"Stop saying that." She had the irrational urge to stamp her foot. "I just let you out of a situation you would have walked away from anyway."

"Is that right?" The pain meds were obviously kicking in, because his face had color to it and the lines around his mouth had softened. "How did you ever get such a low opinion of me, anyway? You hardly even know me."

"I know your type, though. I've seen how men like you behave."

I've had experience up close and personal, too.

Anger flashed in his eyes. "Men like me? What the hell is that supposed to mean?"

Erin bit down on her lip, forcing back the immediate retort. This man was injured and in pain. This was no time to pick a fight with him, even though she was itching to, as obnoxious as he was behaving.

"I'm going to try to reach Ivy. Would you like something besides coffee first? Your sister did say you like juice in the morning." She managed to ask the question in her most politely impersonal voice. "Or would you prefer to wait until after you've had your shower?"

"That's it?" Each word was underscored with irritation. "You're not going to answer my question?"

"I'll take that as a no." She turned and headed out of the room. "I guess that's a no on the juice, too. I'm going to call Ivy and tell her she needs to make other arrangements."

"Yeah. Fine. Okay. You do that." When she didn't say anything he shouted, "I agree with you. This was a huge mistake. I can call a million women who'd maybe even pay me to do this. You hear me?"

"Go ahead. Pick one. Any one. Find one who'd put up with your sweet personality."

"Talk about sweet personalities. Have you looked at yours lately?"

Erin kept on walking, even as Jake continued to shout from his bed. Once she reached the kitchen, she sat down in one of the breakfast room chairs. The first thing she needed to do was pull herself together. She wanted to fix another mug of coffee, but at the moment her hands were trembling too much. She was going to kill Ivy the minute she got her hands on her.

When she had herself under control, she pulled her cell phone from the pocket of her slacks and speed-dialed Ivy. Not surprisingly, the call went directly to voicemail. The little rat was hiding from her, no doubt about it. She left a message.

"Call me at once. Damn it, Ivy. You got me a job with your brother? You gave me a fake name! What's going on here? I can't do this. Call me right now."

Feeling slightly calmer, she got up and fixed another mug of coffee for herself. While she sipped it, she did a search on her phone to find out what happened to Jake. What she read shocked her. This was no simple broken leg. She knew enough about football to be aware that his injury was devastating and could very well be career-ending.

What the hell was she going to do? Ivy had put her in an impossible situation, counting on Erin's sense of responsibility to override everything else. But living in the same house with Jake, who rang all her bells including the warning ones, was a recipe for disaster.

Okay, there's the money. Don't forget the money.

Oh, yeah, the money. How could she overlook that? She was nearly down to the last of her severance pay, and her savings weren't even worth mentioning. She had her check from the last two weeks but not even the barest prospect of a job.

So what were her choices? Working for Jake and getting a fat salary or being unemployed. She was still mulling that when she heard another crash from the master suite. She raced down the short hallway to the open door, stopping short at the sight. Jake had apparently tried to get out of bed again using his walker. Whether he was just off balance or woozy from the meds, he'd fallen sideways against the nightstand and knocked over the lamp. Now he was leaning one hand on the nightstand and trying to fish the walker around with the other.

Great. Just great.

"What the hell did you think you were doing?" She managed to leverage him into a semi upright position, then onto the bed, no easy task when his body was both large and unwieldy.

He flopped back onto the pile of pillows behind his head, the leg in the cast straight out on the mattress, the other one hanging over the edge, his foot on the floor. In that position it was impossible not to notice the fact his cock was swollen and thick and pressing hard against the soft material of his shorts. Her eyes were drawn to it automatically, despite her best intentions.

"Excuse me." The words were polite, his tone not so much. "Do you think you could give me a hand again here?"

His raspy voice startled her and heat crawled up her face. Well, crap.

"What exactly were you trying to do?" she asked as she hefted the other leg onto the mattress and pulled the sheet up to his waist.

"I wanted something, and I figured I'd used up all my favors with you today."

Crap. "It's obvious you can't manage anything by yourself."

"Thanks so much for telling me." Bitterness edged his words. "I guess you'll just have to hang around to make sure I don't get myself into trouble again." The deep grooves in his face and the faint sheen of perspiration on his face were obvious indications of the pain he was in. And yet there was no denying the sarcastically teasing tone to his voice. And damn! Was that a tiny sexual overtone she heard?

Stop that, Erin.

She righted the lamp, thanking fortune that it wasn't broken, and straightened the two books that had also been knocked off. "Tell me what you needed so badly. I'm afraid if you try to do this again you'll kill yourself, and how will I explain away your dead body?"

"You're all heart, right?" His sarcasm was somewhat dimmed by the fact that he was breathing harder than normal and his face sported a sheen of perspiration.

"Maybe I just don't have one. So. What can I get for you, now that I'm here?"

"I wanted another cup of coffee." He shot her a look of irritation and held out the mug that, miraculously, had not been brushed to the floor. "I was afraid you'd be pissed off at me if I asked for room service."

She had to resist the urge to smack him. "Did anyone ever tell you that you're a jackass, Russell?"

He managed a grin. "Some of the nicest people you'd ever want to meet. But then they got to see my winning personality."

Erin blew out a breath of exasperation. She took a minute to remind herself that this was not fun for him. His season was over, although hopefully not his career. He was out of action and out of the loop, in pain and filled with frustration. Okay, she'd spare him one minute of sympathy, but that was all. Surely she could be a big enough person to do that.

"I'm curious," he said. "How is it you were even available for this charade? I thought you were running the spa at that fancy resort outside of Austin."

Erin looked away from him. "It's been sold and the new owners closed it while they do extensive renovations."

"Well that sucks canal water. But I'd think in a city like this there would be other places who'd snap you up in a heartbeat."

"Yeah, you'd think. It's not like I haven't been looking either. I keep getting the same line. 'It's the economy. People aren't spending as much on extras these days.' As if keeping in shape was an extra." She turned her gaze back on him again, making sure her face was composed. "I'm examining my options."

"Which is how you got roped into this?"

She nodded. "Ivy knew I lost my job, and she thought this would be a win/win situation. Your sister can be very persuasive."

"You got that right." The muscles in his jaw tightened. "Sometimes too much so."

Erin planted her hands on her hips, indignant. "No kidding."

Jake grimaced. "Yeah, I would have been more suspicious if I was hitting on all cylinders. I'm completely aware of how persuasive and sneaky my sister can be. She gets an idea and she's like a dog with a bone."

Erin nodded. "Tell me about it. Meanwhile, we need to get her over here to face the music and see how we can resolve this. Having me stay is not a good idea, and you know it."

"I guess." He picked up his cell from the nightstand. "I've left a bunch of messages for her, but it's plain she's avoiding both of us."

"I'll get her." Oh, yes, she would definitely get hold of Ivy. "Not to worry."

"In the meantime, could you see your way to bringing me a fresh mug?"

She swallowed a sigh. "Yes. Just don't move until I get back."

His laugh held little humor. "I'll do my best."

"I'm not staying," she told him again when she brought him fresh coffee.

"Then you'd better get hold of Ivy. And soon."

No, she wouldn't stay; this needed to get fixed right away. Damn Ivy, anyway. She retreated to the kitchen again, trying to figure out what to do. After pulling out her cell phone, she tried the woman yet again.

Chapter 5

Jake muted the sound on the flat screen television and closed his eyes. He was fucking sick of watching anything. Besides, despite the lineup of six hundred channels, there didn't seem to be much of a choice.

How the hell had he landed in this situation with Erin hired to take care of him? He was going to kill his sister the minute he got his hands on her. If he ever did. She'd made herself suspiciously unavailable. Oh, he had her number. He saw her fine evil hand behind this. She was up to her old matchmaking tricks again. Why couldn't he make her understand that he wasn't interested in a damn relationship right now? If his leg didn't heal, what did he have to offer anyone? He had to concentrate on that, and Erin was definitely a distraction.

Then the memory of his night with Erin flashed in his brain and caused sensible reason to flee. He could still remember the shape of her curvy, sexy body, the feel of her satin-smooth skin, the lush silk of her dark red hair that swung easily just below her shoulders. And those eyes. Hazel, with intriguing flecks of gold. They hadn't done a whole lot of talking, but what conversation they'd had at the party let him know she was a smart, savvy woman. Five-foot-five of sex and smarts. A dangerous combination.

And one apparently out of his reach, for whatever fucking reason.

Ivy had been all up in his shit, asking about that night and talking Erin up, as if she was her press agent. Somehow he didn't think Erin knew about it or would be all that thrilled if she did find out. His sister, for whatever reason, was determined to get him coupled up before he retired, as if he couldn't find someone himself.

It was just, well, he was convinced he had nothing to give to a real relationship. When he looked in the mirror, he still saw the scared fourteen-year-old determined to stand up for his mother and sister. Football had given him a life. A new life. But behind that, he'd never gotten past believing he was worthless. Less than nothing. Who would want him?

For a brief few hours, he had believed it would be different with Erin. In one night his emotions had gotten involved. Then her words had knocked him on his ass, words that hurt even more than the ones *he'd* used to reduce Jake to nothing.

Now here he was, a goddamn cripple, at the mercy of the one woman who wished herself any place but here. He wondered what she thought every time she had to help him to the bathroom. Did she see just a useless piece of flesh, the way *he* had?

Maybe not. Despite her attitude she certainly had looked her fill of his dick every time she walked into his room, her eyes fastened to the outline of it beneath the thin gym shorts. Was it possible she still had residual feelings from their night together? That something was brewing between them? Did he dare even hope?

He wished he could figure out a way to get past the steel wall she erected around herself. It was like an imaginary line of scrimmage was drawn between them, the line players could not cross until the ball was snapped. He was on one side, Erin on the other, and no one was calling the plays. This just damn sucked. What did she have against football players, anyway? Something had to have happened for her to have such an aversion to them, such a low opinion. And did he really want to know? Maybe he should just take football out of the equation and see if she'd get to know him as plain old Jake.

He'd have to think of something, because in spite of everything, the attraction he'd felt for her from the very first moment he laid eyes on her seemed to grow stronger every minute. And it was a lot more than sexual. He, the man who'd insisted on no relationships in his life, who could not allow himself to be distracted from football for reasons that had roots in his childhood, was having his life turned upside down by a woman who had told him point blank she didn't like or trust football players. Well, shit. Now what? Maybe while he was lying here like a lump of clay he could think of something. At least it could give him something to do besides feeling sorry for himself.

He found a channel with an old movie, lowered the volume, and set the timer. Then he closed his eyes and prayed for inspiration and relief.

* * * *

Erin opened a bottle of white wine she found in the fridge, searched for a wine glass, and poured a generous drink. Then she carried it out to the patio off the family room. After the day she'd had, she was sure she deserved that and a lot more. Ivy had yet to return her phone calls, which only raised her blood pressure to the danger level. She'd tried calling her office several times, only to be told her friend was out, in a meeting, or with a client.

Uh-huh. It seemed Ivy had this avoidance thing down to a science. Well, tomorrow that would come to an end.

Jake had been Mr. Grouch personified all day, including when the home care man came to help him shower and shave. He had given her no idea what he wanted to eat, and being unable to get a hold of Ivy, she'd made an educated guess for both lunch and dinner. Jake had bitched up a storm but then eaten every bite of his food.

When she brought his dinner, he'd asked in his grumpy way if she thought she was too good to eat with him. She'd told him she had no appetite, which wasn't all that far from the truth. She'd helped him get ready for bed before escaping with her wine to the patio. It was so pleasant out here, the roof a shield from the elements, the screening a protection from insects. Massive plants in colorful pots created a tropical ambience, and with the sun just setting, the magnificent oak trees in the backyard were bathed in the golden glow. It was a scene that under normal circumstances would have been so peaceful and soothing. Tonight she wasn't sure if even every drop of wine would do that.

The damn chemistry between them just threw her out of whack even more than everything else. That kind of electricity had gotten her in trouble with him before, and she didn't intend for it to happen again. Absolutely not. Uh-uh. No way. If she didn't hear from that rat Ivy by the time the home health care person came tomorrow, she'd get in her car, storm her friend's office, and make her take care of business. Getting involved with Jake in any way could only end in disaster.

But wait. That meant she'd be spending the night under the same roof. In one of his bedrooms. In his house. The thought of being in such close proximity to him sent little tremors to her sex and made her breasts ache for the touch of his hands. Her nipples longed for the hot wetness of his mouth.

Holy shit!

What a hot mess she was turning into. She gulped down the rest of her wine and rose to get a refill. Maybe ice water would be a better idea. She might think that Jake and all the men like him were dangerous to her emotional health, but she had been totally unable to wipe the memories of that one night from her mind.

Wine. More wine.

She carried the glass to the room where she'd put her things and decided she'd at least unpack what she needed for the night. She had just picked up her cosmetics bag to carry it into the bathroom when the intercom on her nightstand squawked.

"Erin?" The word blasted out at full volume.

She jumped, nearly dropping the bag in her hands, and hurried back to the nightstand. Turning the volume button down first, she pressed Talk.

"Yes?" She worked to keep her voice low and well modulated. "Did you need something?"

"Yes." This came out much lower. "I need you to come in here." He paused. "I mean please."

If Erin hadn't been so incredibly pissed over the whole situation, she might have laughed.

"I'll be there in a few minutes."

"How many minutes is a few?" he asked.

"More than you'd like if you don't shut up and let me finish what I'm doing."

She waited a few seconds but the intercom remained silent. Dampening her irritation, she took a few things out of one of her suitcases and put them on the little side chair for the next day. She had no intention of unpacking everything. Tomorrow she was out of here if she had to have Ivy arrested and brought to her in handcuffs.

After taking one last fortifying swallow of wine, she headed toward the master suite, detouring on the way to get fresh water for Jake for the night.

He was lying in the same place she'd left him when she picked up his dinner tray, back against the pillows, leg elevated. The big television was on but the sound was muted. The covers on the bed were partially thrown back, but thank goodness they covered him from the waist down.

"I thought as long as I was coming into the room I'd make sure you took these." She used the most neutral tone she could manage.

"Yeah, okay," he growled.

She dropped his sleeping pill into his hand plus the antibiotic, uncapped the water, and handed it to him. He drank almost half of the bottle before recapping it, and she wondered what she'd do if he had to get up in the middle of the night.

"Do you need a pain pill? You look pretty uncomfortable."

He shook his head. "I told you, I want off of them as soon as possible. I can handle pain."

"Just make sure you aren't being foolish about it. Sometimes when your body is trying to fight off pain it can't heal as well." She put her hands on her hips. "Okay, Mr. Russell. What was it you wanted?"

His eyes widened. "Mr. Russell? How about Jake?"

"We have a formal relationship," she said in her primmest voice. "We should maintain it."

He scowled. "Well, aren't you just the prissiest thing. Okay, *Miss Bass*. I hate to disturb you but I wondered if you had any luck getting hold of my suspiciously absent sister?"

"You could have asked me that over the intercom," she pointed out.

"But I wanted to ask you in person." He used his elbows to hitch himself up a little higher. "Well?"

For a moment she couldn't speak, mesmerized again by that strong muscular body, the dusting of golden curls on the planes of his chest, his sexily rumpled hair. And oh, hell. There it was again, that very obvious woody, his swollen cock highlighted by the soft fabric covering it. Her mouth actually watered.

"Well what?" she finally managed to say, hoping the drumbeat in the walls of her pussy didn't sound as loud as it felt.

"Have you managed to get in touch with Ivy?" He shoved the sentence out through gritted teeth.

Okay, that shocked her back to common sense. Ivy. Damn Ivy. She was going to wring her neck.

"If I had," she snapped, "she'd be standing right here explaining this situation to both of us and fixing it. So, no. I have yet to talk to her."

"Me either." He watched her through slightly hooded eyes, his gaze so penetrating it stabbed clear through her, making her feel almost naked.

She wet her lips. "Was there anything else?"

He just kept staring at her. Was she just imagining it or was the sexual tension in the room so intense it was like a living thing she could almost reach out and touch? Her palms were sweating, and she rubbed them on her slacks.

"Jake?" she prompted. "Did you want anything else?"

"Yes." He cleared his throat. "I want to talk to you."

"Talk?" She cocked an eyebrow. "About what? I'm really tired. Besides..." She waved at the giant flat screen on the wall opposite the bed. "You've got plenty of entertainment available."

"I don't want to be entertained." His features were set in a fierce look. "I want to talk to you."

"Oh, so I'm not entertaining?" Holy crap! What was with this guy? He was just as insufferable as she'd figured. "Is that what you're saying?"

"No. Jesus." He rubbed his hand over his face. "That didn't come out right." He reached for the half-filled bottle of water she'd left him and knocked it onto the floor.

Sighing, something she suddenly seemed to be doing a lot of, she picked up the water, uncapped it again, and handed it to him.

"Can you drink it by yourself or shall I hold it for you?"

He pinched his eyebrows together and got ready to make what she was sure was some smart remark, but when he shifted his body on the bed she saw pain cut lines into his face like the ones she'd seen earlier. When Erin was ten, she'd fallen and broken a finger and she still remembered how much it had hurt. She was sure Jake's pain was magnified a thousand times more than that, although he was well past surgery. She'd have to work at toning down the snark in acknowledgment of his situation. At least until tomorrow when she was sure as hell out of here. She forced a smile.

"Sorry. That was uncalled for."

"An apology?" He snorted a laugh. "I might need those pain pills after all to counteract the shock."

Bite your tongue, Erin. Just bite your tongue.

"I've been known to give one now and then," she told him.

He patted the bed next to him. "How about if you sit down and talk to me for a minute."

Really? "Damn. Are you that bored?"

"Maybe I just want to get to know you better." He watched her, obviously gauging her reaction.

Everything in her stilled. "I think we went over this the last time we were together," she reminded him.

"The *only* time." His eyes burned into hers. "If I remember correctly, you were the one who killed it. Right?"

"For very good reasons."

"Yeah? Well, I still don't know the real reason, but I'm damn sure it isn't me."

Her stomach knotted. He was right. He hadn't been the underlying reason, but she didn't want to go into that.

"Pretty sure of yourself, aren't you?"

"So I've been told."

"If that's what you want to talk about, I'm going back to my room. My *temporary* room."

"Fine. Then just talk to me for a few minutes about anything at all. You pick the topic." He gave her the same penetrating stare. "Maybe I just want to know more about you. About who you are as a person."

And that way lies its own dangerous path.

She shoved her hands into her pockets. "I don't think that's a good idea. Besides, you need to get your sleep. To heal."

"Twenty-four hours a day isn't going to help me heal any faster." He spat the words out, each one edged with bitterness. "I feel like a damn cripple. Half a game and my damn season is over. I can't wait to get this fucking cast off and get back on the field. It's killing me lying here like this."

Lord. The man changed with the wind. One minute he was trying to be charming, the next he was grumpy, and the next angry and resentful as hell. Erin was glad she would only be here until tomorrow. She wasn't sure how she'd deal with all his personality changes on a daily basis.

"Jake," she began slowly, "other football players have had serious injuries and survived. You will, too."

"Other players have been injured and it killed their damn careers. Look at me. I'm thirty-two years old. I'm a key player, but I've got maybe two or three more years left before my speed begins to diminish and I get cut back to second string. Coach sends me in for fewer plays. Some games maybe I'm only in for one or two snaps. Then I'm cut altogether. But fuck. I want those last few years."

He picked up the empty water bottle and threw it across the room.

"Temper tantrum much?" She picked up the container. Easy enough to toss it in the kitchen on the way back to her room.

"My broken leg, my house, my right to a tantrum." His tone of voice was far from pleasant.

"Are you always this pleasant?" She shook her head. "Did you ever think this was a sign that you needed to expand your world beyond football?"

"No." He nearly shouted the word, then scraped his hand over the stubble on his face. "This is my life and I'm not apologizing for it."

She tried to weigh her words carefully. As irritated, angry, and frustrated as he was, anything could set him off, as it just had. "I can't begin to know how you feel, and I'm not going to try and argue with you about this—"

"Good," he interrupted. "Because it is what it is. Go back to your room. I was delusional to think we could have a decent conversation here. I just thought as long as you were stuck here, maybe we could clear the air about a few things."

As if this was really the best time to do that. Not with his frustration level so high.

"I think you're right. I should go back to my room. Tomorrow I'll be out of your hair, and you can yell at the person who takes my place."

She turned and walked out of the room as pulled together as she could be, then closed the door firmly behind her. She stopped in the kitchen to toss the empty water bottle before reaching her room and throwing herself on the bed. Holy mother. Just being in the same house with Jake had her mind imagining forbidden things. What was up with that? It wasn't as if she were fulfilling a crush or something. And besides, she'd had plenty of sex before she met him.

But not as good as it was with him.

That was a thought she needed to wipe from her mind. Tomorrow she'd find Ivy if she had to get the cops to track her down. She'd get out of here, back to her own life, and concentrate again on finding a job. She allowed herself one moment of regret. On the surface, this job should have been a real plum. High dollar salary, a beautiful house to camp out in, nobody but one grumpy patient to bother her. If only that patient hadn't turned out to be Jake.

Finally she pushed herself off the bed, washed off her makeup, brushed her teeth, and pulled on her favorite sleep shirt. She lugged in her cell phone charger, hooked up the phone, and sent one last message to Ivy.

Call me ASAP, you rat, or I'm calling the police.

Then she crawled in between the covers and pulled them up to her chin. Burrowing her way into the pillows, she closed her eyes and prayed for sleep.

* * * *

He was waiting for her when she came into the bedroom, lying naked on the bed, pillows propped behind him, legs outspread. He was like a golden god, all toned muscles and carved features. His sun-streaked blond hair was sexily mussed, brushing his forehead and his ears. His face sported a darker scruff, just enough to make her mouth water. She wanted to rub her cheeks all over it, like a cat. Flat abs that she wanted to slide her hand over beckoned her along with the sculpted muscles of his strong legs, the sweep of his lean hips, and a cock that was magnificent in its majesty. It stood out from the deeper gold, thick nest of curls at his groin, its head a magnificent purple. One tiny drop of fluid sat exactly in the center of the slit.

Lying back on the bed, Jake wrapped his fingers around it and stroked very slowly up and down, his eyes glued to Erin. She drew in a long breath and slid her tongue over her bottom lip as if already tasting him. She couldn't stop drinking in the sight of his magnificent athlete's body, the restrained power evident in every cut of muscle. Standing at the foot of the bed, still fully clothed, she practically drooled at the sight of him. The urge to lick him all over, to taste every inch of that magnificence was so strong she had to restrain herself.

The look simmering in his eyes sent moisture flooding her panties and every pulse point throbbed with anticipation. Her breasts ached for the touch of his hands and she wondered how his mouth would feel on her nipples. She had to shove her hands into her pockets to keep from palming her own breasts and squeezing them. Just looking at Jake aroused her more than other men had done with all their talents and tricks.

The sight of his hand very slowly moving up and down his engorged shaft fascinated her so much she couldn't draw her eyes away from it. Her own fingers itched to replace his and stroke him, feeling the hot steel beneath what she knew was velvety skin. Everything they'd done that one night together, the way they had explored each other's bodies, the kisses on erogenous zones, the glide of tongue and stroke of fingers set the pulse in her womb to pounding as hard as a jungle drum.

"Are you just going to stand there looking at me?" he asked. His voice was like warm melted chocolate sliding over her like a sensuous cloak. "Take off your clothes. I want to feast my eyes on your gorgeous body. God, it makes my mouth water just thinking about it."

The sound of his rough voice sent shivers racing over her like millions of minute fingers, and more of her cream flooded her panties. His words were arousing, sensual, plucking at her as if he'd actually touched her. She squeezed her legs together, hard, to still the pulsing in her pussy while her fingers found the hem of her T-shirt. Like a dancer in a club, teasing the audience, she slowly eased the shirt up and over her head, and tossed it to the floor. With the same deliberate, liquid movements, she reached behind her to unclasp her bra, slid the straps down her arms, and pulled the garment free.

Jake stared at her breasts, now unfettered and aching for his touch. With bravado she didn't know she had, she lifted them and offered them to him, her thumbs stroking lightly over her nipples. She felt a boldness with Jake that no other man had ever sparked in her, a desire to take a walk on the very wild side.

"You'll have to come closer if you want my mouth on those rosy, ripe buds," he pointed out. "You're a little far away at the moment."

"Don't you want me to take off the rest of my clothes first?" she teased.

"Damn straight I do." He was still rubbing the length of his shaft with a languorous motion of his fingers. "I love looking at that body. But more than that I want to feel my dick inside you. Feel those hot pussy walls grip me like a vise and squeeze me until we both come."

She trembled at his words, turned on by his blunt talk. It wasn't that she hadn't heard it before, but with Jake, the words danced over her like electric flames, igniting her nerves and sending her heated blood rushing through her veins. With Jake she was learning that words could be as arousing as actions.

She unbuttoned her jeans, lowered the zipper, and slowly eased them down her legs. One flick of her foot and she'd kicked them to the side. Last came the miniscule scrap of lace and satin that passed for her panties. With her eyes still locked with his, she hooked her thumbs in the elastic and shimmied out of them, accentuating the movements of her hips. She'd done a lot of things before, but somehow a deliberate strip tease had never been one of them. Now it would be something she could share only with Jake.

Jake, who looked as if he wanted to eat every inch of her and taste her with slow, delicious licks of his tongue. She was halfway between embarrassment and raging desire. He seemed to bring out her inner wild woman in a way no one ever had before.

"Gorgeous." He breathed the word. "Come closer and let me touch you."

With a deliberately provocative movement, she sashayed over to stand beside the bed. She was close enough that he could reach out his free hand and skim his fingers over her breasts. Just that light touch made her pulse race and moisture flood her sex. When he squeezed each nipple, hard, she sucked in her breath at the exquisite pain that surged through her.

He dusted his hand between her breasts, over her tummy, and down to probe between the trimmed curls covering her mound. When he idly trailed two fingers between her damp lips, she hitched herself forward and rocked her hips back and forth. Every muscle in her body clenched in response and the walls of her pussy pulsed with need. A need that accelerated when he slid his fingers free, brought them to his mouth, and slowly licked them clean one at a time.

"Better than the finest brandy," he told her in his slow molasses drawl. "Get up here and let me taste some more."

She climbed onto the bed and straddled him, knowing this was one of his favorite positions. And now it was one of hers. He gripped her hips and pulled her forward, dragging the lips of her sex slowly over his chest, the soft curled hairs on his chest an erotic tickle on her skin. When he finished adjusting her, the cheeks of her buttocks rested on his upper chest and her pussy was perfectly aligned with his mouth. Erin rested her hands on her thighs to balance herself, digging her fingers into her skin when he lazily spread her labia and stared at her with heat in his eyes. The hunger in his eyes stoked her fires even higher.

Erin didn't remember any man ever looking at her body the way Jake did, as if she were the most delicious morsel in a sensuous feast and he couldn't wait to taste her. Of course, she didn't think she'd ever been as unrestrained with any man before. He managed to push every one of her hidden buttons.

"Keep those hands right there on your incredible thighs." His voice was low and rough. "Close your eyes and feel. Just feel, sugar."

At the first slow lick of his tongue on her clit, she trembled with delight, icy heat racing over the surface of her skin. Beneath her, his body was furnace-hot, searing her sensitive skin. His callused thumbs rubbed gently over the lips of her pussy as he continued to stare at her, the look he gave her as hot as fire. When he swiped an anticipatory tongue over his lip, she shivered, her inner muscles clenching.

Drawing in a long, slow breath, Jake set up a steady rhythm, licking and lapping, never increasing the speed no matter how she urged him or begged. With her eyes closed every sensation was enhanced, every touch of his tongue exaggerated. She was stunned at the way it made every other sense come to life, how every reaction was amplified.

His thumbs pressed her lips open as he fed from her, swirling the tip of his tongue around her clit, then stroking the hot flesh on either side of it. When he finally thrust his tongue inside her, every muscle in her body clenched and she clamped down on him. He hummed against her, the vibrations reverberating through her, like a violin when its strings are plucked. And then there was nothing but the intense all-consuming pleasure as her release uncoiled and surged through her with the force of a wild storm.

She rode it out, focused only on the incredible feeling gripping her, on the spasms that shook her, urged higher and higher by Jake's incredible tongue. When the last of the shudders subsided, every ounce of energy seeped from her body. He rolled her to the side and pulled her against his

*body. She felt his hand skim her back and her arm, slow soothing strokes
as she waited for her heart rate to return to normal.*

*She lay there, cocooned for a long time, his lips stringing kisses along
the line of her jaw, thinking that she'd never felt so complete, so—*

Erin sat upright in bed, her heart pounding, her breath coming in
loud rasps, the pulse in her pussy throbbing with the insistency of jungle
drums. She pulled at her sleep shirt, tugging it away from her sticky skin
that was covered with a fine sheen of perspiration. What on earth?

Then it slammed into her, the erotic dream she'd woken from.

Oh. My. God.

She threw back the covers, and on legs slightly unsteady wobbled her
way to the bathroom. After filling the tumbler on the counter, she drank it
down without stopping. She ran cold water over her wrists and splashed it
on her face, then looked up and stared in the mirror. Her face was flushed,
her eyes slightly glazed with the I've-just-had-great-sex look. What was
wrong with her?

I want to jump Jake Russell's bones. That's what's wrong.

Wrong on so many levels.

Why couldn't he have been a dud in bed? A selfish lover? The asshole
she'd expected him to be? She'd finally stopped having those very sexy
dreams about him and now here she was, back in the soup again. This was
just bad on so many levels. The worst part of it was she had a sneaking
suspicion that underneath that jock exterior Jake was actually a nice
guy. Of course, she'd thought that about someone once before, and she
remembered exactly how that had turned out.

"Ivy, you are so going to pay for this," she muttered.

She dreaded going back to sleep. She didn't need another dream that
left her hot and bothered and hungry for more. Maybe if she was quiet
enough about it she could sneak into the kitchen and fix herself a cup of
tea. The one-cup brewer made tea and hot chocolate as well as coffee, so
she could do it easily. Maybe she'd have hot chocolate instead. That was
her comfort drink of choice.

She did without slippers, afraid they'd make a sound on the hardwood
floors, and she had no idea how soundly Jake was sleeping right now.
Unwilling to turn on any lights, she unplugged her cell from its charger
and used her flashlight app. She had just popped the K-Cup of hot
chocolate in the holder when she heard something coming from her room.
It startled her so much she nearly knocked over the machine.

Wait. There it was again.

She realized suddenly it was the intercom on her nightstand. Should she go directly to his room? Answer the intercom first? She left the mug and took the cup out of the holder, then hurried back to her room.

Pressing the Talk button, she said, "Yes? Do you need help?"

"Of course I fucking need help." The voice was nighttime hoarse and gravelly. "Do you think I'm buzzing you to make idle conversation?"

Well, he was certainly his charming self. Of course, Erin wondered how pleasant she'd be in his situation, forcing herself to forget for the moment that he was Jake Russell and think of him as someone in a bad spot who needed her assistance.

"I'll be right there."

When she reached his room, she took a moment to gather herself, swallowed hard, and opened the door. He was lying back against the pillows, pain edging his face. The lamp beside his bed was on, highlighting the sweat glistening on his body and the rise and fall of his chest. He had one foot on the floor, the leg in the cast still on the bed, and the foldup walker was lying crookedly on its side.

"I need to get up." He spat the words out. "I'm sorry to disturb your beauty sleep. Believe me, I don't like this any more than you do."

Erin took a calming breath to steady herself.

Just pretend he's an anonymous person who needs you. Mr. Anybody. Yeah, right.

"Okay," she said quietly. "We can do this."

"It's the fucking cast on my wrist," he growled. "I can't put any pressure on that damn hand, which screws with my equilibrium. Maybe someone should shoot me and solve all my problems."

He chuffed a breath as she leveraged him to sit up. This close to him she couldn't help inhaling his very masculine scent. She thought irrationally that he was the only man she'd ever met who still smelled good when he was sweaty.

Focus. Be smart and focus.

Using the same method they'd contrived earlier in the day, she got him up and to the bathroom. He pushed the walker ahead of himself and closed the door.

"I'll wait to help you back," she called out.

"Thanks."

But he sure didn't sound all that grateful.

The door opened and he clumped out across the threshold, doing his best with his one good leg and one good hand. Without saying a word,

Erin moved beside him, and they made their way back to the bed with her supporting him as best she could and him leaning on her.

God, he smells so good.

Damn. She gave herself a mental smack.

Once she got him onto the bed, she folded the walker and leaned it against the nightstand.

"It will be easier for you to get to here than stuck between the bed and the nightstand," she told him.

"Thank you." He blew a breath and hitched himself higher against the pillows.

"You're welcome." She helped him raise the leg in the cast to the bed, then stood back, assessing his situation. "I think you should probably take your pain pills so you can get back to sleep. You look like you're not feeling tiptop."

"Ya think?" He gave a short, humorless laugh. "How would you feel with a broken leg and wrist, needing some man to help you get to the bathroom and back?"

"I get your point. Let me get you some water."

She started to back away, but he reached out and grabbed her wrist. A dark flush rode his cheekbones and heat glittered in his eyes, now darkened to a rich espresso.

"I'm going to say something to you, and I don't want you to take it the wrong way."

She tried to free herself from his grasp, but his fingers tightened. "That already sounds like something I'm not going to like. You may want to think twice about saying it."

"I've thought of little else since that night together. Especially when I'm trying to fall asleep." His voice was husky. "You have the most beautiful nipples of any woman I've ever seen."

She looked down and realized she'd run in here in her sleep shirt. No robe. Nothing to cover herself properly. She'd just hurried to see what he needed. If her hands had been free, she would have crossed her arms across her chest to give herself even the tiniest protection. But warm male fingers held her in place.

"Don't be embarrassed," he said. "Please. I mean that in the nicest way possible."

Out of nowhere, her brain flashed back to the dream she'd just had, and the image of Jake twisting her nipples and sending shafts of the most pleasurable pain right to the core of her. Damn! Again she tried to jerk her hand away, but Jake's fingers circled her wrist more tightly. The warmth of the contact sizzled through her blood and set up tremors in the walls of her sex.

Really, Erin? Get your act together.

"Jake, this is highly inappropriate. Please let me go."

"Inappropriate?" He scowled. "A man paying a compliment to a woman is inappropriate?"

"I'm not here as a female, Jake. I—" She stopped. That sounded stupid even to her.

"Could have fooled me." His mouth twisted in a caricature of a grin, evidence that he was riding the edge of pain. "Let me just look at you for a minute, okay? Jesus, look at me. I couldn't do anything if you paid me."

"Jake..." She shook her head. "Can I have my hand back?"

"Just tell me one thing. What did I do wrong that night? I thought we really clicked. What was so bad that you won't even acknowledge how great we were together?"

This was going nowhere. "If you behave yourself tonight," she told him, "I'll answer your question tomorrow. Okay? Now let me get you some water and your pills."

He released her hand with obvious reluctance, but the heated look he gave her burned the surface of her skin.

This is bad, this is bad, this is bad.

She repeated it in her head as she got the water from the kitchen and made her way back to his room. She had to get out of this house before her resolutions disintegrated and her willpower deserted her completely.

Jake was in the same position she'd left him in, sprawled back against the pillows, covers tossed to the side. She made a conscious effort to avoid looking at the thick outline of his cock beneath the flimsy material of his shorts, but her eyes seemed to have a mind of their own. One corner of his mouth quirked up when he saw where her gaze was drawn, but mercifully he didn't make a comment.

He took the open bottle of water from her, waited while she dropped his pills into his palm, and popped them into his mouth. Despite his banter and his obvious state of arousal, just as earlier, the degree of pain he was enduring seemed to be intense.

"Would you like me to call Coach Raymond tomorrow and ask him to check with Dr. Moline and see if he can up your pain meds?"

"No, damn it." He practically barked the words.

Erin flinched.

"Sorry." Jake rubbed a hand over his face. "I didn't mean to yell, but you know how I feel about the fucking pills."

She blew out a breath. "I understand what you're saying. I truly do. I just hate to see you in such agony."

He shrugged. "I've had worse. Believe me."

"I think you're exaggerating, but if you say so. Let me elevate that leg again."

She worked the pillows under his cast as she had before. When she was finished, she folded the covers back neatly and left them at an angle in case he wanted to pull them up later. And she did all of it while doing her best to touch nothing but his cast.

"That should take care of things for tonight. But of course please use the intercom if you need me again."

She backed away from the bed and headed for the door.

"Erin?"

She stopped but didn't turn around. "Yes?"

"Thank you."

"You're welcome." She left the room, closing the door gently behind her.

Chapter 6

At six thirty in the morning Erin wasn't feeling too chipper. She'd had a hard time falling back to sleep after Jake buzzed for her in the middle of the night. By the time she'd got him situated on the bed and elevated his leg again, she'd decided it was useless to go back to bed. Who knew how soon Jake would wake up, and she really wanted to get hold of Ivy.

After fixing herself a mug of coffee, she carried it to her bedroom—*her* bedroom?—unplugged her cell from the charger, and speed dialed Ivy.

"Do you know what time it is?" were Ivy's first words.

"You're damn lucky I didn't call you hours ago. Ivy Russell, I am going to kill you the minute I lay eyes on you, which better be in the next hour. Or else."

Ivy's yawn echoed over the phone. "No can do, sweetie. I'm leaving for Dallas this morning."

"Dallas?" Erin practically screamed the word. "You can't go to Dallas."

Ivy laughed. "You want to try telling that to my boss? I have an appointment with a hot client this afternoon. I expect to be gone for a few days."

"Then you'd better figure out a way to get me out of this fucking mess before you hit the road. I'm not kidding, Ivy. This isn't funny."

The silence went on for so long Erin wondered if her friend had hung up on her.

"Ivy?" she prompted.

Finally she heard a heavy sigh. "Okay, here's the deal. I can't do it because I have a job and as I told you right now I have to leave town. I did try a few people, but there is no one who has all the necessary skills you do."

"Necessary skills?" Erin was outraged. "How skillful does one have to be to help him back and forth to the bathroom?"

"The bathroom?" A peal of laughter erupted. "Oh, that's just too funny."

"Not funny from this end. At least he doesn't expect me to attend to his personal hygiene."

"Really?" Ivy's voice still held a tinge of humor. "That might be interesting."

"Ivy! Damn it anyway." She drew in a calming breath. "So?"

"So there is no one else. At least no one who'll put up with his grumpiness and give it right back to him. And someone who has the skills to deal with the bullshit that's going to come down."

"Bullshit?" Erin squeaked. "Oh, please tell me about it."

"Okay. I'm assuming the phone calls haven't started yet, but be prepared. They will. I know he doesn't want to talk to anyone, especially the players who are out there doing what he can't right now."

"That's the damn truth," she muttered.

"What? What did you say?"

"Nothing. What else?"

"We've gone over all this before, but it can't hurt to repeat it. God knows how many women might have his number and want to pester him, although he's not one to give it out easily. That's not his style."

"Stingy with the number. Got it." Erin took a fortifying sip of the coffee. "So where do they get it from?"

"Some of his teammates have a hard time growing up." Ivy sounded irritated. "They think it's a kick to pass his number around and tell the football groupies they should call him."

"Well that certainly sucks."

"Yeah, he's had to change it a couple of times."

Erin felt a headache coming on. "What else?"

"He does some charity work that he likes to be low key about. I mean, like he wants *no one* to know about it." She rattled off the names of a shelter for homeless women and children and a sports league for underprivileged kids.

Erin was stunned. She never imagined Jake or any other player would be at all interested in philanthropy or volunteer work. Oh, she knew about all the hospital visits these guys made to children, but she always assumed that was more for publicity than anything else. She'd figured the minute the cameras were gone, so were the jocks.

"Why does he want to hide it?" she asked. "I'd think he'd want everyone to know. I mean, not just for his ego but to get other people to contribute."

When Ivy didn't answer at once, Erin began to wonder if they'd been disconnected.

"He has his reasons," Ivy said at last, "and they are very private. Don't bring it up to him."

"Not me. Anyway, I didn't realize he was that, um, philanthropic."

"See there?" Ivy said. "Maybe you've been giving him—and the other guys—a bum rap all this time."

"Ha!" She sniffed. "Remember, I've seen them in action."

"But only when they've been pumped about a game or a victory." She paused. "Make this work, Erin. He needs someone to help him through this, and it has to be someone who can put him in his place when necessary. And put up with his bullshit."

"Well, thank you so very much for throwing me under this bus."

Damn! Damn! Damn!

"You can do this. I know you can. And if you call me, from now on I promise to answer. And I'll check in more frequently. Scout's honor. But please. Just handle this for me. Okay? And for Jake?" Her voice softened. "Erin, he and I—we've only got each other. I'm sorry I tricked you into this, but I wouldn't trust him to just anyone. Please do this for me."

Well, damn. How could she say no to that? She wondered exactly what Ivy meant about having no one. Didn't everyone have relatives of some kind? But this wasn't the time to discuss it.

"I might end up killing him before this is over," she pointed out. "Are you good with that?"

"I'll owe you big time."

"Yes, you will. By the way"—she tightened her grip on the phone—"you didn't say exactly how long this was for. Just a few weeks, you told me. How long should it take?"

"Just until he gets the cast off his wrist and can get around with crutches. Maybe have a walking cast."

"How long, Ivy?" she demanded.

"Um, I think they said about two months. Or maybe three."

"Three months?" Erin screeched. "Are you kidding me? There's no damn way I'll last here three months."

"Sure you will. Okay, gotta run. Bye."

Erin stood there looking at the phone and wondering how the hell she was going to do this. Besides doing all the fetching and carrying, she had to battle this unwanted attraction to him that just didn't seem to go away, no matter how hard she tried.

Too agitated to get any rest, and accepting that she wouldn't be out of this house anytime soon, she decided to unpack her suitcases and set up her laptop. Then, swallowing the last of her coffee, she headed for the bathroom and a hot shower.

Although maybe what she needed was a cold one.

* * * *

Jake looked at the woman spread out before him on the bed. The rosy tips of her breasts complemented the dark thatch of red hair covering her mound. Slowly he pulled one tight nipple into his mouth, sucking on it, then grazing it lightly with his teeth as it hardened beneath his touch. Erin gave a small moan as she arched her breasts up to him, pushing herself up to his mouth. Lord, he could play with these magnificent breasts forever if he didn't have other areas of her body he wanted to taste and enjoy.

He laced a light kiss at the hollow of her throat where her pulse fluttered before laying a trail of kisses down through the valley between her breasts. Her skin was so soft, like brushed satin, and smelled faintly of roses. Her scent traveled through his body right down to his dick that was already painfully hard.

He took a moment to trace his tongue through the circle of her belly button before moving his mouth lower. He inhaled deeply and the scent of her musk filled his nostrils. She smelled like heaven, maybe even better. He thought for sure he could get drunk from the perfume of her body. And when he dipped his head lower and inhaled again, all the blood in his body headed straight to his already throbbing groin.

He ran his tongue between the lips of her pussy, humming in satisfaction at the delicious taste of her. He wanted to take the time to feast on her, but he didn't think he could wait any longer. He reached into the nightstand drawer and retrieved a condom, then ripped the foil open with his teeth and sheathed himself. At the first thrust into her body, he had to stop and hold his breath, afraid it would be all over in a second if he didn't find some control.

Erin wound her legs around his hips and then drew herself closer to him, locking her ankles together at the small of his back. The feel of her was so exquisite, the tightness of her pussy around him so incredible, he wanted to stay like this forever.

But she pulled herself to him a little more tightly, and that triggered his movements. He wove his fingers into the lush red hair tumbling around her face, holding her head in place so he could look into her eyes, seeing the hazel with its incredible gold flecks. Slowly at first, then faster, he drove in and out of her hot, wet heat, sliding against the slickness of her flesh. She gripped him like a vise with her inner walls, clamping down on him with the force of a fist.

Jake was sure he'd died and gone to heaven. The taste of this woman, her scent, the feel of her, were more sensual than anything he'd ever experienced. More, he told himself, and picked up the pace, thrusting into her harder and faster. He locked his gaze with hers, seeing desire in her eyes as strong as his own.

He drove into her again, stronger this time and—

Jake came awake with a start and looked around, confused. Okay, he was in his room, in his bed, with—

With his hand wrapped around his damn dick, about to explode.

Shit, shit, shit.

Then it hit him. The dream. Erin. Her sexy body beneath him, just as he'd dreamed about every night. Just as he remembered from their one night together. Hot and sweet and so sensuous she drove him right out of his mind. This wasn't the first dream he'd had about her, not by a long shot. While he might not have had an orgasm in the dream, tonight his body was more than ready for it. In other circumstances, he would have made his way to the shower and finished himself off there. But he couldn't even get out of the damn bed by himself right now.

Eyes fastened on the door, he worried that Erin would pick this particular moment to barge in—wait, she never barged. Okay, knock on the door and come in to check on him. And his cock was begging for him to finish, for God's sake.

As aroused as he was it didn't take long. He closed his eyes, imagined her delicious naked body again, and three or four quick strokes finished him off. He felt the semen spill over his fingers, felt the racing of his heart, and forced himself to draw slow breaths to control it. At last the tension eased from his body, his breathing slowed, and he opened his eyes.

Just in time to hear a tap on the door and see it opening.

"Jake? I thought I heard you cry out in here and—" She stopped, still as a statue, with her hand still on the knob of the partially opened door. Her jaw dropped and a delicate red flush crept up her creamy skin.

"Uh, sorry. I thought I heard—I'll, uh, come back later."

"Wait!" he practically shouted the word. "I find myself in a very embarrassing position here. Extremely embarrassing." He blew out a breath. "I'm not sure quite how to explain this to you."

She stood in the doorway, her eyes widening as she took in every bit of his situation. "I, uh, think I can figure it out for myself."

He stared at her as he still clutched his now semi-hard dick, his hand damp and sticky, his shorts not much better, and wondered how much longer she would make him suffer. Or continue to be embarrassed. Finally she chuffed a sigh and moved forward.

Despite the fact that he needed to clean himself up and his leg was beginning to hurt like a motherfucker again, he had to give her credit. She wasn't running like a scared kitten.

"Is this considered one of my executive assistant duties?" She was standing beside the bed now and apparently she had a wicked sense of humor. "Because I didn't see it in my job description."

He wished she'd quit staring at his groin and get on with it. The longer she took the more humiliated he felt.

"The home health care person won't even be here for a couple more hours," he told her. "You don't want me lying here in this mess until then, do you? I mean, come on. I'll beg if that will help."

Would she do it? Shit, he hoped so. He wanted to feel her soft hands on him, any way he could get it.

"I think the embarrassment is enough." Her plump lips curved in a tiny smile. "You are embarrassed, right?" Then she gave an exaggerated sigh. "Maybe I'll just pretend I'm your nurse."

"Whatever it takes," he told her. "You know, you could just bring me a cloth and a towel and I could do it myself."

But that wasn't what he wanted. Could he convey the message without saying it out loud? Did she understand just from the way he looked at her that he really wanted her to take care of him?

"But then I wouldn't be living up to my responsibilities, right? Besides, with your casts and your injuries it will be next to impossible."

That was the damn truth. The thought of her soft hands on his cock and his balls was too much to resist. He watched as she walked into the bathroom, eyes fastened on the delightful sway of her hips. Hips he'd held in his grip while he plunged into her and—

Nope. Not going there. He'd be primed for another little accident. He made himself take deep slow breaths while he listened to the water running. Then she was back, a towel in one hand, a damp washcloth in the other. And a businesslike attitude.

Well, hell.

"Okay, then let's play hospital."

He saw a slight tremor in her hands as she sponged his fingers carefully after he eased his grip on his dick. She dried his hand off, then set the towel on the nightstand with the wash cloth on top of it.

"Don't you want to know how this happened?" His voice was low and thick. "I don't normally just lay here in bed and jerk off."

Her face reddened with a delicate blush. "I think I'll pass. Thanks anyway."

"What if I told you I was dreaming about you?"

"Jake, please."

"Please what?" he teased. "Tell you the details?"

"Please don't tell me anything." She made her voice as noncommittal as possible. "Okay. We have to get those shorts off," she told him, "and I don't think that's going to be a lot of fun for you. I'll be as careful as I can."

"Just do what you have to."

She untied the string on his shorts and began to ease them over his hips and down his legs. He sucked in a breath as she bent his uninjured leg so she could free that one first, then eased the fabric down over the cast. He hadn't taken a pain pill since before he went to sleep, and the places in the damaged leg where they'd operated were throbbing like crazy. When she finally got the shorts free and tossed them to the floor, she picked up the washcloth again, and keeping her eyes averted from his, bathed his cock and his balls. She might pretend she was unaffected, but he saw that blush stain her cheeks again and her hands shook just the tiniest bit.

She dried him off and carried the cloth and towel toward the bathroom.

"There's a hamper in my closet," he called out.

Erin made a sharp turn into his walk-in closet. When she emerged she asked, "Fresh shorts?"

"Third drawer in the dresser on the right hand side."

Getting the clean shorts on was nearly as bad as taking off the old ones. Finally she had him settled again, the pillows behind his head plumped, the ones beneath his injured leg rearranged. She took a step back and studied his face.

"Pain pills," she announced, and headed to the bathroom where she'd stashed them.

"Nope," he ground out, when she was back with them. "Still not taking them."

"Tough guy, aren't you? There's no need for you to lie here in pain, Jake. You had a severe injury to your leg and some complicated surgery. You might even do yourself damage if you don't ease the pain."

"Fine. Fine, fine, fine." He was getting pissed off all over again at the injustice of the whole situation, never mind that she might be right. "Just give the cripple his pills and go about your business."

Desiree Holt

He expected a smart comeback from her, but she just shook out two of his pills and handed them to him with the bottle on his nightstand.

She looked at her watch. "It's seven thirty."

He frowned. "Yeah? And you're all dressed. What the hell time did you get up?"

"Early. I'm an early riser. Would you like some coffee and juice? Your home care person will be here at ten o'clock. When he left yesterday he said that's the time he'll be here every day."

"Did you ever get hold of Ivy?"

"Yes." She nibbled her lip, then wiped all expression from her face. Still, he could see anger blazing in her eyes.

Uh-oh.

"I take it that did not go well. When is she coming over?"

She tightened her fists and shoved them into her pockets. Today she was wearing slim jeans and a soft shirt that draped too nicely over her breasts.

"She's not. She's going out of town."

Jake widened his eyes in shock. "She's not coming here at all? To talk to us? To me? What the hell?"

Erin shrugged. "She's your sister. You know her better than I do. I think she's throwing both of us to the wolves."

"And you're offering me juice and coffee. Does that mean you're staying?"

She shrugged. "So it appears. No one's looking for a replacement, and even I'm not rotten enough to walk out and leave you like this."

Well, well, well. This could get interesting. Even with the pain crawling up his body, the possibilities of the situation sent a surge of pleasure through him. He'd have plenty of time to plead his case and see if he could erase this hard-on she had for him and apparently all football players.

Be nice. Play nice.

He wet his lips. "Thank you for that. I really do appreciate it. And coffee and juice would be nice."

"I thought I'd wait to fix a meal until after your shower and everything. Unless you want something now with the coffee."

"No. I'm not much of a breakfast eater, anyway."

"Fine." She drew in a breath and let it out slowly. "It would probably be good if we sat down together after that and went over things I should know. Any activities of yours you'll be missing, people you need to contact. People you don't want coming to the house."

"You're going to be my bodyguard, too?" He couldn't resist the tease.

She gave him the tiniest grin. "Like you said, I'll just think of it as another guest relations job. I'll be back in a minute with your stuff."

He held in his smile until she was gone from the room. Then, when there was no chance she'd turn around and see him anymore, he pumped his fist in the air.

Yes!

Maybe this broken leg would be good for something after all.

Chapter 7

Erin reread the e-mail Ivy had just sent, with key telephone numbers she might need and more instructions regarding Jake's personal activities. This person can visit him, keep these people away, don't let just anyone speak to him without asking him, etc. etc. etc. She was going to kill her friend. Or maybe just torture her until she begged to be killed. How was she supposed to deal with it, when Jake pushed every one of her sexual buttons, and it seemed he was having the same trouble?

She'd finally accepted she wasn't going to be able to leave. Jake wouldn't even discuss the possibility of the team hiring someone—his damn ego again, as if he had something to be ashamed of—and her conscience wouldn't permit her to just up and walk out, telling Ivy to get her ass over to Jake's and fix things. So here she was, determined now to use all her skills to excel at this job she was stuck with so when she walked away she didn't have any regrets.

Regrets? Does that apply to the sex also, missy?

Deliberately putting anything related to s-e-x out of her mind, she finished separating the big stack of mail she'd placed on the kitchen table. She'd found it on the counter just dumped into a big carton, probably by Ivy the night she'd stayed here. It was obvious no effort had been made to sort through it. She took the liberty of ditching all the unsolicited advertising and solicitation letters in a big trash bag. She discovered people with any kind of notoriety got mail from everywhere and everyone. The rest of it she tried to sort alphabetically, by sender's name. After lunch she'd bring them into the bedroom and go through them with Jake, see if there were any she needed to handle for him.

Handle for him? Okay, so Ivy had told her she'd be kind of an executive assistant. Ha! Talk about putting lipstick on a pig. But she was here, she was doing it, and she'd accepted the fact that wasn't about to change. She needed to pull up her big girl socks and get on with it. The money was good and much appreciated in her situation.

At least they'd gotten past the embarrassing episode where she'd had to clean him up. The rest of the day hadn't been nearly as uncomfortable as she'd expected it to be. Still, although they hadn't mentioned it again, every time she was in his room she saw him watching her through half-closed eyes. Sexual tension hummed in the air. Jake hadn't helped things by lying there all day with his covers thrown back, his swollen cock obvious beneath his flimsy shorts.

"I'm hot," he'd told her every time she suggested he cover up. "It's fucking hot lying in this bed."

She'd offered to turn up the air conditioning, but he told her with blatant hunger in his eyes that air conditioning wouldn't fix his problem. She certainly didn't intend to ask him what would.

Had he really been dreaming about her? What would he think if he knew she'd had an erotic dream about him? When she'd thought about it last night, after she finally got into bed, she'd been hot and cold by turns, her breasts aching and the walls of her sex thrumming. She could not give in to whatever attraction she felt for him. For one thing, in his condition, not much would be possible. For another, and most importantly, she knew she'd be just another notch on his bedpost and she was tired of men like that.

The trouble was, even in the short time she'd been here, she was beginning to have conflicted feelings about Jake Russell. Okay, sure, he was injured and in pain and reluctantly dependent on her for everything. But as bad as he was being, it wasn't nearly as obnoxious as she'd expected.

Wait. No. She wouldn't go there. If she allowed herself to feel sorry for him or make excuses, she'd be—

She'd be nothing. Because she was going to put up an invisible wall between them and keep it there.

She was just putting the rest of the envelopes in a neat stack when the phone rang. It startled her, mostly because there had been so few phone calls since she'd arrived. Coach Raymond, Jim DiMarco, Scott, the doctor's office, innocuous calls like that. Apparently, Ivy had passed the word about her because no one seemed startled that she was answering the phone. But those were the only calls that had come in since she'd arrived a little more than forty-eight hours earlier. No personal calls. She thought that very strange for a man in Jake's position.

All the calls she'd been expecting today had already come in this morning. Should she answer this? She hadn't seen a landline phone in Jake's bedroom, making it obvious he was not taking any calls. Ivy had said this would be part of the job, so when the phone rang twice more she figured she'd better pick up. She just hoped it wasn't some airhead groupie or a glamour girl looking to give Jake her own special brand of healing medicine.

Oh, wait. Ivy had been specific about telling her the number was unlisted. Still, Jake could have given it out and—

Oh, answer the damn phone, idiot.

Lifting the receiver, she cleared her throat. "Jake Russell's residence."

God, didn't she just sound like a prissy housekeeper. What was next? A uniform and starched apron?

"Who the hell is this?" a gravelly sounding man demanded.

"This is his—" His what? "His personal assistant."

The man on the other end of the call laughed so hard she could hear him wheeze. "His what? Are you shitting me?"

"I am his personal assistant," she repeated, digging her nails into her palm. "May I ask who this is?"

"It's—" *Wheeze, wheeze.* "I'm—" *Wheeze, wheeze.* "Tell him Santos is on the line."

"Santos," she repeated, and all her hotel training kicked in. "May I ask if that's a first name or a last?"

"You mean you don't know Golden Legs Santos, the Mustangs' hot wide receiver? Who are you, anyway? Do you live under a rock?"

Erin silently counted to ten. "Not all of us are addicted to football, Mr. Santos."

"Oooooh." He made a teasing sound. "Putting me in my place, right? So, honey, if you don't like football, what are you doing with Big Jake? And why the hell isn't he answering his own phone?"

"Mr. Russell is recovering from a serious injury and complicated surgery." She put as much authority into her voice as she could muster. "He doesn't wish to be disturbed."

"Oh, honey, you sound like you could be disturbing him a lot. Wanna disturb me for a change?"

Erin reached for her self-control. This was exactly why she hated all jocks and wished them sailing off on a garbage scow. "I'll tell Mr. Russell you called."

"How about telling him I want to speak to him?" Now the man was getting belligerent. "What's the matter? Doesn't he want to talk to his friends?"

"If you're such a good friend, why didn't you call his cell? Don't you have the number?"

"I, uh..." A pause. "I lost it. But it's all good. He'll take my call. Just tell him it's me."

Erin had an idiotic desire to reach through the connection and smack this guy. She wondered if both he and his ego fit in the same room together.

"Fine. Hold, please."

She tromped off down the hall to Jake's bedroom. He was lying there with the television on but muted, his eyes closed. She waited a moment, then started to turn away.

"I'm awake," he told her. "Who's on the phone?"

"Someone named Santos. When I asked for his full name he wanted to know why hadn't I heard of Golden Legs Santos. He says he wants to talk to you."

Jake's eyes flew open and anger flashed across his face. "That asshole. Absolutely not. Not even if he was the last person on earth."

"Wow! What did he do to you?"

"Not to me specifically but to everyone in general. He's an immature jerkhead who things he's God's gift to the world. Tell him I'm asleep."

"Okay. If that's what you want." She trudged back to the kitchen. "Sorry, but Mr. Russell is asleep."

"But—"

"I'll tell him you called." She barely restrained herself from slamming the receiver back in the cradle. What an ass.

She looked at the clock. It was almost lunchtime. Jake always slept after his shower and shave and whatever else the guy did for him. She was sure with his inability to handle himself physically he was exhausted by everything. But he'd said earlier he wanted lunch so she walked back to the master suite.

"Did you get rid of the jackass?" Jake wanted to know.

"I did, but I don't think he was happy."

"Tough shit." Jake made a rude sound. "He thinks he's a one-name celebrity, like that singer, Prince."

"So what *is* his name?"

"Gary Santos, but he thinks that sounds too ordinary." Jake grunted. "He doesn't even qualify for ordinary, if you ask me."

She bit her lip. "I hate to say this, but I think he needs some etiquette lessons."

Jake laughed, a rusty sound as if he hadn't done it for a while. She was sure he hadn't had much to laugh about lately.

"That asshole. I hope you put him in his place."

Oh, yes, she certainly had. "I told him you weren't taking calls. I also suggested that if he was really a friend, he'd have your cell phone number."

Jake grinned at her, a panty-melting smile that had her biting her lip. *No, no, no.*

"You are so damn right. I don't want to talk to him or see his ugly face."

"I take it you don't like him?"

"No shit." He shifted his position slightly, hitching himself up a little higher against the pillows. "He's another wide receiver on the team with an ego bigger than the whole city of Austin. He thinks my injury is his ticket to stardom."

She lifted an eyebrow. "How so?"

"He's not a regular starter, so he figures he'll get more playing time now that I'm out of commission. He wants to come here and stick it in my face."

"Nice guy." She studied him. "By the way, he's the first personal call you've had. Mostly it's just been your agent and people from the team office. How come your phone isn't ringing off the hook?"

Jake rubbed the thigh of his injured leg above the cast. Erin was sure it ached a lot.

"Coach Raymond put out the word to the team members to lay off for a few days. I asked Ivy to tell the same thing to our friends." He closed his eyes for a moment. "I really don't feel like talking to anyone."

"I can understand that. So what did you do with the phone from this room? You do have one in here, don't you? Although I'm sure you don't get many calls on it."

He pointed to the drawer. "Stuck it in there. I told you I'm in no mood to answer phone calls." He lifted a shoulder. "I believe that's your job, right?"

"Sure. Whatever." She frowned. "And your cell? Did you decide to hide that away, too?"

"Same place. As a matter of fact, why don't you just take it and keep it with you. That way if it rings you can answer it and tell whoever it is to go to hell."

"Jake!" She was appalled. "Why would I want to do that?"

"I told you. I'm not in the mood to see anyone. They've all been asked to give me some space." He grimaced. "But I guess we're out of space."

"I'm sure people are concerned about you."

"Yeah, yeah. Right. I don't want anyone to tell me everything's going to be okay when I know there's a chance it won't. I don't want anyone fussing over me or telling me how much they miss me on the field. And I don't want any of the guys showing up with big-breasted, little-brained females thinking they'll cheer me up. I'm in no mood for bullshit. Period."

"But they're your friends," she protested.

"Ha!" Anger cut lines in his face and flashed in his eyes. "I'm really not that close to any of the guys. And the others? Only when I'm a big star on the field. Otherwise they're just going to come pay their obligatory visit, then go out and tell everyone what a mess I am right now."

She wanted to tell him that he was all wrong, that his friends would not do that. But she'd seen enough of these guys in action to know the only thing important to them was their ego. A major reason why they—and Jake—were on her No-No list.

She didn't know if she wanted to smack him for his pity party or feel sorry for the mess he was in through no fault of his own. More than that, she'd noticed that as they talked, his cock, which had been blissfully at rest, was again swollen and pushing against the flimsy fabric of his shorts.

Deliberately averting her eyes, she opened the nightstand drawer, making sure to stand as far away from the bed as she could. Sure enough, next to his cell was the landline phone, just tossed in. She lifted out the cell and stared at it.

"Are you sure you don't want to keep this in here? I feel funny with your phone."

"There's no one I want to talk to," he said.

"What about all your little cuddle bunnies? I expected them to be swarming all over you."

"I have a fucking broken leg," he snapped. "And I haven't had any so-called cuddle bunnies. They bore me."

"Uh-huh. That's what they all say." Like Trace McKay. She bit her lower lip. "Okay, we have some other things to go over. I thought I'd order some lunch. Maybe we could eat together and talk."

"And where would we do that?" He waved at his leg. "I have trouble enough just getting to the bathroom and back."

She glanced at the sliding doors that led out to a patio. "I thought it might be pleasant to eat out there. I can help you."

Desiree Holt

Frustration flashed in his eyes again. "And if I fall? Are you going to pick me up?"

"Jake, you could fall when I'm helping you to the bathroom. Quit being such an ass."

"I'm not an ass, I'm a cripple."

"Oooh! Time for a pity party?"

"I deserve one." He pounded his hand on the nightstand, then winced.

"Go ahead," she told him. "Break your other hand."

He glared at her. "Could I have a little sympathy and understanding here? This isn't exactly a picnic."

Erin shook her head. One minute she felt sorry for him, the next she wanted to kill him. She knew his emotions were all over the place as he tried to deal with what was happening to him. Despite her lingering resentment at being here, she could empathize with him and his predicament. But enough was enough.

"I don't think sympathy is what you need right now. Are you in a shitty situation? Yes. No question about it. Could it be worse? Yes. Could you deal with it better? I happen to think so."

"You're all heart," he snapped. "Thanks for being so understanding."

Erin had to stifle the urge to smack him. Okay, he was in a bad situation, but he didn't have to act like a little kid whose party had been spoiled. "I do understand. I even understand why you might not want to see people, although I think your closest friends might cheer you up. But..." She held up a hand. "You have two choices. You can sulk and rage and feel sorry for yourself. Or you can be pissed off but make the best of it. If I'm going to do this job properly we have things to discuss."

"Yeah?" He scowled at her. "Like what?"

"Stuff. I thought it might change your adorable attitude if I got you outside for a little while. It's a nice day and fresh air does wonders for the disposition."

"There's nothing wrong with my damn fucking disposition." Irritation laced his voice.

Erin burst out laughing. "I rest my case." She managed to swallow her smile. "Ivy said in her notes that you like Mexican food. I found a menu from a Mexican restaurant near here, so I thought I'd place an order. They menu says they deliver. That work for you?"

"Yeah. Fine, whatever."

"When the food gets here," she told him, "we're eating on the patio. No more bed trays for you. End of discussion."

She turned to leave the room, but Jake reached out and grabbed her wrist. His fingers seared her skin like individual brands. Once again, when she tried to tug her hand free, he tightened his grip.

"Why do you always want to run away from me? Why are you afraid to let me touch you?"

"I'm not." She yanked and he released his grip. "I just don't think we need to have a lot of touching here. Except, of course, when I help you move around."

"I don't bite." His voice was soft, like a caress. "Or maybe I do, in the right places."

First he wanted to take her head off, and then he wanted to seduce her. He was all over the place, and she had to figure out how to deal with it. She stuck his cell phone in her pocket and headed for the door. "I'll be back when the food gets here."

* * * *

Jake watched her leave the room, eyes fastened on the delicious sway of her hips and the curve of her delectable ass. His good hand curved automatically, as if cupping its nice roundness. He itched to touch her again, to caress her smooth skin and inhale her spicy scent. He'd relived that night over and over and over again, the memories ingrained in his brain. Witness the embarrassing evidence of a wet dream she'd caught when she walked in on him still fisting his cock. When he'd calmed down after discovering this little situation his sister had engineered, he'd hoped maybe they could pick up where they left off, or maybe start again, if that was what it took.

Not only did Erin Bass have a very low judgment of football players, she had a temper to go with it. Which, in turn, spiked his own. Being laid up the way he was, his season on the field down the drain, didn't do much for his disposition, which he was sure only added to her opinion of him.

He wondered if Ivy had bothered to tell her exactly how long this job would last. He'd hardly been able to believe it himself. Three months in the cast. Three fucking months before he could even begin to start therapy. No matter that during that time, if the x-rays showed him healing properly, he could graduate to a walking cast. Never mind that in another week he might get the soft cast off his wrist.

Oh, and that would be another pleasant interlude. He had to go to the doctor's office to get both the leg and wrist x-rayed to check the progress. How the hell was Erin going to manage that? Getting him back and forth across the room was hard enough.

Shit, shit, shit.

He closed his eyes and leaned back against the pillows, trying to calm himself before he burst a blood vessel. His leg hurt and his wrist ached, but he wasn't going to take the damn pain pills. It had been three weeks already, and he wasn't going to let himself become dependent on them. He'd had worse pain when he *hadn't* had broken bones, so he could gut it out.

He did his best to clear his mind and focus on something pleasant. Immediately, the image of Erin naked beneath him popped into his mind, and that certainly wasn't going to relax him. *Water*, he thought. *Water is soothing and calming. I'll try that.*

While he was mentally searching for something peaceful to focus on, he dozed off, startled awake when something touched his arm. He blinked and saw Erin beside the bed, gently touching him. As soon as she saw him open his eyes, she pulled her hand away.

"I knocked," she told him, "but you didn't answer. I worried that something had happened to you."

"Like what?" He looked as if he wanted to chew nails. "Hasn't enough happened already?"

"I'm glad to see a nap juiced up that sweet personality of yours. I came in to tell you the food is here. I'm going to set up everything on the table outside before I help you to a chair."

"Fine. Fine, fine, fine. Whatever."

"Everything will be set up in a minute."

He watched her as she fetched lunch from the kitchen, then drinks, and finally a large stack of mail and her iPad. Getting outside was just as much fun as moving always was, especially since he needed to make a quick pit stop first. To her credit, Erin never complained, never said a cross word about it, even though he knew juggling his unwieldy body wasn't easy for her.

Out on the patio, she pulled over another chair to rest his leg on and made sure he would be able to eat as comfortably as possible before settling herself.

"Just FYI," she told him. "The maid is here cleaning the rest of the house. She's going to do your bedroom and bathroom while we're out here. I figured that man cave needed airing out."

"Thanks. I guess."

"I'm overwhelmed with your graciousness."

Jake made a rude noise and turned to his food.

He eyed the plate in front of him. Tamales, rice, and refried beans. One of his favorite meals, and easy to eat with only one functioning hand.

Good. He'd told her to get Mexican, but too many women would have ordered food that required a dexterity he didn't have at the moment.

Erin pulled his cell phone from her pocket and set it on the table beside the other things she'd brought.

"What's all that?" He indicated the things next to her as he cut off a piece of tamale.

"Mail." She chewed a bite of food and swallowed. "I threw out all the junk mail, and this is what's left. I think it's a three-week accumulation. I hope there isn't anything important in it."

He shrugged. "Probably not. If it was urgent they would have called my agent or the team office."

"Oh, by the way." She picked up his cell phone and looked through the messages. "I hope you don't mind. I checked your calls, since you've had this turned off. I figured that if someone really needed to get hold of you they'd have called the landline."

"I told you, they know better than to bother me." He forked another bite of tamale into his mouth.

"Still. I assumed you didn't mind me looking, since you told me to take the phone."

"So what did you find? Nothing important, I'm sure."

"Joe Reilly called. Said to get back to him when you felt like talking." Erin glanced at him. "Wasn't he injured, too? I seem to remember he had to retire."

"Good shot." His fingers tightened on the fork he held. "Maybe he wants to tell me being gimpy and out of the action isn't so bad after all."

"Quit it." She said the words in a normal voice, almost as an afterthought. "Stop feeling sorry for yourself. I think it's great that you have friends interested in what's happening to you. Maybe share their feelings with you."

"Guys don't share their feelings." He stabbed at the food on his plate.

"Oh, right, right. I forgot. Maybe you don't even have feelings."

"What else?" he demanded.

"Someone named Mandy called five times and left messages. Apparently it's very important that you call." She grinned. "She stressed the word 'very.' I'm surprised she didn't call the landline."

"She doesn't have the number." Bubbly Mandy, with the big breasts and the little brain. Why the hell had he ever given her his cell number? Oh, wait, he hadn't. "I hung out with her a few times but that's all."

"Hung out?" She cocked her head. "Define hung out."

He shrugged. "You know. Hung out. Some joker probably thought it would be a cute idea to give her my number." He shook his head. "Assholes."

"That seems to be your latest favorite word." Erin chuckled. "Shall I call her back for you?"

"Hell, no." The answer popped out automatically but then he thought better of it. "Yes. Call her. Tell her I'm out of commission, you're my personal assistant, and I won't be seeing her again."

He wasn't looking at her, but he could feel her eyes boring into him.

"Are you for real? You want *me* to break up with your girlfriend?"

"She's not my girlfriend." He shoved a forkful of rice in his mouth, hoping to deter further discussion.

"Well, she's something. She has your cell number, and she apparently thinks it's okay to keep calling."

"Mandy was a mistake. She—"

"See?" she broke in. "That's what I mean about all you guys. You want to know why I didn't want to pursue anything with you after that night? This is a very good example."

Jake took a slow drink of his iced tea. "What we had that night is so far above anything I had with Mandy they aren't even on the same planet. I would have made you see that if you'd given me an opportunity."

"Easy for you to say now." She picked up her iPad and made a note. "Call Mandy. All right. Some of your teammates want to come by and see you. The team is on the road for the next two weeks, but they'd like to stop by after that. Would you like them to come at the same time or separately?"

"What makes you think I want to see them at all?" Just what he needed. Guys still active delivering a dose of sympathy. Or worse yet, obviously relieved that it hadn't happened to them.

She looked as if she wanted to say something, then changed her mind and made another note. "I'll let them know I'll get back to them when the team is back in town. Maybe your pleasant personality will return by then."

Jake glared at her. "You know, I can do without the snarky remarks, Miss Bass."

"And I can do without the temper tantrums, Mr. Russell." She spoke in a cool, even tone, gave him a phony smile, and delicately took another bite of her food.

They ate in silence for a very long moment. Obviously she was prepared to outwait him for as long as it took. He forced himself to swallow another bite of food, then another. Finally, he put his fork down.

"Okay, I'm sorry that I'm an ass. I apologize. Can we get on with this? Please?"

Was that a teeny smile crooking one corner of her mouth? If it was, it disappeared almost at once. She picked up her iPad and turned to the Notes section again.

"Coach Raymond called while I was in the kitchen. He wanted to know if you had lost your cell phone."

"What did you tell him?"

This time she actually grinned. "I said no, only your mind."

"Ha ha ha. So what did he want?"

"You have an appointment with Dr. Moline next week." She looked at her notes again. "They want to take x-rays to make sure your leg is healing properly. Also, he is hoping to remove the soft cast from your left wrist. You might be graduating to crutches."

"Stop the presses." He took another swallow of his tea. "I can hardly wait for that three ring circus."

"I appreciate your enthusiasm."

"Tell me something." He waited until she looked at him. "Exactly how am I going to get to the doctor's office when it takes all we've both got just to get me to the bathroom? Did your boyfriend Coach Raymond tell you that, by any chance?"

"As a matter of fact, he did. He's sending one of the trainers to take you. I'm sure he'll be able to handle you a lot better than I do." She took another bite of food. "The appointment is next Tuesday at eleven o'clock. Coach is going to schedule your home care for your shower and shave earlier than usual that day."

"Good. I'd hate to show up at the doctor's dirty and smelling."

Again a smile teased her lips. He wondered how hard he'd have to push her to get her riled up again. Did he even want to? She wasn't any happier with this situation than he was, so maybe he should cut her some slack. Except she wasn't in this fucking cast, and she obviously wasn't half as horny as he was. Damn it.

He slogged through a few other messages with her, and then they attacked the mail. He gave mostly one or two word answers until they came to a letter from Lynne Corday at The Good Shepherd House. No, he wasn't discussing this with Erin. He could just imagine her comments. Instead he held his hand out for it.

"I'll handle this one myself."

She raised an eyebrow. "Really? Must be pretty special if it trumps the coach, your agent, your teammates and—oh, yeah—Mandy."

"This has nothing to do with anything." He tried to grab the letter from her, but she held it just out of his reach. "Give it to me."

Her eyes widened at the rough tone of his voice. "What on earth is this? Are you doing something you're ashamed of? When I talked to Ms. Corday she spoke very highly of you."

"You called her?" He stared at her, unbelieving.

"I returned her call. She left a message on your cell, saying it was important. You didn't seem in a telephone mood, and no, I did not put her on the same list with Eye Candy Mandy."

Jake actually had to laugh. "Eye Candy Mandy. I'll have to remember that one. I will say, you certainly nailed it."

"Let me guess. Double D breasts, Botox lips, and clothes two sizes too small."

He chuckled, the tension broken slightly. "You've been peeking."

"I didn't have to. I know the type. So what's with Lynne Corday? Come on, 'fess up. How bad can it be?"

"It might ruin my asshole image," he pointed out.

"It would have to be pretty drastic. Come on, my curiosity is really ramped up now."

He sat back in the chair. He really tried to keep this part of his life out of the limelight. He wasn't one of those guys who hogged the media or did things for attention. He had a reason for the things he committed to, a very personal reason he had hardly ever discussed with anyone. His agent, Scott, knew. Coach Raymond. A couple of his close friends. That was all. He had moved way beyond that, a lot of it with the help of the Granite Falls Coyotes. He didn't think he was ready to share it with a woman who pushed all his buttons from behind an invisible wall.

"Well?" she prompted. "I didn't think this was such a hard question. I can look them up on the Internet, you know."

"No." He nearly shouted the word. "No, I'll tell you." He held out his glass. "Can I have some more iced tea first?" He waited while she filled his glass and took two healthy swallows. "The Good Shepard House is a shelter for abused women and children. We give them a safe place to stay and provide support until we can relocate them."

Erin lifted her gaze from her plate, a stunned look on her face. "But that's fabulous. Why wouldn't you want to let people know about it? Why don't you let everyone know what you're doing?"

"I have my reasons."

"Like what?" she pushed.

Controlled anger rolled off him in waves. "Like reasons that are my own. Okay? Can you just tell me what she wants, and we can move along here?"

She raked her fingers through her hair. "I don't understand, but okay. I guess it's not my business. She wants to know if she can come by and meet with you for a little while. Any time in the next couple of weeks, she said. At your convenience."

"Oh, great. She'll see me all wrecked up like this."

"Jake, I'm sure she's seen people with broken legs before. It doesn't diminish you." He could feel her stare. "She said she had some key things to go over with you."

Damn. There was no getting away from it. He knew what Lynne Corday wanted. He had created a special fund for some renovations and expansion of The Good Shepard House. There were details that needed approval. He also wanted to beef up security and add to the clothing and other items they provided for the women and kids who showed up most times with literally nothing.

"Make it for after I come back from the doctor's," he told Erin. "And I'd appreciate it if you just did not mention any of this to anyone."

"Not that it's any of my business," she said, "but are you planning a fundraiser for them?"

He shook his head. "We don't do public fundraisers."

"Why not?" Curiosity was stamped all over her face.

"A few of us fund it privately. No one wants publicity for it. Can you please leave it at that? Please?"

He'd very quietly managed to gather a small group who provided the financing for the place, since keeping it under the radar was essential. No one, not even Erin, who made every nerve in his body twitch, was going to pry it out of him.

When she didn't answer, he threw his napkin on the table. "I think that's it for today. Can you bother yourself to help me back to the bed?"

Her face instantly sobered. "I'm sorry. I didn't mean to push. It's just I was so surprised that—I mean—"

"That a jackass like me could do something so serious? So worthwhile?"

"You're right." She tucked her hair behind her ears. "It was thoughtless and rude of me. Let's just finish the rest of this pile."

"I'm done for today. I need to get back to my bed." When she didn't move, he added, "Now."

"I'm sorry. Of course."

He cursed silently until he was settled back in his room again. He clenched his fists while Erin fussed with the pillows supporting his cast, brought him a fresh glass of iced tea and set it on his nightstand, turned on his big screen television, and handed him the remote.

"I'm fine. Just clear off the patio table and leave me be." He was exhausted from the effort of moving around and irritated that he found himself in a situation where someone had to answer his phone, read his mail, and pester him with unwanted questions.

She paused on her way out to the patio and turned back to him. "I'm sorry. I didn't mean to offend you. I was just surprised…I mean…never mind. I disrespected your boundaries and I'm sorry."

He watched from beneath lowered lids while she cleared everything off the patio table and carried it back to the kitchen. When she came back to close his door, she looked as if she wanted to say something again, but he closed his eyes in a deliberate signal to leave him alone. He heard the soft click of the lock and let out the breath he'd been holding.

He had no intention of publicizing anything about The Good Shepard House now or ever, nor did he plan to unload on Erin about it. Erin. What the hell was he going to do about her? He wanted her with a fierce hunger. At least the little set-to over lunch had effectively defused his cock so it rested limply against his body.

His only question was, for how long?

Chapter 8

He was waiting for her in the same position and the same state of undress—naked—as he usually was. Heat burned in his eyes as he watched her adjust the pillows beneath his cast. When her bare breasts brushed against his good leg, he let out a soft groan that brought a smile to Erin's lips.

"Easy, stud," she murmured.

He was always so primed, his fingers wrapped around his thick, swollen cock as if holding it in check. And maybe he was, because it never took long for that first orgasm.

They had to be very careful because of his injuries, but it amazed her how inventive they'd become. Their lust, or whatever they might call it, was always on a hair trigger. It seemed no matter how often they were together, how many orgasms they gave each other, it was never enough.

She still carried the image of the scene when she'd walked into his room after he had what was obviously a major wet dream. Copious semen spread over his fingers and hand and even dripped down to his balls. When she'd cleaned him up that day, she'd had to call on all her willpower not to use her tongue to do it, to lick every drop from his skin.

Looking at him now, she licked her lips at the memory of her first taste of him. Pleasantly salty and tart, like a great bedtime snack. It had become one of her favorite things to do with him. And it was the first thing on her agenda tonight.

"Straddle me backwards," he told her in a rasping voice.

Usually she knelt between his thighs to give her access to every area of his groin.

She frowned. "Why?"

"Because I want my hands all over that gorgeous ass of yours. One of these days when I'm back in one piece again, I'm going to take you back here and give you the best orgasm of your life."

Shivers skated over her spine at his words, and the walls of her pussy fluttered with need. That was one thing she'd never done with anyone, always believing it was too personal to share except with someone very special. But Jake was steadily becoming that "someone special" to her, despite her initial resistance to him. Now the image of that act ramped up the desire surging through her.

"I'll have to sit on your chest," she warned him.

"Exactly what I had in mind." He moved his hands to give her room. "Come on. Bring that sweet ass up here to me."

With very precise movements, she arranged herself so she sat squarely on his very hard, very firm chest, legs on either side of his hips. Licking her lips in anticipation, she curled the fingers of one hand around his very hard shaft and leaned forward to lap the soft velvet of the head. Teasingly she dipped the tip of her tongue into the slit, bringing a gasp of pleasure from Jake.

"Like that, do you?" she asked.

"You know it, babe. That tongue of yours is a magic wand."

"Oh," she teased, "I think you're the one with the magic wand."

She bent to her task again, a most pleasant one, sliding her fingers from root to tip and back in a steady rhythm, punctuating the strokes with swirls of her tongue around the head. With her other hand she cupped his balls, loving the feel of the soft skin that contained them. She worked his cock, and she manipulated his balls, humming against him in satisfaction.

The contact of his hands on the cheeks of her ass sent an electrical shock through her, one that intensified when he trailed his fingertips through the hot crevice separating those globes. When he pressed the tip of one finger hard against her rear opening, she sucked in a breath, dragging her teeth the length of his hard dick.

"Jesus, babe," Jake gasped. "I'm so primed I can come any second."

"That's because you can't wait for me to get here," she teased, "and always start without me."

"Actually, it's because just thinking of you naked like this with your mouth on me gets me so hot I have to squeeze tight to keep from going off by myself again."

"I should have licked you clean with my mouth that day instead of just cleaning you up."

His body tightened beneath her. "Well, here's your chance. Do it hard, babe. Real hard."

She took him in her mouth again and sucked, pulled, and squeezed until in seconds he erupted, spurting into her mouth like a geyser. Her throat worked rhythmically as she swallowed the thick semen, relishing its taste. When she had milked him dry, she drew her mouth slowly up the length of him, gave the soft head one last lick, and sighed.

Moving carefully, she turned herself around and knelt between his thighs. His face was flushed with the aftereffects of his release, and his eyes had darkened almost to a rich chocolate. His chest heaved with the effort to breathe steadily, and she was sure his heart rate was above the normal line on the chart.

Her own body was already aroused, even more so as she licked her lips to catch the last lingering taste of his cum. Her pussy throbbed with need and her nipples just begged for his mouth or his hands.

As if reading her thoughts, he lifted his hands, albeit a little unsteadily, cupped her breasts, and pinched her nipples between thumb and forefingers. She sucked in a breath, leaning into his touch, wanting—

Erin sat up in bed, heart racing, her breath trapped in her throat, stunned to find herself pinching her nipples.

Holy shit!

This was so not good. Not good at all.

She had to stop having these erotic dreams about this man. Surely she had more discipline than this. Maybe she should have brought her vibrator with her, but Mr. Big Guy had somehow seemed inappropriate for this situation. Instead, she existed in a constant state of sexual frustration for a man she couldn't allow herself to care for.

Just like before, she threw back the covers and headed for the bathroom. Water. She needed a cold drink of water. Always did after one of these intense, scorching dreams. Then she dampened a washcloth and ran it over the clammy skin of her face. She really could use a shower, but when she checked the time on her cell phone, she saw it was two o'clock in the morning. The shower would have to wait until she got up for good.

She slid back beneath the covers and pulled them up to her chin. Her body still throbbed with need, and her brain whirled with the images from the dream. Images she had not been able to block since the day she'd walked in on Jake with his dick in his hand. What the hell was she supposed to do? How had she ever thought she could last all this time? Bad on her for letting Ivy play on her sympathy and her financial situation.

Since the ill-fated lunch, they had been tiptoeing around each other like two tigers in a cage, waiting for the first one to pounce. They'd established a routine and never varied from it. He'd gone back to having his meals on a tray in bed, exchanging only the minimum amount of words with her. He watched television, napped, or sulked. Those seemed to be his main activities. Even when she helped him across the room to the bathroom and back, they might as well have been two strangers.

Well, she told herself, *isn't this what you wanted?*

They had added one activity to their routine that was both good and bad. Dr. Moline had sent a therapist to show her some of the simple exercises Jake needed to do with his uninjured leg and wrist so he wouldn't lose his flexibility. Of course he bitched about everything and touching him set off fires raging along her nerves and in her very susceptible pussy. Keeping her objectivity was getting to be harder and harder. Talk about torture.

Still, she wondered what kind of hot button The Good Shepard House was. It had certainly sent him into full retreat, deep into a shell she had been unable to breech.

Lying there, she ticked off the chores she'd completed. She'd called Eye Candy Mandy back, blocking out the sound of the screech when Erin told her Jake was not accepting calls or visitors.

"But he'll see me," she'd insisted. "He always wants to see me. Are you sure he knows I called?"

"He was very specific that he's not taking phone calls or seeing visitors," Erin had told her with as much patience as she could muster. "He asks you to respect his wishes."

"Hmmm." Silence. "Okay, maybe I'll wait a few days and then just show up." She'd laughed, low and sultry. "I promise he won't turn me away."

"That's a very a bad idea. I'd hate to call someone to throw you out."

"Wait. Just who did you say you were?"

"I'm his personal assistant," Erin had told her in a smooth voice.

"Well, he gets personal with me, too," Mandy had snapped. "We'll just see who calls the shots here." She'd clicked off.

Erin shrugged. Oh well, if the bimbo showed up, she'd figure out what to do with her. Anyway, first she'd have to get past the gate code.

She'd also returned the other calls Jake had agreed to let her handle, including the one to Joe Reilly.

"We sort of lost touch with each other," Joe had said, regret in his voice. "We were tight in high school, but then we went to different universities and got drafted by different teams. He should know there are a lot of the Coyotes still around in San Antonio and Austin. Not all of them are still playing. Some of them didn't even go pro. But we're trying to reconnect with each other."

"I'm sure he'd love to be included," Erin had told him.

"My wife started a Facebook page. Coyotes Win." He'd chuckled "A little corny but it works for us. I'll check and see if he has a Facebook account and send him a message."

"I'll tell him about it, too."

"So when do you think it would be okay to come by?" Joe asked. "The Coyotes are going to retire his number the last game of the season, and I'd like to do some prep on it."

"I'd say call me back in a couple of weeks. He's really not into company right now."

"I'll bet this injury really rocked him," Joe had guessed.

"Yes, it has. He's sure his life will be over if he doesn't get to play his last couple of years."

"I may be able to help him out with that." Joe had given a short laugh. "Show him there really is life after football."

"That would really be great. How about if you call me back in two weeks and we'll test the waters?"

"Good deal. Talk to you then." Jake was going to be very busy two weeks from now.

Yesterday she'd gotten a text from her bank about a deposit processing in her account. She'd given the account number to Ivy who told her she'd be paid by direct deposit. Even knowing what she'd been promised, the amount still astonished her. It also nagged her conscience. For that much money, surely she could put aside her prejudice against football players in general and Jake in particular.

But that was easier said than done, especially since the nagging surge of lust that she felt every time she was near him completely clouded her judgment. The most difficult times for her were whenever she had to touch him, like helping him exercise his uninjured limbs. And he sure didn't make it easy for her, knowing every touch pushed her buttons. By now her nerves were stretched tighter than rubber bands.

Today was his doctor's appointment. Hopefully he'd get the damn soft cast off his wrist, they'd fit him with crutches, and he could at least get himself back and forth to the bathroom. She was torn between saving her sanity and living up to her bargain.

And you aren't ready to let go of Jake Russell yet, kiddo.

Now where had that come from? Her inner self? If so, her inner self needed a stern talking to. She also needed to figure out how to stop these stupid dreams.

Sighing, she pulled the covers over her head and set her inner alarm clock for four hours. Jake's helper would be here early today to get him ready for the doctor, and she had things to do.

* * * *

Jake came awake slowly, blinking his eyes at the sunlight slanting into the room. He had told Erin to leave the blinds open so he could enjoy the light. At the moment, getting out of bed to adjust them himself wasn't an option. He lay back on the pillows, drew in a long breath, and let it out very slowly.

He knew he was acting like a real shithead to Erin. It wasn't her fault. Anyone would have asked the same questions she did. It was his sore point. There was a part of his life buried so deep he refused to discuss it with anyone. As far as he was concerned, his life began when he and his mother moved to Granite Falls. Her job and the football team had been his saviors. And Coach Fenelli. The team had been like a brotherhood, and even though he had lost touch with many of them, they were still and always would be his family.

They had quite literally saved his life. Made him who he was today. Gave him the first and only sense of self-worth. That was why football was his life. Without it, he had no idea who he was. Or who he would then become. How could he ever be worthy of Erin or someone like her? If he lost that validation, what would become of him?

He really ought to try reconnecting with some of the guys. Maybe while he was lying here, feeling sorry for himself, he'd at least try to look them up and see where everyone was now. Scott had mentioned something about a Facebook page, but he hadn't paid a lot of attention. It wasn't as if he actually had to contact them, but he could satisfy his curiosity about what path everyone had taken.

Maybe, if he presented it to a select few of them, those who would not probe and ask personal questions, he could tap them for Good Shepard. No publicity. That was definitely not in his wheelhouse. But there had to be others who would do it just for the good of the cause. To help people who really, really needed it.

It might even get his attention off Erin.

Ha! Fat chance.

Then he needed to figure out how to get in her good graces, if that was even possible now. He was starting even lower than square one. Okay, he'd see what the doctor had to say today and get an idea of his mobility. Then he'd think about what to do.

* * * *

"Well, I'd say you got good news today." Erin poured coffee into two mugs and carried them to the kitchen table. "No soft cast. Exchanged the walker for crutches."

"Yeah, hurray." Jake lifted his mug in a mock salute and sipped the hot liquid.

He had insisted she go with him to the doctor, and she hadn't wanted to upset him when she didn't know what the results of the visit would be. The driver DiMarco had sent to pick them up was very pleasant, joking with Jake as he wrestled him in and out of the car.

She sat down across the table from Jake. "Your wrist has healed nicely. Your leg looked good on the x-rays. I'd count that as positive. And look. You're sitting at the kitchen table instead of back in your bedroom." She waited as long as she could for him to answer. "Right?" she prompted.

"Yes. Right." He looked over at her and—damn!—he actually managed an almost-smile. "Look, I apologize for the other day. You pushed some buttons you didn't know about and I reacted badly."

"Yes, you did." She wasn't letting him off the hook. She waited to see what else he might say. Then she sighed. "Okay, okay. It's your business and I'm not going to get into it. You've had a pretty rough morning, been hauled around and jostled a lot. How about a little nap before lunch?"

"Nap?"

She grinned. "I changed your sheets while Nurse Charlie had you in the shower this morning and sprayed freshener in your bedroom."

He spewed his coffee. "Nurse Charlie?"

She giggled. "My little name for him." God, it felt so good to have that angry tension gone.

"You didn't have to change my sheets, you know. Delia comes again tomorrow. She could have done it when she does the laundry."

"Darn." She snapped her fingers. "And I was so looking forward to playing with your shorts."

He stared at her, and then his mouth curved in a wide grin. She suddenly realized what she'd said and wanted to slide under the table. Instead she took both their coffee cups, carried them to the sink, rinsed them, and stuck them in the dishwasher.

"Come on, let's get you back to bed."

Again that wicked grin. "Are you coming with me?"

Right. Think before you speak, idiot.

"Not exactly. Here's a chance to try out those new crutches." She frowned. Could he handle them? "You feel good about using them after you practiced at the doctor's office?"

"I guess we'll find out."

Erin got them from where she'd leaned them against the wall, helped him up from his chair as best she could, and guided him until he had them properly under his arms. It was impossible to do anything without touching him, and the mere contact with his body, even through the soft material of his shirt, sent fingers of flame whisking through her bloodstream. She bit down on her bottom lip in an effort to control her errant, unwanted feeling of sexual need that always seemed to consume her whenever they made contact.

Although their progress down the hallway was halting, it was a major improvement over the walker. She was sure his ability as an athlete and his training had a lot to do with his adaptability to this. Even so, they were both a little breathless by the time they reached his room. He balanced himself on the crutches while she folded back the covers and rearranged the multitude of pillows, waited while he lowered himself to the bed, and leaned the crutches against the nightstand. He managed to bend down and pull off his dock shoe he wore on the undamaged foot, but he needed Erin to help him swing both legs up on the bed again.

She'd thought this would be easier now that he could use both hands, but he couldn't seem to hitch himself into the center of the mattress. She did the thing with the pillows for his cast, but today she felt extra clumsy, a situation emphasized by the fact she kept bumping her breasts on the cast as she bent over him. What was wrong with her?

She did her best to avoid touching him anywhere but his leg, but no luck there either. As she tried to straighten up, her arm brushed against his crotch. She jerked back as if she'd touched a lit flame. Jake's fingers closed over her elbow, and he tugged her toward him.

"Don't," he said when she tried to pull away. "Look at me."

She let her gaze travel up the length of him until it locked with his. His face was flushed with desire, the late day scruff so temptingly delicious she wanted to rub herself on it like a sleepy cat. His eyes were now the dark color of espresso, and the hunger in them was so evident he might as well have worn a blinking neon sign. He stroked his fingers lightly along her arm, the barest of touches but enough to ignite even more flames. He caressed her gently, slowly, as if he expected her to bolt.

Or smack him.

Walk away. Tell him to let go of you. Be smart about this. You know this is a huge mistake.

But smart apparently wasn't on her agenda today. All those erotic dreams flashed in her mind like a naughty movie, and without warning moisture flooded her panties and her nipples hardened. Damn! The man was lethally dangerous where she was concerned, because try to deny it or not, she wanted him. Badly.

What was the old saying? You'll hate yourself in the morning?

Maybe. But being this close to him, inhaling the clean male essence of him, remembering the magic of his touch and the heat of his kisses, the feel of his thick cock inside her—common sense fled and all her other senses took over. Despite her good resolutions, she was totally lost, giving herself over to the pull of desire between them.

Jake slid his fingers into her hair and pulled her head down so her mouth was aligned with his. His hot breath fanned her cheeks.

"Give me your mouth, sweet thing." His voice was thick with need. "Just one kiss. I need to celebrate getting that cast off my wrist and moving to crutches. Don't you want to help me?"

"I think a glass of wine might do the same thing, now that you're off your pain meds."

"Come on. One kiss. I promise not to be grouchy for the rest of the day."

"Yeah, right."

This was a bad idea. One kiss would lead to more, because she stupidly had no willpower where he was concerned. With a sigh of surrender, she moved her head the extra tiny space until their lips touched, his so warm and firm. He licked the closed seam of her lips, one smooth glide back and forth.

"Open for me," he whispered. "Now."

Tossing all her reservations aside for one wild moment, she braced her hands on either side of his head and let his tongue sweep inside and lick every surface of her mouth. He coaxed her tongue to dance with his, twisting and twirling, tasting every bit, a sensual tango that she wanted to go on forever.

She was so lost in the taste and heat of him it barely registered when he tugged up the hem of her short-sleeved sweater. He slid his hand smoothly along her rib cage until he reached one breast. When he cupped it gently and squeezed, she couldn't hold back a tiny moan.

"Get down here with me," he said in a low tone. "I want to feel your body next to mine."

She had one last moment of sanity, piercing the erotic fog surrounding her. This would be the time for her to break away and tell him this wasn't such a good idea. Instead, her traitorous mouth said, "There's hardly any room next to you."

Desiree Holt

"You could go around on the other side, you know. I have a whole half a bed that's not being used."

"No, that's the side with the broken leg. I can just see you knocking me out with it." She swallowed. "I'm not sure—"

"Don't you have any sympathy for an injured man?" He grinned, humor in his eyes. "You're supposed to see to my needs, right?"

Her laugh was slightly hysterical. "I'm not sure this is in my list of duties."

"Then I'm adding it on. Come on, be adventurous."

She tried again, her last chance to escape. "It will be uncomfortable for you."

"You let me worry about that. Dr. Moline said I don't need to keep that leg elevated all the time, so let's see what we can do."

The hunger in his eyes wiped away the last of her restraint. He managed to maneuver his body so he was lying on one side, sort of, tugging Erin down so she was lying next to him, albeit in a very narrow space. The feel of his heated body set her nerves on fire, especially when he rucked up her sweater more and opened the front clasp of her bra. When his fingers teased her nipples, pinching them lightly and stroking her aching breasts, jolts of electricity shot straight through her to her pulsing sex.

He still wore the shirt he'd put on for the trip to the doctor, and impatiently she yanked it up from his shorts enough to bare his chest so she could slide her hands over the crisp curly hair covering his hard wall of muscle. Finding his hard male nipples, she scraped her fingernails lightly over them, eliciting a harsh intake of breath from him. They lay there, teasing each other with sensual caresses until she wanted to scream at him to get on with it.

"We'll probably have to be a little inventive," she warned him.

"Inventive is my middle name. I promise you."

"Good." She smiled.

"I want to undress you," he growled softly, "but I think I might need a little help here. How about it?"

"If you'll do the same." She wanted to see him naked again, see his glorious muscular body. Not even the cast could detract from his athletic male beauty. Not that she hadn't seen most of it every day, but this was different. A lot different.

"No problem." Desire and hunger flared in his eyes.

As she eased off the bed, the memory of her striptease in the dream popped into her head and her inner adventurous devil took over. With slow movements, she discarded the bra and sweater, unzipped her slacks, and eased them down her legs to step out of them. The last piece to go was the tiny scrap of satin that passed for her panties. She wiggled her hips as she slid the insubstantial fabric down, stepped out of it, and held it up like a trophy before dropping it with the rest of her things.

"Jesus." Jake sucked in a deep breath. "Your body is even better than I remembered. Come here."

He gestured with his hand, and she stepped close to the bed. Sliding his hand between her thighs, he nudged them apart to give him easy access to her already throbbing pussy. He stroked his fingers through her folds, just skimming the tip of her clit enough to draw a slight gasp from her. When he lifted his hand away from her, his fingers glistened, and he gave her a knowing smile.

"Soaked." He licked each finger with a slow lap of his tongue. "And delicious."

He repeated the movement twice, leaving her trembling and craving more. She wanted him to plunge his fingers inside her, to rub her aching clit and relieve this agonizing tension rippling through her body. She rocked her hips forward slightly, coaxing a lazy grin from him.

"You want more, sweet thing? So do I. But you haven't finished your chores yet." He pointed to his body. "Didn't you say I have too many clothes on?"

"Yes." She licked her lips. "So I did."

It was an awkward process, but the very awkwardness was exciting. Jake pulled himself up to a sitting position, and together they made short work of his shirt. The shorts were a little more difficult, the cast an awkward obstruction. She leaned over him, unbuttoned and unzipped the shorts he'd worn, and started tugging them down over his hips. He braced himself on his elbows to lift his weight as much as he could. She did okay getting them past his ass, and he bent his uninjured leg to free it. The cast was another matter. Finally, she climbed up onto the foot of the bed and tugged from there until she could pull them off completely.

The boxer briefs were even more of a challenge. By the time he lifted his hips again and she dragged the briefs off, almost falling onto his cast while she did, they were both huffing and puffing. She wasn't sure this whole thing was worth it.

He grinned at her and said as if he could read her mind, "Yes, it is."

"Is what?"

"Worth the effort."

Maybe he was right. Apparently all this wasn't a mood killer, either, because she was still highly aroused and greedy for him. Ditto for him.

He was gloriously naked now, his thick cock swollen with need, the head a dark purple, the sac with his balls lying heavy against his thighs. The sight was even more than the memory, even beyond what she'd dreamed, and her hands flexed with the desire to touch him. When she tore her gaze away from his groin to look at Jake, his mouth curved in a knowing grin.

"Go ahead. You can touch it. God knows I've dreamed enough about you doing it."

"Y-You have?" she stammered.

His mouth curved in a grin that could only be called hungry. "Don't you remember what I said before? Or did you want to push that out of your mind?"

She felt a blush creep up her cheeks at the remembered image of him lying in bed, fingers wrapped around his cock, semen spilling over them. And his tension as she'd carefully cleaned him with as much objectivity as she could muster.

"Go ahead," he urged. "Touch me again." He wet his lips. "Please."

She pressed one knee on the bed next to him and then reached for him, curving her fingers around him, feeling the heat of the steel-like shaft through the soft skin. Beneath her touch, the ropy vein wrapped around it pulsed with the blood coursing heavily through it. She brushed her thumb over the velvety head, spreading the tiny bead of pre-cum sitting on the slit.

God! This was so much better than any dream. Even better than she remembered it from that one night. His very male scent mixed with whatever aftershave he used—something woodsy—was such a turn-on. She wanted to bury her face against his skin and just inhale. Touching him sent little slivers of electricity sparking through her, ramping up her own pulse. She leaned forward and took just the head in her mouth, loving its lush velvet softness, and traced her tongue around the furled skin surrounding it.

"I want to watch." Jake swept the curtain of her hair away from her face and tucked it behind her ear. "I want to see it all."

She hummed against him as she slowly lowered her mouth to the root and then drew it all the way back to the tip. Beneath her, Jake shuddered so she did it again. And again. His shaft flexed beneath her fingers so she squeezed, eliciting a deep groan from him. She worked him with her fingers and lips, moving slowly and steadily, feeling him swell and harden and throb beneath her touch.

She jerked when she felt his hand skate over the curve of her ass, up and down, before he trailed his fingers through the hot crevice. Just like in the dream. And just like that night. She'd tried to bury so much of it so she could walk away from it—from him—but the feel of him now brought everything back with growing intensity.

As she worked his cock, sucking and pulling, he rubbed his fingers up and down in a steady rhythm in the warm space separating the cheeks of her buttocks. She shivered again when he slipped his fingers lower to find her pussy, stroking the wet flesh and sliding the moisture back to her other opening.

Oh God!

"I'm not gonna last long," Jake told her in a rough voice. "Not long at all. This feels too damn fucking good."

The faster she worked him, the faster his hand moved, massaging her own moisture into her hot tissues. She squeezed his balls rhythmically in cadence with her attention to his shaft, so she knew exactly when his climax began its climb from deep inside his body. She increased pressure and speed, felt the surge beneath her fingers, and took him full into her mouth as his release roared through him.

With that first hot surge, one finger pressed into her anus, and she felt the walls of her sex spasm. Because she had to balance herself with one foot on the floor, she couldn't give in to the urge to squeeze her legs together so the walls of her sex clenched convulsively on nothing but air.

Oh God!

She kept her lips sealed around him until the last spurt had filled her mouth and she swallowed it. The reality was way better than the dream. Then she eased her lips up, gave one last lick to the head, and turned to smile at him. His cheeks were dark with the heat of his orgasm and his eyes heavy-lidded, lust still crackling in them.

"Come here." He tugged on her arm. "Straddle me."

"Jake, I don't want to hurt you—"

His laugh was edged with sexual desire. "I don't think anything could hurt me right now. And I wouldn't be much of a lover if I left you unsatisfied after you did such a good job for me."

"But—"

He pressed his fingers to her lips. "Ssh. We'll figure it out."

Except it took much longer to figure out then he obviously expected. She tried to straddle him across his groin so he could slide into her, leaving her to do most of the work, but when he tried to move his leg to get in a better position he knocked his cast into her.

"Ouch!" She rubbed her hip. "That thing weighs a ton."

"You should try it from my side of the fence," he grumbled.

When she tried to reverse positions, she found herself with no place to brace herself. One good thrust and she'd fall on her face. Now *that* could definitely be a mood changer. She moved herself around to try yet another position, but when Jake shifted to help her, the muscle in his good thigh cramped and his face contorted with agony.

Erin flopped back down beside him, laughing. "Our intentions are good, Jake, but that's about all."

"I'm useless," he complained. "Just damn useless."

"It's okay." She placed soft kisses along his chin. "Really."

"No, it's not." He looked at his leg. "Fucking cast. Fucking linebacker. Fucking useless offensive line. This is just a bitch."

She lay on her side next to him, propped on an elbow, fitting into the narrow strip of bed next to him. "I said it's okay. Really, Jake."

And a lot better than a dream.

He closed his eyes for a long moment, and she wondered if he was mentally retreating from her. She lay there, schooling herself to be patient and preparing herself for it, even as she regretted getting herself in this position again.

Finally, he opened his eyes and looked at her.

"Like I said, I can be inventive. Do you believe me?"

Oh, yes, indeedy. She certainly did. That night together unreeled in her brain like the replay of a movie.

"I do."

"All right then." He ran his thumb over her lips and along the line of her jaw. "Just lie here and close your eyes."

In an instant the dream came back to her, the one where she was straddling his chest and his tongue was doing wicked things to her. Every nerve in her body was on fire, and her erogenous zones thumped with need. She had to force herself to relax, to let the sensations roll over her. She trusted him in the dream, so could she not trust him in reality?

"Why?" What did he have in mind?

"Just do it, please? For me?"

She giggled. "I thought I already did something for you."

"And now it's my turn. Just lie here and close your eyes. Don't open them for any reason."

"Should I be afraid?"

"Yes." He chuckled "Be very afraid." He hitched himself just enough that he could turn slightly in her direction. "Close them."

Obediently she did as he asked, blocking everything from her mind but this moment. She felt his hands at her breasts, cupping one, then the other, cradling them in his palms. His thumb rubbed lightly across each nipple until she felt the flesh harden and peak. He put his mouth close to her ears, licking the edge before gently probing the inner shell. A shiver of delight skimmed over the surface of her skin, and the pulse in her sex beat insistently. Without the sense of sight, every touch, every sensation was magnified a thousand times.

Arousal raced through her, hot and fierce, and a little whimper escaped her lips.

"That's it." His mouth was close to her ear, his breath a warm breeze against it. "Just lie there like that with your eyes closed nice and tight."

His fingers trailed down between her breasts, paused to trace the indentation of her navel, before drifting down to her pussy. She tried to open her legs wider to urge him to touch her *there,* but she didn't have much room to maneuver. And Jake didn't seem inclined or able to give her more room, not with that heavy cast to move around.

He caressed the inside of her thighs, smoothing his hands over the skin, gently brushing her pubic curls before dancing his fingers over the line of her hips and back to her thighs. Her breasts felt heavy with need, her nipples aching, and her pussy demanded attention. Her skin actually felt as if it had been sandpapered, all her nerves exposed and raw.

"Please," she whispered.

"Please what?" His fingers were still brushing her skin everywhere.

"Please touch me." She let out a long breath.

"I am touching you, sweet thing." His laugh was low and sensual. "Where would you like me to touch you?"

"You know."

"No, I don't think I do." He licked the shell of her ear. "You'll have to be specific."

"Touch—touch my breasts."

"Like this?" He pinched each nipple gently. "Or this?" She felt his breath on her breasts just before his hot wet mouth closed over one hard peak and sucked.

She felt the pull clear to her womb. "Oh, yes," she breathed. "Yes."

He grazed his teeth over them, nipping lightly, then soothing with his mouth. Every nerve in her body snapped and sizzled and she moaned again.

"Feel good?"

"Yesss," she hissed.

"What else would you like? Tell me." His palm cupped her mound, squeezing gently before he sifted his fingers through her pubic curls.

Desiree Holt

"You know." Why did she have such trouble saying this?

"No, I don't think I do. And unless you tell me, I don't think it will happen." His busy fingers were back at her nipples, tweaking and twisting, ramping up her need.

Oh, God!

"Put your fingers inside me." She whispered the words.

He licked the side of her neck. "I'll see if I can make that happen." His voice was low and rumbled through her.

He was in no hurry, while her body cried out for relief right now. She pushed her legs apart, silently urging him to move his hand where she wanted it. Without her sight, she couldn't see where to move, and the leg she'd pressed against him now clunked against his cast.

Ouch!

"Shit!" Jake growled the word.

"Oh my God!" She yanked her leg back, pain shooting through her heel. She opened her eyes. "Are you okay?"

"I'm fine. I think you got the worst of it." He stroked his palm over her face. "Close your eyes again. I'll take care of this."

"But—"

"Close your eyes." He nipped the lobe of her ear. "That is a damn mood killer. Let's see if we can get it back. In a second, you won't even think of your foot. I promise."

It didn't take too much effort on his part, since not even nearly breaking her heel could erase the raging need consuming her. She closed her eyes, took a deep breath, and let herself fall into his touch.

He nudged her legs apart to give him access and cupped her with his palm. She loved the feel of his hand as he brushed the inside of her thighs, the heat of his fingers as finally, finally, they moved to her pussy. He slid one digit through the length of her slit, stroking up and down, circling her clit with each caress. The walls of her sex spasmed and a whimper of need rose up from her throat.

Jake closed his lips over one nipple and bit down gently on it just as he slid two fingers into her wet, waiting channel. He licked her tormented nipple and then slid his tongue over the other one.

"God, I love how wet you are," he breathed. He worked his fingers in and out of her, setting up a rhythm, pressing her clit with his thumb each time he thrust completely into her. "I love the feel of those slick walls around my fingers. If I wished for anything, it would be that it was my cock inside you instead."

"Me, too," she whispered.

She was having a hard time talking now as sensations raced through her body, everything so much more intense with her eyes closed. She trembled as heat consumed her and tried to push down on Jake's hand.

"Slow, Erin. Real slow."

But she didn't want to take it slow. She wanted it fast. She wanted it hard. She wanted it now. Jake, however, seemed to have his own agenda, because he never varied the tempo of his strokes, adding a third finger and dragging the tips over that very sensitive spot inside her channel.

The tremors began and her entire body focused on what was happening. Her pussy clamped down on Jake's fingers, and she hitched her hips, riding him as her climax roared up from deep inside her. The tremors became spasms and the spasms became intense shudders, her entire body shaking. Jake took her mouth in a deep, hot kiss, his tongue probing and searching while he drove his fingers in and out of her again and again and again, riding her through the sensual storm.

Slowly her body relaxed, her limbs leaden, her pulse returning to a normal rate.

"You can open your eyes now," Jake murmured.

When she did, his face was right there and his coffee-dark eyes were looking directly into hers.

"I love to feel you come. I just wish I was inside you."

She gave him a lazy smile. "I'm not complaining."

He gave a low, rumbling laugh. "Yeah, but I am. This damn cast is a pain in the butt."

She studied him for a long moment. What on earth had she gotten herself into here? How was this going to work going forward? She might be intensely attracted to this man, cast and all, but she still didn't trust his ability to sustain a relationship. If she ever got her life back on track, she wanted to find that one right man to build a future with. She was pretty damn sure Jake Russell wouldn't be that man.

Besides, while he might have been Mr. Hot and Sexy today, focused on her pleasure as well as his, there was no guarantee that tomorrow he wouldn't revert to the same grouch she'd been tending to every day.

"I can smell your brain burning." He brushed his lips softly over hers. "Give it a rest, Erin. Let's just see what happens, okay? Can you do that?"

Could she? She guessed she was about to find out.

Chapter 9

Never have sex with a man in a cast.

Erin sighed as she rubbed cream into the abraded areas on her arms. The heel could wait until she got ready for bed. Being acrobatic in any way when one of the participants had a full length cast on his leg presented more problems than she wanted to remember. Even though what she referred to in her mind as "the incident" had happened four days ago, her body still carried reminders of it. At night in bed, it was all she could think of.

And dream about. Oh, yes, the dreams came nightly now.

Well, she'd gone and done it again, only now she had no place to run. She was stuck here with a man she was so strongly attracted to she wanted to jump his bones every minute of every day. The memory surrounded them, the sexual tension crackling and filling the room. It was impossible not to be aware of it and it complicated everything.

Okay, smartass, what if he doesn't feel the same way? What if he's just playing with you, waiting for his leg to heal? Could she take a chance again, knowing disaster might lurk?

He's different than Trace. You know that. In so many ways. Pay attention to that.

After taking her cell from her pocket, she checked to see if there was a new text from Ivy. There were certainly plenty of old ones, checking on Jake's condition and dropping little bits of information.

Jake likes this special coffee cake.
Jake likes fresh bagels.

Erin had to stop herself from texting back.

How about stopping to pick some up when you come by to see him.

Jake needs to be reminded to answer his e-mail.

It was a blatant cue to Erin that she had yet to approach this subject with Jake. That ought to be fun.

But the text she sent tonight? Not even a one-word answer. Nada. Zip. Zippo.

No different than when she called the office. There someone answered, but she got such a runaround she felt like she was on a merry go round.

"No, sorry, she's on an appointment."

"Oh, I apologize but she's in an all-day conference off site and can't be disturbed."

"No, I'm sorry. I have no idea where she is."

Okay, so Ivy was avoiding her. Big surprise. Not that she had a lot of time to chat. All her time was spent waiting on Jake, sorting his mail, answering his landline as well as his cell phone, an instrument she was ready to pitch in the trash. This morning she'd started letting all the calls go to voicemail and sorting out the ones she thought might be important. Jake was no help. He still didn't want to talk to anyone.

She had just started fixing the salad for dinner when the buzzer at the gate sounded. Who on earth would come by at mealtime unannounced? She checked the video in the hall, saw it was Jim DiMarco, and opened the gate for him.

"Good to see you, Erin," he told her as she let him into the house.

"Ditto," she said.

"How's our patient today? Grouchy as ever?"

She gave a slight laugh. "Does night follow day?"

"Well, let's see what's going on." He glanced into the kitchen. "Oh, sorry, I didn't realize how close to dinner time it was. I was about five minutes away and thought I'd take the opportunity to stop by."

"No problem," she assured him. "It's nothing that can't wait. Come on, I'll take you back to him."

"Still hiding in the bedroom?" he asked, as they walked down the hall.

"Yes. If you have a solution for that, I'm open to hearing it."

"We'll see."

As usual, Jake was lying on the bed, the flat screen television on but muted.

"Look who's here." She tried to put a cheerful note into her voice.

Jake waved at him from his semi-prone position but made no effort to get up.

"I'm just going to turn the oven down," she said. "You two need a chance to chat."

"No. Come back," Jake insisted. And what was that all about? Was he afraid to be with the general manager alone?

"In a second," she called back at him.

But she intentionally gave them several minutes, hoping DiMarco might have a fix for Jake's mood. But when she returned, she could tell Jake had been something less than cordial. DiMarco still had a smile on his face, but he was already shaking Jake's hand in preparation for leaving.

"I know you're about to eat," he was saying, "so I'll let you get to it. But I'll stop by again."

"Yeah, thanks," Jake grunted and turned his gaze back to the television.

"I wish I could find a way to pull him out of this funk," Erin told the GM as she walked him to the door.

"I can understand it," DiMarco told her. "His whole life has been turned upside down. His future is uncertain, and he's having trouble handling it."

"But other players get injured," Erin pointed out. "They survive."

"Jake's more than just another player," the man told her. "He's one of the stars. He's had a great career, and this was supposed to be his best year yet. Now he sees it moving forward without him."

"If he doesn't figure a way to deal with it, he'll have a real problem."

DiMarco sighed. "Don't I know it. I'd like to get him some counseling but—"

Erin waved a hand in the air. "Forget it. Not with the mood he's in. He's not ready to hear anything like that right now."

Saying the words out loud to DiMarco made her realize how right she was. Whatever was driving him, Jake was in no way ready for anyone to even hint that he wouldn't return to the playing field. Whatever his fixation on football as his defining image, he wasn't about to let go of it. Again she felt the enormity, and sympathy for whatever drove him engulfed her.

"I'll just keep trying," DiMarco told her. "He's more than just another player to me."

"I keep thinking I'm missing something." She shook her head. "I get the feeling it's more than just being out of action. It's as if football is the only thing that defines him. Without it, he's nobody."

DiMarco frowned. "You know, I get that feeling sometimes, too. Coach just sees it as a tremendous drive to succeed, but I think it goes deeper."

He gave her a half smile. "I was hoping if there was something, he'd open up to you about it."

"Oh." She laughed. "Trust me. If Jake is going to open up to anyone, it certainly won't be me."

"But the two of you seem to have reached a sort of détente. I thought…"

Erin shook her head. "I think you can forget about that."

"Too bad. Well, you've done great keeping his uninjured leg and wrist flexible, but now he has to start rehabbing that wrist." He pulled a business card from his shirt pocket. "We use this clinic all the time. I've arranged for someone to begin work with him tomorrow afternoon. He'll be here every day, except weekends."

Erin twisted her lips in a wry grin. "That ought to be fun."

DiMarco smiled. "I'm sure. I should have called first to let you know, but I didn't want to give Jake too much time to pitch a fit. Will three o'clock work?"

"That's fine." She chuckled in spite of herself. "It's not like he's going anywhere."

* * * *

She finished dinner preparations, then carried their food out to the patio off Jake's bedroom. When it was ready, she walked into his room. Since their clumsy attempt at sex, he hadn't shown an interest in a repeat performance. Had he lost interest in her? Was he frustrated by the situation with his cast? She could certainly sympathize with that. But dammit, now *she* wanted a repeat performance and had no idea how to let him know without backing down on all her principles.

Oh, yeah, Erin. Principles give you great orgasms, right?

Shut up, she told the voice in her head. *Just. Shut. Up.*

She helped him with the minor exercises every day, but that seemed to be the extent of his interest in anything. For whatever reason, he was retreating from her. The careful lack of expression on his face and the indefinable look in his dark eyes were signs to her that something was festering deep inside him. She just wished she could figure out what it was. If he had no interest in life, he'd have no life to get back to.

She pointed to the patio. "Dinner's waiting for you at the table. Time to eat." Since he got his crutches, she'd bullied him into taking his meals on the patio. He still gave her grief about it, but she thought it had become more of a game than anything.

"Is that any way to treat a cripple?" His tone was still tongue-in-cheek, although she sensed the bitterness at his situation underneath it as he gave her his usual comeback.

She laughed at that one. "You're getting to be less and less a cripple every day."

And like that, the playful tone was gone.

"Do you see me on the football field these days?" Anger flared in his eyes. "If I'm not out there, I'm a cripple. The cast tells everyone."

"You can't let football define you," she tried telling him, remembering her conversation with DiMarco. As she'd gotten to know Jake, she had to admit, albeit grudgingly, that he was so much more than that guy on the field.

"Yeah? Well, news flash. It does."

"Okay, enough with the pity party." She pointed to the patio. "The table's set and everything is ready. Get your ass out of bed and come eat."

Mumbling under his breath, he levered himself upright, grabbed his crutches, and maneuvered himself out to the covered patio. When he'd made it into one of the chairs, he leaned his crutches against each other.

"Looks good," he told her, eyeing the food. "I didn't think chicks liked to cook anymore."

"I don't know what kind of *chicks* you hang out with, but I enjoy cooking. It's relaxing." She paused. "Be truthful. Isn't it better eating out here instead of hugging a tray in bed?"

"Maybe." He said the word grudgingly.

She'd thought he might clump his way into the kitchen for meals now that he was more mobile. However, it seemed Jake was going to push every one of her buttons. Getting him out to the patio off the master bedroom was an alternative for her.

Over dinner, she told him about the physical therapist DiMarco had arranged for.

Surprisingly, he didn't argue about it. Instead of biting back, complaining that his hand was no good when his leg didn't work, he surprised her.

"It's a beginning," he told her. "I'm a running back. My ability to take the handoff of the ball is almost as important as my ability to run with it. First I get my hand to work, then my leg. Right?"

"Of course." She smiled encouragingly. "It's all good." She hoped with the new changes Jake would be in a good mood.

After dinner, she got him settled for the night. She wanted to tell him he could fetch anything else he needed from the kitchen, but she reminded herself everything was baby steps.

"I have some things to do in my room," she told him. "Do not use the intercom unless it is a vital emergency or I'll break your finger."

"But you're supposed to be my caretaker," he reminded her.

"For anything you can't do for yourself," she said. "You can certainly get yourself to the bathroom and the kitchen."

Before he could say anything else, she headed down the hall.

With Jake settled for the night—she hoped—she was ready to carve out some time with her laptop and get back to job hunting. She had plans and a new determination. Four hours later, she'd found only a few opportunities worth exploring, but it was better than nothing. And she needed to get to bed. The day started early in the Russell house.

She came awake the next morning with a feeling of trepidation. In addition to ordering the therapy, the doctor had also pronounced Jake well enough with his wrist healed to shower and shave.

"He'll need to wrap the cast completely in cling wrap," Moline had said. "You know, to protect it."

Today the man who'd been helping him with his routine was going to show both of them how to do it. Oh, joy. The cast extended clear up his leg almost to the top of his thigh. And his balls. And his cock. Erin knew she'd have to be the one to help him. She could just imagine his grin as she did her best to avoid grazing them with the back of her fingers.

The smart thing would have been to never have sex with Jake at all.

That horse has already left the barn, Erin. Put it behind you. Get your head in the game. Forget those urgent signals every time you're in the room with him.

She knew all the pitfalls of a repeat performance in Jake's bed, but couldn't stop thinking about it. Wanting it. She hadn't had an attraction to a man this intense since…since… Well, just since all that shit happened in her life.

She kept glancing at the intercom, waiting for Jake's voice to come bellowing from the little speaker despite her threat to him. It stayed strangely silent. By the time she finished dressing, she was edgy, wondering if something had happened to him. What if he'd fallen and hurt himself? No, he'd have shouted and called for her. What if he was still asleep? Well, too bad. He had people coming. And she had to learn how to be his handmaiden in the bathroom.

She detoured to the kitchen to get a breakfast tray ready. She was still bringing him his coffee in the morning, but today started a fresh chapter in his life. Yesterday, while Jake was getting his shower and shave, she'd run up to the nearest market and picked up a few things. She'd grabbed some fresh bagels and a box of pastries from a great bakery even she had heard of. This morning they'd eat out on the covered patio, where they took the rest of their meals. And maybe today she could sweeten his disposition with a fresh pastry.

His door was closed, but when she knocked, there was no answer. She rapped again, a little louder.

"Come."

A bad choice of words on his part because she was sure he was ready to. She knew *she* was every time she looked at him, a very difficult situation. She opened the door and looked in. Jake was lying in his usual place against the pillows, covers thrown off, body exposed to her eyes.

Hello, morning boner.

"Don't hang out in the doorway." He motioned her forward, unsmiling. "Did you bring my coffee?"

Okay, so Mr. Grumpy was still hanging around.

"Not today, smart guy. Today we're getting you out of bed right away, getting your blood moving before you get your first lesson in taking a solo shower."

He snorted. "That will be an interesting change."

"Whatever. I'm getting your juice and coffee, but you won't get it in bed. It's a nice day. I'm taking it out onto the patio. And I have a treat for you."

His eyes widened slightly and a corner of his mouth ticked up in a hint of a grin. Was Mr. Grumpy leaving? "A treat? Are you going to have breakfast with me in the nude?"

What he said didn't bother her half as much as the fact that she sensed he was only pretending to joke. The slight buoyancy he'd gotten from the removal of the soft cast and the news he could start wrist therapy and showering by himself had dissipated. At first she'd chalked it all up to him just feeling sorry for himself, but as she got to know him better, she had a sense it went much deeper than that. She understood that football was a big part of his life, but what was going to happen if it turned out it could only be a small part from now on? What would he do?

In that moment, it became a goal of hers to show him that there was life after football. That there were other things, like this Good Shepard House and more opportunities she'd come across in his mail. She almost laughed at her thoughts, but at least it would give her something to focus on besides the void her life was currently in.

"Erin?"

Jake's voice snapped her out of her reverie. She grinned.

"Uh, no, I'm not dining in the nude with you. But I did get fresh bagels, banana nut muffins, and cinnamon streusel coffee cake from Take the Cake." She forced a smile. "Ivy texted me it's one of your favorites."

He eyed her for a long moment. "Is that supposed to sweeten me up?"

Her lips quirked up in a smile. "As if. But you might enjoy it. Come on. Out of that bed."

"Wow." His forehead creased in a scowl. "No more Miss Sweetheart, right?"

Erin had to chuckle. "She forgot to show up. Now come on. Get your ass to the bathroom like a good little boy, and I'll get breakfast. I also have some more stuff to go over with you."

Still scowling, he pushed himself upright and reached for his crutches. "I'm telling Ivy on you. She promised me someone nice."

"Yeah? You'd have to get her to talk to you first. And I can be nice when I want to." Now why the hell had she said that? "See you in a few."

"Wait. What happens if I fall on the way to the bathroom or out to the patio?"

She sighed in exasperation. "You've been doing just fine for the past few days. But if that happens, I'll call someone with a forklift to haul your ass back upright."

Knowing that was her best exit line, she left the room and headed for the kitchen.

Chapter 10

"You know, I'm actually beginning to enjoy breakfast out here." Jake helped himself to a banana nut muffin, cut it precisely in half, and took a bite.

"That was the point," Erin told him. She refilled both their mugs from the carafe of coffee. "Getting you out of that bed."

"And do you have a plan for me getting you back into it?" The words were out before he even realized it, but he wouldn't have taken them back. He was pleased to see a soft blush creep up Erin's beautiful cheeks.

"I think that ship has sailed." She took a sip of her coffee. "Things seem to be going along okay without it. Why rock the boat?"

Well, crap.

Jake kept hoping he could scale that big wall that was back in place around her, and he planned to keep trying. With his future still uncertain, it gave him something to focus on.

She nodded at her ever-present iPad, now sitting at her elbow. "We need to get at the e-mails and messages after breakfast. You'll be happy to know I cleaned out most of what was in there."

"See?" He grinned. "I knew you were perfect for the job." This one and a few others.

What are you doing, Russell? What will you even have to offer her if you get the death blow when the cast comes off? Talk about being selfish. But he just could not seem to help himself.

"Ivy finally called," she told him.

"Damn nice of her," he grumped.

"She wanted to check on your progress." Erin bit off a piece of muffin, chewed, and swallowed.

"Did she at least apologize for getting you into this mess?" And me, he wanted to add.

Erin shook her head. "Not a bit. She did say she'd be by to see you when you stop wanting to rip her head off."

He didn't comment, so she looked at her iPad again. Today's list, he was sure.

"After breakfast we have to do your toes."

She said the words so primly he actually burst out laughing. "I'm sorry if that offends your sensibilities. Don't you work with the appendages of your regular clients?"

"I work in a *spa* or a *resort*." She emphasized the words. "Their toes don't usually come into play."

"No? Well, maybe they should." He saw the muscles in her jaw tighten. He was really getting into pushing her buttons. "The therapist said they were getting swollen. You'd hate for me to have swollen toes, wouldn't you?"

He loved the feel of her slender fingers on him as she worked each individual digit the way the therapist had shown her. It might not be on her list of favorite things to do, but she sucked it up and handled it. He got the distinct feeling that sticking this out to the end had become a point of pride with her.

"I could see you were developing a problem. I'll take care of it." Another sip of coffee. Another bite of muffin.

Alrighty!

He could hardly wait until the guy showed up later to show them how to wrap his cast. Would she have to cover his leg all the way to his balls? Would her fingers brush against them? Touch his dick? The thought of that intimacy made him painfully hard. It took every bit of discipline he possessed to push the images out of his brain. "Do you have time in your busy schedule to watch a movie this afternoon?" he asked.

"My schedule is busy with you," she reminded him, "so yes. If that's what you want to do." She pinned him with a look. "In the great room, though."

He burst out laughing. "Afraid to watch it with me in my bedroom, are you?"

One corner of her mouth twitched as she tried to hide a grin. "Just aware of your ulterior motives."

"Maybe they wouldn't be so ulterior if you would just remember how hot we are together and give us another chance."

"There's a Mustangs game on tonight," she told him. "How about watching that with me?"

Just like that, his rare good mood vanished. "Way to kill a nice buzz," he snapped.

"Are you planning to boycott them forever?" she asked.

"When I'm back in the harness, I'll have plenty of time to watch game films."

"Not the same thing," she pointed out.

"Don't care. Just forget it." He pushed back from the table. Obviously, though, she was through letting him just lie in bed, feeling sorry for himself. He had to admit she nagged almost as well as Ivy did.

"Let's do my toes. I can hardly wait."

"You know you've been a real bear the last few days," she told him as she rose from her own chair. "I was beginning to miss that side of your charming personality."

At this particular moment, he was in no mood for her snarkiness. The frustration of his situation like a sore spot that he kept pushing at, as if to remind himself exactly how rotten this whole thing was.

"I suppose," she went on, "this means you still don't want to take any phone calls?"

"There's no one I want to talk to," he insisted. "I'm not in the mood to handle that stuff myself. You agreed to do it, so do it."

When they were finished with his toes, and Erin went to clean up after breakfast, he clumped his way to the den where he fired up his laptop. No one ever entered this room except him. He made his way into the room early enough to put away all the things he didn't share with others. Personal mementos that had little to do with the game or his career. Things that reminded him of very intimate parts of his life. It took him a while, but when he finally collapsed back into the desk chair, the only visible signs of his life and career were a few framed photos that had been published everywhere.

Seated at his desk, he decided to check out the Coyotes Facebook page. For kicks, he got an account of his own, something he had resisted until now. Despite what some would call a flamboyant lifestyle, with a string of Eye Candy Mandys, he didn't flaunt himself the way a lot of the other guys did.

"Nice picture."

He looked up and realized Erin had walked into the room.

She'd spotted the photo of the state champion Granite Falls Coyotes team, the one where they'd hoisted the big trophy, front and center on his desk.

"You know what it is? Oh, of course you do. What else would it be?"

"I did a search for them the other night," she told him.

"You did? How come?" That was interesting. According to everything she said and did, she had zero interest in him. Zip.

She shrugged. "How could I not? I have the usual dose of human curiosity. You guys were apparently the talk of the state for a long time. Not just for winning but for the community service work you did and for how tight you were together."

He managed a smile. That was true, every bit of it. "Yeah, we were like family. It was great."

"So how come you haven't kept in touch with them since then?" she persisted.

He shrugged. "We all went in different directions after graduation. Then we all got busy with whatever we were doing."

"So, are you checking Coyotes Win on Facebook now?"

He nodded. "Shay Reilly did a very good job setting it up," he noted.

"She did," Erin agreed. "I see she's got head shots of all the players from the yearbook and current ones for some of you guys. And bios when she was able to get them. Some of you still play in the NFL, some others are retired for a variety of reasons. And then there are those who never played after college."

"Uh-huh." He studied the shots.

She moved into the room. "You know Joe Reilly does a show on Fox Sports."

"Mm-hmm." He was well aware of Joe's program, *Inside the Helmet.*

"Rafe Ortiz works security for the owners of the stadium," she continued. "Hank Beckham is an engineer."

He thought about sending Shay a message to ask where he could send stuff about himself, but since he had no idea where he'd be after this season, he decided to wait.

Quit feeling so sorry for yourself.

But it was damn hard. Without football, he really didn't know who he was.

"Well, I'll leave you to it. I have some things to take care of."

He was still engrossed when she called him for lunch. He said little, and Erin, sensing he was in no mood for conversation, left him to his silence. His meeting with Lynne Corday was that afternoon and he wanted to prepare for it. He crutched back into the den, realizing he was actually getting much better on the clumsy things. The physical therapist had told him to practice with them daily so they became easier to use. Still, every time he propped them under his arms he cursed the circumstance that made them necessary.

He wanted to see today's visitor in the den, though. Other than his bedroom, it was really the only room in the house that gave him the situation he wanted. Needed. He could close the door and their conversation could be completely private.

He leaned back in the big upholstered chair, his foot propped on an ottoman, crutches leaning next to the desk at the ready, and forced himself to relax.

"Knock, knock."

He looked up to see Erin in the doorway, holding a large tray.

"I thought you might like to serve something to your guest," she told him. "I ran to the bakery for some special cookies and fixed a pitcher of iced tea. Is it okay to set it on this little table?"

"Sure. Thanks for this." He watched her place the tray and rearrange the plates and glasses. "You do good work. Maybe I could hire you full time."

There was more truth than poetry in his words. With each passing day, he realized how important she was becoming to him. It went way beyond the sex. Somehow he had to make this work between them, because he wanted her in his life and for more than just sex.

"To be your personal caretaker? Ha!" She made a face. "We both know how well that would work out. Well, if you're all set, I'll just hang out in the kitchen until your guest gets here and I can let her in."

"And what do you plan to be doing in the kitchen?"

She shrugged. "Working at my laptop."

"How's the hunt for job openings going?" He asked the question casually but he damn well didn't want her finding something.

"Still nothing. But I'm eternally optimistic."

He cocked an eyebrow. "Just out of curiosity, what will you do if you find one before your obligation here is up?"

"I guess I'll cross that bridge when I come to it. But even if I find something, the process takes forever, so I don't think you'll need to be placing a classified ad just yet. Is there anything else I can get for you?"

He studied her for a long moment. God, she was so prickly. So edgy. So independent. And so damn sexy. She was everything he wanted in a woman, and he'd managed to make himself into something that was the total opposite of what she wanted.

She looked so appealing standing there in her slacks that fit her butt and her hips so well and the short-sleeved sweater that draped over breasts that made his mouth water. Her soft, plump lips were slicked with a pale lip gloss. Other than that, she wore no makeup. God knew she didn't need it.

The other night she'd been into it as much as he was. No way could she fake her responses. But the damn cast had been a mood killer, and since then she'd acted as if nothing happened. Still, the heat never stopped simmering in her eyes. Oh, yeah, she still wanted him, no matter how much she tried to deny it, just as much as he wanted her. He sure didn't plan to make love to her only in dreams, especially since she'd admitted she'd had dreams, too.

"Jake?"

She stood there, waiting expectantly for an answer, so he gave himself a mental shake.

"No, nothing else. Thanks for this."

"All right then. I'll show your guest in when she arrives. Enjoy your afternoon."

She obviously wasn't about to hang around and make idle conversation with him.

Lynne Corday arrived promptly at three thirty. Erin showed her in, nodded at him, and closed the door.

"Nice companion," she teased him. "Although I have to say she doesn't seem quite your type. Or the type to be a housekeeper."

Jake ground his teeth. "She's not."

"Oh?" Lynne lifted an eyebrow. "That sounds interesting. Is there a story behind this?"

"I needed some help here until I can manage by myself, the team wanted someone who was a buffer between me and the public, and my sister is trying to play matchmaker and pissing both of us off. And, well, she needed a job."

Lynne chuckled. "From my few conversations with her, I'd say she'd have no trouble getting one."

"She wants to stay in training and spa work. It's what her degree is in, and there doesn't appear to be any openings around here at the moment. Anyway, I'd rather not discuss Erin Bass, if it's all the same to you."

"Of course." She looked at the tray Erin had left. "If these are for me, you get high marks. I love the cookies from Take the Cake."

"Help yourself, please."

She poured iced tea for both of them, helped herself to a cookie, then opened her briefcase.

"The reason I asked for this meeting is I have the estimates on the renovations and addition you asked for." She took another quick bite of cookie before pulling out a folder and handing it to him. She took out a similar one for herself. "I'd like to go over the figures for you and get a feel for what you want to do and when you want to proceed."

"This is all just between you and me, right?" he asked. "Not even anyone on the staff knows?"

"Yes. Just the two of us." She lifted a shoulder. "But it still puzzles me why you are so determined to be completely anonymous. What you're doing—have done—is so wonderful. You've helped so many people. Why don't you want people to know about it?"

"For the same reason you don't publicize the house itself. To protect the safety of the women and kids who come to you there. They don't deserve to have their privacy invaded."

"I agree." She nodded. "But at least let us recognize you within the organization. I mean, for goodness sake, you spend time there during the off-season with the kids when I know you must have other things to do. And I can't count the number of boys you've coached on the mini football field you had built for us."

"Just leave it be, okay? It's my choice. Let's go over these estimates and drawings."

By the time they'd gone through everything in the folder and debated the items on the list, making adjustments as they went, they'd finished the tea and the cookies were gone. And Lynne Corday wore a pleased smile on her face.

"So you'll get the new contracts drawn up and bring them by?" he asked. "And get me the start date. The earlier the better."

"I'll try to have them by the end of the week."

"Good deal."

She put everything back in her briefcase and snapped it shut. "As usual, you're outdoing yourself. I can't tell you how thankful we are."

"The results are worth it," he told her.

"Well, the addition will give us more suites for families and both play and classroom areas for the kids. You know how grateful we all were when you bought that property four years ago and built the new facility for us. This is way beyond what we ever imagined. We certainly could never have done it without a lot of help."

Jake leaned back in his chair, shaking the remnants of the ice cubes in his glass.

"It beats having a public fundraiser for it. Like you said, anonymity is so important for the mothers and children who come to us. And it helps us ensure their safety, too. But it's quite a financial obligation for you."

He gave a short laugh. "What else would I do with my money? Between my contract with the Mustangs and my endorsements, I certainly have more than I can ever use. And this is something I feel passionate about."

Her features softened. "I know it is. And it's personal for you as well. While people give back to us when and how they can, you should know that we don't often get a response of this magnitude." Her lips curved in a smile. "Of course, not all of them achieve the success you have."

He lifted one hand, let it fall back to the desk. "It's what I want to do. Let's leave it at that."

She sighed. "Fine. If that's what you want."

"I do. I'll have my accountant transfer money to the Good Shepard account so you can write out a check for the deposit."

She studied him for a moment. "Doesn't he ever say anything about all this money?"

Jake laughed. "He gets paid a lot of money to keep me honest and not ask questions. Period."

"How's the leg coming?" she asked.

Jake grimaced. "Don't ask."

"Any word on when you'll be able to get the cast off?"

"I wish." He raked his fingers through his hair. "I did get the soft cast off my wrist, though, and I'm doing therapy for the ligaments and the hand. I have another doctor's appointment next week. I'm hoping when they take their x-rays they might move me up to a walking cast."

"Don't rush it," she cautioned him. "That's the worst thing you can do. Let it heal properly."

"Yeah, that's what everyone says." He made a sound of disgust. "But none of you are sitting here watching who they are go down the drain."

"Jake." She leaned forward in her chair. "You are so very much more than a running back for the Austin Mustangs. So very much more. You're a very smart man who is also filled with compassion and blessed with a big heart. And more."

"Except if I weren't out there making the big plays no one would care. Admit it, Lynne."

"Maybe some people," she agreed. "But you find that in any industry. Besides, you have a very sharp mind and a college degree that backs it up. You could put both of those to use doing a lot of different things. The world would be wide open to you."

"I'll bet those kids at Good Shepard wouldn't be quite so wide-eyed and eager to see me come around without the headlines and fame."

"Now that's where you're wrong. Oh, maybe some of them, but the rest of them? Uh-uh. They see right to the heart of you."

"Nice sentiments," he said. "But that's all they are. Anyway, can we please put that subject to bed?"

"Of course. I'm sorry, I didn't mean to upset you."

"Not to worry. I'm good. Just get me those construction contracts to sign."

"I will. Thanks again." She held up her hand when he reached for his crutches. "Don't get up. I'll see myself out. Thanks for the delicious cookies."

"You can thank Erin if you see her. She did the shopping."

"I will. See you soon." She opened the door to leave, then stopped and turned. "You know, you've got quite a treasure there, from what I can see. Maybe you should do something to try and hang onto her."

He blew out a breath. "Don't I know it. But somehow I don't seem to be her cup of tea."

"Well, just try making yourself into another blend. Be a shame to lose her. See you."

Jake sat in his chair, staring at the empty doorway for a long moment, Lynne's words replaying in his head. He wished Erin could see him the way Lynne Corday and the people at Good Shepard did. But then he was a different person when he was there.

Damn it! He wished he knew exactly what it was that had soured her on football players in general and him in particular.

He slammed his hand down on the desk hard enough to make the metal dishes holding paper clips and pens jump and rattle. But all he got out of that was a sore hand, and he couldn't afford any more injuries.

* * * *

Erin had just finished setting the alarm codes after showing Lynne Corday out when she heard the clinking and rattling in the den.

Lord, what now?

She hurried down the short hallway and into the room in time to see Jake holding his right hand and grimacing.

"What did you do?" she asked, and hurried over to inspect the damage. "Let me see."

"I'm fine." He pulled his hand close to his chest.

"Then why are you making such a face? Here, let me look." She grabbed his hand before he could protest and turned it over so she could inspect it for damage. "Well, it's a little red on the edge, but it doesn't appear you've broken anything."

"Lucky me." He sounded like a wounded bear.

"I'm going to get you some ice to put on it. Keep it on for ten minutes, then ten off, back and forth for about an hour and you should be good. If it still hurts later, we'll do it again."

"What's with the 'we' business? It's my hand."

She nodded. "Which you banged up by doing something stupid, I'm sure."

"I want to go back to my room," he told her.

She gave a short barking laugh. "You sound like a little kid. If you don't want to stay in here, how about going out to the patio? The one off the living room for a change. It's a really nice day, and you've been pretty much hiding from the fresh air. Come on, I'll bring your ice out there." She grinned. "And if you're a good boy, I'll bring you some more cookies."

"If you make that a beer instead, you've got yourself a deal."

"A beer? Sure. You've been off the pain meds a while so I don't see any harm." She had to restrain herself from offering to help him with his crutches. The doctor had said he needed to do as much for himself as possible and hopefully the sore hand he'd hit wouldn't make things difficult for him.

"That would be a real treat."

"I'll meet you out there." *Don't ask him if he can make it by himself. Don't ask him, he's okay.*

She picked up the tray, carried it into the kitchen, then set it on the counter. Before she refilled the plate and got the drinks, she hurried to open the slider to the patio. She had visions of him reaching out with one hand to push it open and taking a tumble. Images of him lying on the floor with only her to help made her shudder.

She had just placed everything on the tray again when she heard him clumping into the kitchen behind her.

"Hand doing okay?" she asked. "I'm getting the ice for you now."

"I don't think I need it. I can tough it out."

"Don't be such a guy." She found a plastic baggy and filled it with crushed ice from the freezer. "It's okay to say it hurts."

"Fine." He barked the reply like an angry dog. "It hurts. Got my beer?"

"Of course. Go sit down and I'll bring everything out."

By the time she had them both situated, with a cushioned ottoman for his leg and his hand resting on the bag of ice, he was huffing a little from exertion and stress lined his face.

"Holy fucking shit," he cursed. "I thought I was in damned good shape. I feel like an old man, and all I did was move around the house a little today and talk to someone."

"Every effort is stressful." She twisted off the cap on one bottle of beer. "You were flat on your back for two weeks after the surgery. Then, when you finally got home, you couldn't do much because of your wrist. Give yourself a break."

He took the beer she handed him and drank a long swallow from the bottle. "It's gonna be hell getting back in shape when this cast comes off. I'll have to work twice as hard as I ever did in spring training."

Erin sat down across from him and helped herself to a cookie. She bit down and chewed slowly while she tried to figure the best way to answer him.

"I think that's a bridge you can cross when you get to it."

He leaned forward. "You sound like you're not too optimistic about it."

"Of course I am." She chased the cookie with a sip of beer. "I just want you to be prepared for whatever it takes."

"I'm prepared. I'm guessing you're like everyone else, certain this injury will finish me, but you're wrong. All of you. I'm determined the crowd will see number twenty-four running out on the field just like always."

Erin held her tongue. She'd been reading up on his type of injury, very similar to the one that had ended Washington Redskins quarterback Joe Theismann's career. She didn't want to hold out false hope to him, but she thought he should be prepared for the same results. Yet he stubbornly refused to even discuss it.

There was something else driving this obsessive need. She just wished she could get him to tell her what it was, because the Jake Russell she was learning about every day was—surprise!—a really good guy. She thought about how miserably he could have treated her, how obnoxious he could have been, and that would have been exactly what she expected. But there didn't seem to be a trace of arrogance or entitlement, and when he wasn't bitching about his situation, she actually found herself enjoying his company.

And something else. Something she didn't even want to recognize or acknowledge or give a name to. That was a dangerous path she didn't want to follow.

"So," she said, changing the subject. "What's on the entertainment schedule for tonight?"

Ouch! That didn't come out the way she wanted it to. She could see him taking it as a double entendre.

He shrugged. "We'll see." His words had a distinct lack of enthusiasm.

"Okay, I'll go inside, turn on the set, and see what's on right now." She pushed her chair back from the table.

"Check Pay-Per-View. Maybe they have something R rated on tonight. Or how about the adult channels?"

She looked at him and he was grinning at her.

"I'll see what's available. We can watch in the living room. I can make you real comfortable in there." She winked. "I'll even make popcorn."

"Still afraid to be with me in the bedroom, sugar?"

"Of course not." *Yes, I am.* "I can sit with you in any room in the house." *Liar, liar, pants on fire.*

He gave a long, penetrating look, one that seemed to strip off every inch of clothing and leave her bare to his voracious look. Heat crept up her cheeks, and she took another swallow of the cold beer, hoping it would return her temperature to normal.

But not as long as he kept looking at her that way, undressing her with his eyes.

"I'll tell you what," he said at last. "I'd like to offer you a little deal. A truce, kind of."

She lifted an eyebrow. "A deal? A truce?"

"Uh-huh. Let's forget when we're alone that I'm a football player and you're a football player hater." His lips quirked at that.

"And what will that accomplish?" she asked.

"We're taking the conflict out of the equation. Cross that invisible line of scrimmage you've drawn in the sand. Let's pretend we're two people who find themselves sharing a house and who enjoy each other's company."

Erin took another bite of her cookie and chewed it slowly. "Do you think we can do that?"

He held out a hand, palm up. "I don't know, but I think it's worth a try. We won't talk about football; we won't talk about anything related to it. We'll put away the boxing gloves and see if we can just enjoy each other."

She mulled that over for a long moment. "And we'll quit sniping at each other?"

One corner of his mouth quirked up. "I will if you will." He leaned forward, as much as his position allowed him to. "If you promise not to throw this in my face, I'll tell you that I like you. You're smart, savvy, sexy, snarky. All the things I like in a…friend."

She laughed. "You were going to say woman, right?"

He grinned back at her. "Damn straight. Because there's no mistaking you are a woman for sure. So what do you think? Want to try this?"

She thought about it for a long time. It would be nice to finally relax. But the sex would always be simmering in the background. How did they handle that? It was there, underlining every word, scoring every touch and every movement.

"It's not going to go away," he told her, as if he'd read her thoughts. "It's up to us if we act on it."

"Both of us?" she pushed.

He nodded. "That's the way it works best."

She nibbled on her lower lip, letting everything tumble in her mind. She'd be taking a real chance here. Being combative with him was the safe way but it was also mentally and emotionally exhausting. Maybe she should try it his way for a while. They could always go back to square one. She hauled in a huge breath and let it out slowly.

"Okay. I'll give it a shot."

The grin on Jake's face did funny things to her nerve endings. He held out his hand to shake, and when she took it, heat pulsed through her body like an overheated furnace. Maybe this would be a lot harder than she thought.

What would she do if he knocked down all her barriers and she gave into everything with him? How would she handle it when it all self-destructed? Because she knew damn well that's exactly what would happen.

Chapter 11

"Looking pretty good, Jake." Joe Reilly shook Jake's hand, then looked him over from head to toe. "That's some fancy cast you've got."

Jake had worn khaki shorts since the only way to get jeans or slacks over the bulky device was to cut the seam down the side.

"Bigger than the one you had, I'm thinking." He tried making a joke out of it.

"Yeah, you have all the fun. Looks like you get around okay, though." He nodded at the crutches. "Those are a bitch to get used to. I know you'll be glad to get rid of them."

Jake was very glad the other man didn't ask him what the prognosis was. The doctors weren't saying yet, and Jake was reluctant to ask at this point.

As with Lynne Corday, Jake had chosen to meet in the den, where he could have complete privacy. Not that they were discussing anything that required secrecy, but knowing Erin's opinion of football players, he didn't feel like discussing his history with her listening in.

"Thanks." He gestured to the carafe and mugs on the tray. "Erin decided coffee would be a lot better for us than beer."

Joe grinned. "Yeah? So this is working out well for you?"

"Uh, it's working. Let's leave it at that. Have a seat."

Joe dropped into the big armchair, putting his briefcase beside him. "Your wrist seems to be fine. What does the doc say about the leg?"

"He's x-raying it again tomorrow to see what the progress is. If I'm lucky, I'll get a walking cast. These crutches are a pain in the ass."

"Don't rush it," Joe warned, unconsciously echoing what Lynne Corday had said. "That's the worst thing you can do."

"I know." Jake exhaled. "It's just so…frightening, I guess. I mean, what the hell am I going to do if in the end I'm done playing ball?"

"I'd say you're borrowing trouble before you need to. But even if that's what happens, you've got a lot to contribute to the world. You could do something like the coaches conference I put together to train high school coaches on how to grow responsible athletes. You could coach young kids. You could get involved in a lot of the youth programs. If I remember when we were in high school, you used to spend Saturday working with the pony league kids. Leaving football isn't a death sentence."

Jake rubbed his forehead. "I guess. It's just, well, different for me than it is for you."

Joe frowned. "If you say so, although I don't see why. Anyway, you've got time to worry about that. Let's talk about this piece I'm doing on you. I got your promo packet from the Mustang media relations director. We'll go through the outline so I can fill in the blanks. I also plan to interview Coach Fenelli. He's pretty excited about the whole thing."

Jake wasn't sure how excited the coach would be if by the time the event took place his football career was over, but he decided to hold his thoughts. He enjoyed the meeting with Joe and was actually surprised how much time had passed when they wrapped it up.

"I'm excited about this." Joe stashed everything in his briefcase and snapped it shut. "I've reconnected with some of the other guys who live in San Antonio and I may get them involved, too. They think this is a great thing."

Jake wasn't sure he wanted anyone else from the team involved if he was a has-been by the time this thing happened. But again he swallowed his words and just thanked Joe for everything. He noticed when the other man rose from the chair he rubbed his thigh, grimacing as if in pain.

"Leg still bother you?" he asked.

"Not so much. Just now and then, especially when I sit for a long time without stretching, but I'm good. Really."

Jake wondered if he'd ever be able to be so offhanded about his own injury.

He managed to haul himself to his feet, despite Joe's insistence he didn't need to, and balance himself on his crutches.

"The least I can do is see you to the door," he joked.

Erin must have heard him clumping down the hall because she came out from her room to say good-bye. "We haven't been watching much in the way of sports," she told Joe, "but I think we need to start watching your show." She looked at Jake. "Right?"

"Oh, sure." He nodded. "Absolutely."

What he really wanted to say was not in a hot minute, but that would sound surly and ungrateful, and probably earn him a few snarky remarks from Erin.

"Okay, then." Joe shifted his briefcase to the other hand so he could shake hands with both of them. "Jake, I'll be getting back in touch with you as we get closer to fill you in on more details." He looked from one of them to the other. "Maybe when you get a little more mobile you could join Shay and me for dinner. We're back and forth to San Antonio a lot and Austin's just ninety minutes away. An easy drive for us."

Erin smiled. "I think that would be nice." She looked at Jake. "Right?"

"Yeah, sure. Of course." *Not in this lifetime.* "When I get rid of this damn cast." He turned to Erin as soon as Joe left and she reset the alarm. "Why did you do that? I don't want to parade the cripple around in public."

She stood there, glaring, hands on hips. "Will you please get over yourself? You aren't the first athlete to be injured and sadly you won't be the last. What makes you think everyone will be staring at you?"

He glared back at her. "What makes you think they won't?" He was *not* going to make a spectacle of himself for anyone.

"Fine," she said at last. "Maybe we can work up to it."

"Like how?"

"Let's get you sitting down again and we'll talk about it. I could—"

But whatever she was going to say was abruptly cut off by the ringing of the doorbell.

Shit.

"Are you expecting anyone else?" Erin asked.

"I'm not. Definitely. Are you, by any chance?"

"Please." She flapped a hand at him. "Give me a break. Who would I be expecting, especially without checking with you first? Let me check the monitor."

"We'll both check it. It can't be anyone I want to see; I'm not in the mood for anyone else."

Silently cursing, he made his clumsy way to the kitchen to see what the security monitor showed. No one from the team had called today to say they were stopping by and he'd avoided everyone else. With Erin's reluctant help, of course. So who the fuck could possibly be at the door?

* * * *

Erin watched Jake as they caught the images on the screen. The concealed camera on the porch was positioned to catch anyone in front of the door. Although, how the hell anyone could get in over the high stone wall or through the electronically controlled gate without the alarm sounding was a mystery.

Standing there were two busty redheads who could have stepped off the pages of Groupies R Us. Their hair was teased into a ridiculous bouffant style, cascading down past their shoulders. Both sported heavy eye makeup and bright red lipstick that clashed with their hair. They wore the shortest shorts and tightest tee shirts she'd seen in a long time, emphasizing toned legs and breasts that could in no way be considered natural. They were obviously identical twins.

Great. Just great.

The doorbell rang insistently three more times.

"Get rid of them." Jake clumped out of the kitchen. If it was possible to make the sound of crutches sound angry, that was exactly what he was doing.

"You weren't expecting them?" Erin asked.

"Fuck, no. Chase them away."

Could she believe Jake? He'd spent enough time working to convince her women like these weren't his style. First she'd get rid of them, and then she'd get to the bottom of things.

Irritated, she headed back to the foyer and pushed the Talk button on the intercom.

"Yes? Who's there?"

In a moment a sexy feminine voice said, "Can we come in, please? We have something for Jake."

I'll just bet you do, Erin thought, and counted to ten. "I'm sorry, but Jake is not expecting visitors. If you give me your names, I'll tell him you came by."

"Oh, we can tell him ourselves, if you just let us in." This was followed by the squeal of giggles.

Okay, she wasn't going to stand here playing games with a couple of idiot groupies. She was pretty sure they wouldn't rush her if she opened the door, but nevertheless she'd be prepared. After shutting off the alarm for the moment, she eased open the front door, pushed the button to unlock it, slid out through the narrow space she created, and shut the door behind her.

The twins grinned widely.

"Hi," one of them said. "I'm Lisa."

"And I'm Lucy," the other one told her.

"We want to see Jake," they chorused, then looked at each other and giggled.

Swell. Just swell.

Erin looked past them to the high stone wall that fronted Jake's house and ran all around the perimeter, and the tall iron gates controlled by a box with a code.

"How did you even get up to the door?" she asked. "That wall is pretty high."

Again they looked at each other and snickered. "That's our secret. But we promise if you let us in, we'll make him feel better."

"What part of 'you aren't getting in' didn't you understand?" Erin was rapidly losing patience. Looking at these two females reminded her of the scene with Trace where—

Nope, not going there again. Not now, not ever.

"I told you." Lisa stamped her foot. "He wants to see us. He'll be mad at you if you send us away."

"Then he'll just have to be mad. I can handle it. And the answer is still no."

Lucy cocked her head and studied Erin. "Aren't you a little, um, old for him?"

Okay, enough was enough.

"And aren't you a little young for him? He's graduated from kindergarten." She looked from one to the other. "One more time. Jake is not receiving visitors. I'll open the gate for you to leave. Otherwise I'm calling the police and I'll have you arrested as trespassers."

She would, too. These women were exactly like the ones Trace McKay hung out with when he was supposed to be exclusive with her. Just the sight of them made her hackles rise and a bitter taste flood her mouth.

The twins stared at her.

"The police?" Lisa's mouth formed a round O. "Are you for real?"

"You have no right do that." Lucy stamped her foot again. "Jake will be glad we're here. You'll see."

"No, I don't think so. I'll give you until the count of three to get going or your ass is grass."

"Jake will be mad at you." Lisa tossed her head and her hair cascaded down her back in a red waterfall.

"Jake will give me a raise," Erin snapped. "I promise you."

"He might fire you," Lucy added. "*I* promise *you*."

"Okay, enough." Erin glared at them. "Now scram."

"We'll make sure he knows how mean you were to us," Lisa told her.

"Good. Be my guest. Just leave. Now. I'm going inside, and if you aren't at the gate by the time I close the door, the cops will definitely be here."

Lucy tugged at Lisa's arm. "Come on, let's go. She's just a bitch. We'll figure something out."

"Not likely," Erin told them.

She stood on the porch, watching, and when she saw they'd reached the end of the driveway she slipped inside and hit the remote. They stomped out onto the street, anger in every move. Erin closed the gate as soon as they were clear, locked the door, and reset the alarm.

Crap, she thought. Obviously someone had contacted those two idiots, given them Jake's address, and probably even driven them here. Maybe even got them over the wall onto the grounds. Was it that asshole Santos, mad because Jake wouldn't talk to him? Or someone else who thought it would either be a good joke or a little gift to cheer him up?

Jake was still in the kitchen, leaning against the counter.

I won't be mad at him. He didn't know the bimbos were coming. I will talk to him like an adult.

"Your cheering section was determined not to leave." She said it in an even-toned, casual voice. "They wanted to make you feel better."

"My cheering section? Not damn likely."

"Are you sure you didn't call them when you weren't having any success getting me to hit the sheets with you again?" She studied his face. "I think they said they were Lucy and Lisa? Ring any bells?"

"Lucy and Lisa?" He shook his head. "I have no idea who the hell you are talking about."

"They said you'd want to see them. You'd be mad if I didn't let them in." She paused and watched him carefully. "Very mad, as a matter of fact."

Jake made a rude sound. "I'd be mad if you did. I don't know who the hell they are except part of the ditzy fluff balls who hang around the team every chance they get." He made a face. "I'll bet it was Santos's idea of a joke. That's just his style. He has the maturity of an adolescent teenager, and he's probably pissed I won't talk to him."

Erin blew out a breath. So she was probably right about that.

"Would he really do something like that?"

"In a hot minute. I guess I'm surprised some idiot on the team hasn't done something like this before now. Half of them can't seem to control either their hormones or their brains."

"You're kidding. They think you'd enjoy this?"

"Apparently." He gave her a penetrating stare. "I keep trying to tell you I'm not the insensitive playboy you think I am. I avoid females like those two, the—what did you call her?—the Eye Candy Mandys. It's not my style. I wish you'd believe me."

"I'm surprised you don't have a better security system, one with sensors on the perimeter at strategic locations."

"Didn't think I'd need it," he told her. "I have a reputation for being pretty inhospitable when it comes to partying and shit like that, despite today's little disaster."

"But you have such a beautiful house," she remarked. "I guess I'm surprised you don't entertain a lot."

"Not my style," he repeated.

Okay, discussion ended. She could take a hint.

"Well, then, we need to call people and let them know what happened." She was surprised he'd agreed to that.

"Damn straight," he agreed.

"Really?" she persisted, just to make sure he meant it.

"Absolutely. Get hold of Jim DiMarco. He'll take care of this. Probably read everyone the riot act."

"I thought by the time guys got to the NFL they were too old for fraternity pranks."

"Some people never grow up." He turned around. "I'm going to sit out on the back patio. How about joining me with a cold beer? After this you deserve it. And we'll talk."

"Talk?"

He nodded. "Talk."

Okay, then!

"Go on," she told him, fishing her cell out of her pocket. "I'll make my call, then meet you out there."

DiMarco was furious. Erin could hear it in his voice. But he was controlled with her. Businesslike. "Some of my players think this is a big frat party. Tell Jake I'll fix it. And I'll come by sometime tomorrow. Let me know if there are any more problems in the meantime. And you can bet I'll pass the word to all the team members to keep their playmates in line."

He told her she'd have nothing more to worry about. She decided she wouldn't want to be whoever was responsible for this. She thanked him very much and hung up.

After snagging two cold bottles of brew, she carried them out to the patio. Jake was waiting for her at the table, leg propped as usual on an ottoman from one of the outdoor lounge chairs, curiosity evident in his gaze.

"I called DiMarco, and he'll take care of it on his end. He also recommended, however, getting your security system beefed up."

"Yeah, yeah, yeah. The security company tried to talk me into it when they put in the system, but honestly, it's been a while since I've had stalkers so I didn't think I needed it when I moved in here."

"Well, it seems you need it now. Can I take care of it for you? Call them? Set something up?"

"Call Scott Manchin, my agent, about what happened today and tell him you notified the team office. He'll call the security company, and he'll also make sure Jim puts the hammer down with the team. He'll tell the guys to have their bimbos lay off or we'll have them arrested for trespassing."

"Are you sure you don't want to talk to him yourself?"

"Nope. I have every confidence you can handle this."

"All right, then. I'll take care of it."

"Sit down," he told her and nodded at the chair opposite him. "And please listen to what I have to say."

She sat, still irritated by the twins but determined to hear him out. She didn't want to break both legs jumping to the obvious conclusion but old impressions died hard. She folded her hands around her beer and waited, back straight, feet planted together.

One corner of his mouth kicked up in a tiny grin. "Could you manage to not look so much like a school teacher about to send me to the corner? Especially since I'm pretty damn sure none of this is my fault. Although you'd make a cute teacher with that beer."

She couldn't help smiling back. "Okay. I'll do my best." She forced herself to relax and take another sip of the cold brew. Then she sat up straight again. "Would you like something to go with? Maybe crackers and cheese?"

He held up a hand. "I'm all set. I don't need any more cookies or anything else. I want to get this straightened out, so just sit. Please."

"Fine." She sat back again, holding the bottle in her lap. "Go on. I'm all ears."

Jake actually laughed. "With a healthy dose of temper." Then his smile disappeared. "I don't know where you got your strange perception of me, but I'd like to put it to rest once and for all. Listen carefully. Please." He took a swallow of beer. "Unlike a lot of the guys in professional sports, I never thought it was great to have half-naked women hanging all over me, ready to fulfill my every need. That was never my style, for…for a lot of reasons."

"Honestly?"

He nodded.

"Isn't it kind of designated behavior in football?" She couldn't help asking.

"For some people. But not everyone. There are guys who never mix it up with the groupies, and for very good reasons." He gave her a pointed stare. "And believe me, I know all those reasons."

"Why?" she asked. "Because you've been there, done that?"

He shook his head. "Because I never wanted to be there, but I saw plenty who did. I had goals to achieve; I was focused. I had a life plan, so to speak. When I was drafted by the Mustangs, I thought I'd won the jackpot. I don't know if you're aware of this, if Ivy's said anything, but it was just the two of us and our mom since I entered high school."

"No." She shook her head. "She never has. But, well, where was your dad? Had he passed away?"

Jake's face hardened and something bad flashed in his eyes. "Not in the picture. Let's leave it at that."

What was that all about? "Okay," she prodded. "Continue."

"I saw what irresponsible behavior did to others. Hell, you can read about it all the time. It wasn't for me. For one thing, these females go from guy to guy, sometimes more than one at a time. You never know who's clean or not, and what's gonna be carried back to you." He chuffed a laugh. "This will sound strange, but my mom gave me a big lecture about it."

"And you listened to your mother?"

A sad look flashed in Jake's eyes. "My mother was an incredible woman. I respected her more than almost any other woman on earth. I didn't want to embarrass or disappoint her. Besides, she made good sense."

Erin couldn't squelch her curiosity. "You speak of her in the past tense. Come to think of it, so does Ivy, although she always mentions little things about her."

"She passed away three years ago. Cancer."

Sympathy bubbled up inside her. "Oh, Jake, I'm so sorry."

"The people Ivy and I are today is because of her." He was silent for a long moment, and then he looked straight at her. "Have I been with other women? I'm not a monk or a saint, just damn discriminating."

Erin hated what she said next, but the words just seemed to drop out of her mouth. "It didn't take much for you to come home with me. So what does that make me, anyway?" Thank you, Trace, for the damaged self-confidence.

He leaned forward as much as he could, lifted one of her hands from her lap, and held it in both of his. "It makes you a very special person, someone I wanted to be with right away. A lot."

She wanted to pull her hand away, but it felt so good cradled in his warm ones. And she really did want to believe every single word he said. To trust that he was different than Trace and all the other jocks still playing in the field of groupies. She had promised to try, even though since Trace that kind of trust came very hard to her.

He waited, and when she didn't comment he said, "Well? Don't you believe me?"

"I want to. And—okay, I'm giving it my best shot. But let's take care of the immediate problem first. If those two idiots showed up, what's to say no one else will?"

He drew his brows together. "Nothing I suppose."

"Okay. I'll call Scott as soon as we're finished here and put him on it. I'm sure having Eye Candy Mandys all over the place isn't what he wants for your image."

"Damn straight."

She took a sip of her beer. "I also think we need to chat about having dinner with Shay and Joe."

Jake picked up his bottle of beer and drained the last of it. Erin caught herself watching the flex of muscles in his neck as he swallowed, the sensuous play of them beneath the skin just showing a late day scruff.

"And *I* think I'm going to lie down." He gave her a slow grin. "If you want to talk, I'll be in the bedroom, waiting."

Heat flashed over Erin, searing her nerve endings. She got the distinct feeling he had more in mind for the bedroom than just lying down, and anticipation wiggled through her body. Could she resist him? Did she even want to at this point? Hadn't he just proved to her that he wasn't at all what she thought he was?

She pushed away from the table and stood up, gathering the empty beer bottles. "Do you need help getting to the bedroom?"

He gave her a slow grin. "I'd love to say yes, but I think you need to make those phone calls. I can manage to clump my way in there."

Still, she waited until he heaved himself to an upright position, gathered the crutches and stuck them under his arms, and began to maneuver his way off the patio. Erin opened the sliding door for him, and when he was safely inside, headed for the kitchen. After tossing the bottles in the recycle bin, she dug Jake's cell out of her pocket and began punching numbers.

She could tell Scott Manchin was pissed at the incident.

"I'll fix it," he told her, not one bit of humor in his voice. "Some of my clients roll in that stuff, but thankfully Jake never did. Could be one of his idiotic teammates thought they'd send him a present."

"That's what he said," she told him.

"He's right. I'll get on this, and come by and see him tomorrow." His voice softened slightly. "Besides, I want to meet the woman who can handle taking care of the grizzly."

"The grizzly?"

"Yeah." He chuckled. "When Jake gets irritated, he's like a bear with a sore paw. Anyway, don't worry, either of you. I'll put a stop to any more of this."

His words made her feel better, but still…

He let her know he'd call the security company and get them out there at the crack of dawn to beef things up. He thanked her for calling, told her he'd just arrived in Austin, and repeated that seeing Jake was high on his list, so she could look for him sometime tomorrow. He'd call before he arrived.

After she hung up, she stuck the phone back in her pocket, let out a slow breath, and headed for Jake's bedroom. Butterflies beat a rapid tattoo with their wings in her tummy and moisture flooded her panties. The pulsing in her pussy spread to every erogenous zone in her body. All her receptors told her Jake wasn't lying down because he was tired. She was sure what he wanted to do had no relationship to another getting-to-know-you talk.

Besides the signals her erotic dreams were sending her, every hot detail of the other night kept replaying in her head. The sex might have been awkward, but it was no less enjoyable because of it. Wait. Enjoyable didn't begin to describe how she'd felt.

Should she stop trying to ignore what was happening, or on the verge of happening? No matter what her opinion of football players in general, the intense physical attraction between her and Jake Russell had electrified the air right from the beginning. She'd be lying through her teeth if she denied that her desire for him, practically a craving, was escalating almost daily, despite her determination and best intention.

Well then, if acting on that attraction again was what he had in mind right now, maybe they had danced around this long enough. Maybe it was time to just go for it and get it out of her system once and for all. Kind of like overeating so you could start a new diet.

Yeah. Like that was going to happen.

Chapter 12

Jake watched Erin walk into the room, her attitude signaling a mixture of desire and trepidation. Days ago, when his anger had finally settled down and the pain in his leg had died to a faint, dull ache, he'd spent time plotting how to move things forward with her. The invisible line of scrimmage was a barrier, and he needed to find a way to snap the ball and initiate the play.

The chemistry between them was so damn intense it practically lit up any room they were in together, especially after their one clumsy attempt the other night to satisfy it. It had been there from the beginning and nothing had happened since then to change that.

Now, however, he realized his sister might have known all along what she was doing. Maybe she'd seen a spark that night at the party. Maybe— who the hell knew what. But she was always on some kind of mission where he was concerned.

He still had no idea what had gone wrong the night he and Erin spent together, or even what was behind her attitude toward him. Try as he might he couldn't get anything out of her except her standard "hate jocks" line. But now they'd circled around this, tested the waters, and silently seemed to agree that they needed to get it out of their systems or see if it moved them forward. When he'd told her he was going to lie down and she said she'd see him in his bedroom, something had snapped and ignited in her eyes. A spark that he hoped had been simmering in there all this time.

He hoped. Damn, how he hoped. His avid gaze took her in as she walked toward him.

God, she was so damn hot. He wanted her now. Right here.

Okay, spark, here comes the lighter.

"You're still sitting up," Erin commented as she came close to the bed. She swiped her tongue slowly against her lower lip, making his balls tighten in reaction. "I thought you wanted to lie down."

He pointed to the crutches leaning against the nightstand. "That's as far as I got. I need help getting the shoe off." He winked at her, casual, although he had to admit he was a little nervous. "And maybe the same with the clothes."

A hint of a grin teased at her lips. "You want me to help you undress?"

"If you think you're up to the task."

She creased her forehead in a mock scowl, but he saw amusement dancing in her eyes. "Are you planning any funny stuff here, Mr. Russell?"

"And if I was?" he asked in a low voice.

The look she gave him was so intense he felt it clear to the core of him. All her questions and doubts and reservations were clear as crystal in her eyes. Jake waited for a long moment for her to decide what to do next, holding his breath. He saw the moment she made her decision and gave in to the situation. When she spoke, her voice was soft, like a caress.

"Then maybe I can just take care of this for you."

He cupped her chin and scanned her face, looking for any last vestige of doubts, but finding none there. "I wish you would."

She knelt down and removed his single shoe, and placed it carefully to the side. Catching her bottom lip between her even white teeth, she unbuckled his belt, drew it through the loops, and placed it next to the shoe. Next came the snap on his shorts and a fumbling tug on the zipper of his fly. Her fingers brushed against the burgeoning thickness of his cock, and heat zipped through his veins.

"I think we need to do the shirt first," she decided.

He groaned, wanting his cock free and her hands on it.

He'd put on a soft collar shirt for his meeting with Joe, rather than his usual tee shirt. Now he pulled it over his head and tossed it to the other side of the bed. Deliberately he leaned back on his elbows, legs hanging over the side, waiting for her next move. She swallowed hard, throat muscles flexing, but forged ahead, tugging down the zipper the rest of the way. He had to grit his teeth at the touch of her slim fingers on him but he managed.

"Can you lift up your hips?" She asked the question without looking at him.

"Like this?" Careful with his injured leg, he braced himself up enough that she could pull the khaki shorts free. She was careful sliding them down over the cast, then added them to everything else on the floor. He waited to see what she'd do next.

"Um, are we leaving the boxers on?" she asked.

"I don't know." He grinned. "You tell me."

He watched her gaze at his groin for a long time, fixated on the heavy thickness of his cock. Then she slowly maneuvered the boxers down over his hips, waiting while he pushed his butt off the bed just enough so she could pull them down farther. Again she was careful moving the fabric over his cast.

Then she just knelt there between his legs and stared for a long moment at his shaft. She reached out a hand that shook just slightly and wrapped her fingers around it, her eyes bright with desire. Oh, yeah, that's the look he wanted. She slipped her hand up and down the length of him once, slowly, and he held his breath, waiting to see if she stopped. She stroked him again and again. When she slid a hand between his thighs and lightly cupped his balls, he groaned at the pleasure of it.

Jesus!

He threaded his fingers in her hair, tugging it back from her face so he could lock his gaze with hers.

"Much more of that and this party will be over before it starts. I've been thinking about this for a long time, sugar. I want to take it slow."

She gave him a saucy grin. "Think we can figure out what to do about the cast this time?"

"Maybe. I'll give it some serious thought." He stroked a finger down the satiny skin of her neck, stopping at the hollow where her pulse beat wildly, and couldn't help licking his lips. "I, uh, think one of us has too many clothes on."

"Really? What do you think I should do about it?"

"How about getting rid of yours so I can see every inch of that sexy body?"

Again he waited, watching her for any clues or signals. When she rose to her feet, backed away a couple of steps, and pulled the hem of her blouse from the waistband of her jeans, he let himself breathe again. She was going to do it! Would it be like his dream? Better? Automatically he reached his hand out for his cock, lazily stroking it as he stared at Erin.

Her lips curved in a knowing, sensual smile as she slowly popped each of the buttons on her blouse. Just watching the simple act of her shrugging the fabric down her arms and off made him harden even more. The creamy mounds of her breasts were restrained only by a confection of lavender and lace that cupped them the way his hands itched to. Erin stood there, chin lifted slightly, the hint of a come hither smile on her lips, as she released the clasp and those luscious breasts sprang free.

They were even more beautiful than he remembered, from either the dreams or their last abortive attempt to have sex. The nipples that topped them looked like dollops of pale chocolate frosting. He wanted to draw them into his mouth and suck on them until they were hard as candy and their sweetness coated his tongue.

She tossed the bra aside, stepped out of her shoes, and eased down the zipper of her slacks, the hiss of it loud in the room. She kept her eyes on his face the entire time she slithered out of the garment. The pulse at her throat was beating so hard he could see it against the delicate skin. His own pulse had ratcheted up so his entire body throbbed with it.

When Erin was down to only the tiniest pair of bikini panties he'd ever seen, in the same pale lavender as her bra, she turned around so her back was to him. The scrap of silk and lace barely covered the sweet cheeks of her ass, their shape making his palms itch to hold them and caress them. Then, hooking her fingers in the edge of the panties, she very slowly shimmied them down past her hips and thigh. The movement of her ass as she rocked it from side to side with the grace of a dancer had him mesmerized. Sliding his thumb over the head of his cock, he wasn't at all surprised to discover fluid sitting at the peak. Slowly he massaged it into the sensitive skin, wishing like hell it was the cream from Erin's pussy he was spreading.

Jake had trouble keeping his tongue in his mouth when she bent over to tug the teeny tiny panties all the way down her legs. She stepped out of them and then bent over to pick them up, giving him a mouthwatering view of not only her ass but also her pussy that he knew was incredibly delicious. She straightened, yanked the barrette from her hair, and shook loose the tumbled masses of dark red curls. Tossing that red mane, she gave him a seductive look over her shoulder. Then she gave a little wiggle of her hips.

Holy shit! He could feel his shaft swelling even more.

She turned and started toward him, then stopped, the bold tease suddenly gone, a look of hesitation washing over her face. If she stopped now he'd back away, although he was afraid if he did, his cock would self-destruct.

"Are we really doing this?" she asked.

"Not if you don't want to." *Please want to.* "It's all up to you." Still, she stood there, poised on the edge of uncertainty. "Come here, sugar." He gestured with his fingers. "Please."

Then the vixen was back, and she walked slowly back to the bed until she stood between his outstretched legs.

"Is this what you want?"

God! The husky sound of her voice sent every single one of his nerves dancing, all of them sending the charge straight to his groin. He raked his gaze over her body, taking in every inch of her creamy skin, his mouth watering so much he was afraid he would drool.

"It'll do for a start."

She bent low to press her mouth to his and Jake took over immediately. Anchoring his fingers in her hair, he held her head in place while he sketched the seam of her lips with his tongue and lightly touched the corners. She opened for him easily, sucking in his tongue and dragging her teeth over it oh so lightly. Damn! Lightning shot through him straight to his balls. He clamped her head more tightly, sealed his mouth to hers, and danced with her delicate tongue. He traced lines in the hot liquid cavern, reveling in the erotic taste of her. She was just as aggressive, sliding her tongue along every inch of his inner surface and moaning softly with pleasure. Kissing her was pure pleasure, an indulgence he was sure he'd never get enough of.

When they broke the kiss, they were both panting.

"Let's do that again." He ran his knuckles lightly over the soft skin of her cheek and down along the line of her jaw.

"Mmm," she hummed and pressed her mouth to his once more.

This time the kiss was more leisurely, gentler, softer, but no less erotic. He wanted to take his time with her, kiss her some more, explore her body as he'd done on that long, erotic, magical night they were together—at least that was how he remembered it. He wanted to listen to her sighs and her little moans again, sounds that signaled what gave her pleasure so he'd know what was good, what she liked.

The unexpected anticipation had been building day by day since the first moment she'd walked into his bedroom and her eyes had unwillingly dropped to the outline of his engorged cock. He considered it lucky he hadn't just torn off her clothes and ravished her. Yeah, not too smooth there. And the broken leg and the cumbersome cast had certainly been a problem the one night she'd dropped her guard. Not that he didn't love her sweet mouth sucking him hard or her hands lightly rubbing his balls. But he wanted the real deal, his dick inside her sweet pussy, her inner walls gripping him like a vise and milking him until there was nothing left.

With superhuman effort, he forced his mind back to the here and now. Bracketing her waist with his hands, he tugged her closer, leaned forward as best he could with the fucking leg in the way, and placed a string of kisses from her navel to the top of her delicious mound. If the damn cast wasn't getting in the way, he'd run his tongue lazily through her slit, sucking up her cream and teasing her clit until she begged for mercy. He'd taste the skin of the crease where hip and thigh were joined, remembering how much that had turned her on.

Instead he did the best he could. Sliding his hands down to the curve of her hips, he leaned forward and pulled one plump nipple into his mouth. It pebbled and swelled immediately at his touch, so he clamped his teeth lightly on its tender surface. Her low moan vibrated through his body, and she arched into him, hands on his shoulders to brace herself. Her scent drifted up to his nostrils, teasing and tantalizing him, a mixture of flowers and pure woman.

He worked first one nipple, then the other, holding her firmly in place but at the same time being extra careful not to rub his cast too hard against her tender skin. From her nipples, he moved his lips in a trail of wet kisses down to her navel and lower. He shifted one hand to slide the fingers between the lips of her hot pussy, finding her slick and wet. He wanted so desperately to slip his fingers inside her and feel those tight muscles clench around them. But more than that, he wanted to feel her around his cock. That one night had made him crave a repeat.

Erin threaded her fingers in his hair and rocked her hips slightly, urging him to stroke and tease her. He could have, too, for a long time, exploring every crevice of her delicious body, but he'd been dreaming about and remembering the feel of his cock in her tight little channel for too long. Slowly he lifted his hand to his mouth, ignoring her soft protests at the loss of his touch, and carefully licked each finger clean of her juices.

"Jesus, you taste good. Better than anything I can remember. I could probably live off your cream for the rest of my life. But..." He set her slightly away from him. "I want inside you as soon as we can figure out how to do this."

The fucking cast was going to be the death of him.

The rise and fall of her chest and the flutter of the pulse at the delicate hollow of her throat told him she was as aroused as he was.

"Let's see what we can do here, sugar."

"Lie back," she told him. "Go on. Here. I'll help you."

He wanted to tell her not to touch him or he'd spill all over himself like he had the other day, but her slender hands were already giving his shoulders a gentle shove and guiding him to turn enough to lie back on the pillows. He tried to be matter of fact as she helped him arrange the leg with the cast but every time her fingers brushed the inside of his thigh or his groin his cock throbbed with insistent need. By the time he had himself settled in a good position, he had to grit his teeth to find any control.

"Take off one of the pillow cases," he told her.

Erin stared at hm. "What?"

"They're king-sized. The only way we can do this is if you climb on top of me, and I don't want to injure you. Wrap one around my cast so you don't bruise your sweet, sweet body."

When she bent over him to do what he asked, her breasts brushed against his naked thigh and he sucked in a breath. But more than that, when she arranged herself on top of him, her wet cunt brushing against his skin, the top of his head nearly came off. He ran his hands over the gentle curve of her ass, dipping his fingertips into that tempting crevice between her cheeks. With his middle finger, he found the hot pucker of her anus and pushed lightly against it. Damn, he wanted to fuck her there. It wasn't an act he indulged in with many women. For him it was the definitive personal connection and he saved it for special situations. He knew if he could penetrate her ass with his dick, the ultimate joining, it would bind them together as nothing else did.

But one step at a time.

"Can you hurry a little?" He nearly bit the words off.

The smile she gave him, a sultry curve of her lips, heated him clear through his body. "A little eager, are we?"

He touched her outer lips with the tip of a finger. "I'd say you are, too." He caught her gaze with his. "Right, babe?"

"Yes." The word was almost a whisper. She held out her hand. "Condom, please."

Shit. He was so far gone he'd totally forgotten. After reaching into the nightstand drawer, he pulled one out and handed it to her. His self-control stretched to the limit as she ripped open the packet and her slim fingers slowly rolled the latex down the length of him.

"Have mercy," he rasped.

"I think I'm fresh out." She moved forward a fraction, rubbing her slick flesh against him.

Jesus!

"Lift up," he told her, urging her with his hands at her hips.

She did and he eased her slowly down on his very swollen, aching cock. He sucked in a breath as her tight, slick sheath clamped around him, squeezing him. When the head bumped against the mouth of her womb, he nearly lost it.

"You good to go?" he asked, hoping like hell she said yes because he didn't have much left of his frayed control. Looking at her, he could see she was in almost the same state.

Erin leaned forward, bracing herself, and slowly began a delicious up and down movement. Each rasp of her soaked flesh against his dick pushed him closer to orgasm. Each squeeze of those muscles nearly made him explode.

"Faster," he groaned. "Please, Erin. I'm begging you."

She licked her lower lip, that sexy little habit that drove him nuts and gave him the magic smile again. "Don't you want to enjoy every minute of it?"

"Believe me, sugar, you have no idea how much I'm enjoying it."

Even worrying about hurting her with his cast didn't take the edge off. Finally, out of desperation for his control, he moved one hand around to find the wet velvet of her clit, just barely touching his chest, and rubbed it and squeezed it until she sped up her rhythm. Her eyes glazed with hunger and those wonderful breasts danced in front of his eyes. The harder he rubbed the faster she moved, her body now racing toward release. He burned with the need for her, every nerve and muscle poised on the edge of detonation.

Jake ground his teeth together until he thought his molars would crack, but he was determined to wait for her. She rode him with fierce intensity, her rich, silky mane of hair swirling around her head, mouth slightly open. Harder, faster, his cock begging for mercy as he tried to wait for her, tried to hold on. As they moved together he had the feeling more than just their bodies were connected. He felt their very souls merging, an electric melding that made them one. He wanted it to last forever, even though his body was begging for release.

Then she was there, her cunt squeezing down hard on him, tremors racing through her inner muscles. The orgasm spiraled up from deep inside his body, like the unwinding of tightly coiled steel, pushing its way through him. Now. Now, now, now. They exploded together, bodies shaking so hard he wondered for one crazy, fleeting moment if his cast would crack and fall right off. Then he was flying, whirling in space, Erin's hot body pulsing in time with his. The muscles of her cunt contracted and squeezed every drop of cum from him until he was sure he had none left.

Finally the last of the intense spasms subsided. Erin leaned forward and collapsed onto his chest, her firm breasts pressing into him, the nipples like hard, little dots. Her heart thudded against him, almost in time with his own, and the only sound for a long moment was the rasp of uneven breathing. Jake banded his arm around her, holding her to him, unwilling to break the connection between their bodies.

With his free hand, he stroked her hair, inhaling the sweet scent of her shampoo. God, she was in his blood, in every part of his body. He'd had plenty of damn good sex, but this was way beyond that. It was more than the mechanics, more than instant gratification. Erin Bass had well and truly spoiled him for any other woman. Ever.

He had no idea how long they lay there, bodies slick with perspiration nearly glued together. He coasted his hands over the lines of her body, loving the feel of her satin-smooth skin, the dips and swells of her curves. Sliding his fingers into the thick mass of her silky hair, he inhaled its flowery fragrance, drawing her scent deep into his body. He thought he could stay like this forever.

At last she lifted her head, her face so close he could count her eyelashes, and gave him that smile that just undid him.

"You okay, sport?" Her voice was low, vibrating gently against him.

He chuckled, his chest jostling lightly against hers. "I don't think I've ever been better. Oh, maybe without the broken leg, but otherwise? I'm damn fine." He kissed her forehead. "How about you?"

She waited so long to answer him he was almost afraid to hear what she said. Then she brushed her lips lightly against his.

"Good," she told him. "I'm good. No, not good. Great." She giggled. "The broken leg didn't seem to slow you down a bit."

"And thank God for that because, Erin? I don't think I've ever wanted anyone the way I want you."

She touched his lips with the tip of a finger. "Let's not get ahead of ourselves, okay? We're still kind of finding our way here."

He knew that. He just wished he could figure out a way to find it faster.

"Whatever works for you. We'll take it one step at a time." He chuckled. "As long as we take a lot of steps like this."

He wanted to grab her and hold her tightly to him again when she pushed up and eased herself from his cock. She balanced on her knees on either side of his body, the spicy scent of her cream drifting up to tantalize him. Jake couldn't help himself. As she was poised there, he ran the tips of his fingers through her slit and again took a healthy lick of her juices.

"Better than whiskey, sugar," he said, and it definitely was. He could get drunk on her on a regular basis. "Okay, you'd better let me help you."

"No, you stay still," she insisted. "The last thing we want to do is more damage to that leg. Don't move."

"But—"

"I can do this."

It was torture watching Erin ease herself completely off his body. When she lifted one leg very slowly to swing it over his cast and rest it between his thighs, completely exposing her delicious cunt with its well-trimmed cap of curls, Jake had a hard time not reaching for her. He wanted so badly to place his mouth on her sweet sex as he'd done before, and lick and suck and lap until he'd drunk his fill of her. If, that was, he ever did get enough, which he had an idea was highly unlikely.

Finally she was standing on both feet at the side of the bed.

"Don't move," she told him with a mischievous grin.

"As if I could," he huffed on a slightly hysterical note.

"Good. I'll be right back."

But when she turned, he got a good look at the side of her body that had been closest to his cast, and he frowned.

"Come over here." He tugged her closer. "Let me see this."

"I'm fine." She tried to pull away from him, but he held on tightly.

"Just hold still a minute, will you? I'm not exactly too flexible right now." He ran his hand over the lower curve of one ass cheek and the outer side of her thigh. "Looks like that pillow case didn't work so well. You'll be sore here in the morning."

She looked down at herself over her shoulder. "It's not so bad. I'll put some cream on it."

Jake heaved a sigh. "This fucking leg and the fucking cast are ruining my life."

Erin threaded her fingers through his hair and caressed his cheek. "We're doing just fine, Jake. The cast will come off soon enough. And think how inventive we can be in the meantime."

"Well, yes, there is that." He gestured at his cock and the condom. "Can you give me a hand here? I have to, um…"

"No problem. I was just about to take care of things for you." She headed for the bathroom. "I'll be right back."

She returned with some tissues and a washcloth and went to work. He forced himself to lie completely still while she tended to him. After easing the condom off over his now only semi-hard dick, she wrapped it in the tissues and set them aside. Then she proceeded to clean him with a warm cloth as she'd done that time he'd—no, he didn't plan to dwell on that. He also didn't want her to spend much time doing this right now. The orgasm had sapped most of his energy, but at her gentle touch, the stupid Little Head was trying to come to life again.

"That's enough." He wrapped his fingers around one wrist. "Besides, with the condom there isn't much to clean up."

"I know." She giggled. "But I wanted to do it again and this time enjoy it."

"Are you saying you didn't enjoy it last time?" he teased.

"Just making sure. Maybe we can wake up our friend here again."

He tugged her hand away. "Nice thought but save it for the next time." He reached up and cupped her chin. "There will be a next time, right?"

Her now familiar slow smile cut right to the core of him. "I expect so. If you're a good boy."

"Wait until you see just how good I can be. Bring that gorgeous face down here." When she did, he planted a gentle kiss on her lips, no tongue, just a symbol of emotion. "That's my thank you."

She studied him, then gave him an answering smile. "You're welcome."

Chapter 13

Scott was as good as his word, and the alarm company had shown up bright and early the morning after the incident with the twins. With the system they brought to install, not even a SEAL team could have gotten into the house or grounds undetected. Well, she laughed to herself, okay maybe a SEAL team. But no one else.

Both he and Jim DiMarco had been irate about the incident and had their own ideas about who had put the girls up to it.

"Who do you think it was?" she asked.

"I'll check it out," DiMarco had said. "And I'll put a stop to it. Unfortunately not everyone in the NFL achieves the level of maturity we'd all like. I know how some of these guys are. But don't worry about it. It's as good as taken care of."

Erin hoped so. She knew first hand some of these guys, too, and they might not be put off so easily.

Scott Manchin also promised to keep an eye on things. Erin liked the man immediately. He was all business, no nonsense. But personable at the same time. And it was obvious he was very worried about Jake. When he left, she walked outside with him to have a few words in private.

"You don't really have to answer me," she said. "I realize you know nothing about me and—"

He held up a hand. "I know that you're doing a great job taking care of Jake, a job not many people could or would handle. I know you're smart, sharp, and have his best interest at heart." He smiled. "And I know Jake's crazy about you, even if he's too hardheaded to admit it."

She stared at him. "All that from one visit?"

Scott laughed. "Studying people and reading them is my business. I'd be no good at my job if I didn't." His face sobered. "Jake's got a tough row to hoe here. I hope he can depend on you. I hope *I* can depend on you."

"Listen." She blew out a breath. "This is just a temporary gig for me. I'm, uh, between jobs."

He nodded. "I know. Jake told me all about it." A smile tipped up the corners of his mouth. "He also told me how it came about. I'm just asking you to keep your options open."

Since job offers weren't flooding her inbox she had no reason not to agree to that.

"But I won't always be here," she reminded him.

He took a moment to reply. "How about this? I'm not sure what Jake's final prognosis will be, but if it's bad, he's going to hit a downward spiral. If you can hang in there until we get past that, I'll use every contact I have to get you into any hotel chain or freestanding in the world. Your choice."

"Whoa. Wait a minute. I don't take handouts."

"And I don't give them. But anyone who can handle this situation the way you are rates top marks in my book. So do we have a deal?"

What could she lose, right?

"Okay, but no more Eye Candy Mandys."

Scott burst out laughing. "Can I put that in my cell memo? I love it." He laughed again.

"Sure. Be my guest."

They shook hands and she watched him drive away, wondering just what on earth she'd managed to get herself into. If Scott Manchin harbored any thoughts about something long term between her and Jake, he was definitely on the wrong path. She was going to enjoy it while it lasted, but when she was done, she was done.

The days actually began to move forward more smoothly. The weather was still nice so Erin served all their meals on the patio. They actually had pleasant conversations. But while she told Jake everything about her life growing up in a household filled with testosterone, he said very little about himself. She knew he and Ivy were close, and despite Ivy's little game plan here, it was obvious Jake cared about her a great deal. He also said little about his mother except she'd been a strong force in their lives.

He did, however, tell her a lot about the Granite Falls Coyotes championship team and the four years of stardom. He talked about Coach Fenelli, who apparently had been a strong influence, and the team members he'd been close to.

"I know I've said this before, but it's possible talking to these guys might give you a perspective on life after football." She paused. "Don't you think?"

"I'll put it on the list." But he didn't sound all that enthusiastic.

So that was a little stumbling block, but she joked him out of it, and they moved on. She decided she'd just have to figure another way to make that happen.

During the day, she helped him with his e-mail, which he'd finally decided to take a look at. "Ivy said it was one of your responsibilities," he reminded her, "and I hate dealing with it." Then he winked. "Besides, you can filter it and sign everything as my executive assistant."

She was glad at least he joked about it.

The phone calls became more constant and she handled those, too. Her personal evil satisfaction came from the few calls he got from groupies who managed to get either his cell number or his landline. She enjoyed telling them that Jake was not interested in them, now or ever, and to shake their booties in front of someone else. Whenever Jake overheard her on these calls, he laughed.

"Where were you years ago?" he asked.

She shrugged. "Years ago you probably weren't interested in getting rid of them."

"Damn it, Erin." Anger and frustration mingled in his voice. "I told you those girls didn't appeal to me. What will it take for you to believe what I say?"

Good question, she thought, but at the moment she had no answer.

Then there were the nights. How on earth to describe them? Sometimes they watched movies and ate popcorn, but the other nights? Even in his situation, Jake was an incredible lover. It took a lot of planning and maneuvering, and some positions produced more laughs than satisfaction, but they'd finally figured out ways to make all the body parts work. He seemed totally focused on her every response, her pleasure, her sexual fulfillment. She'd never had a lover so dedicated to her.

At first the memory of the tantalizing striptease she did for him made her face flame when she thought of it. She wasn't usually that bold. But as she became more comfortable with him in bed, as he focused on making her understand how important her pleasure was to him, the embarrassment disappeared, replaced by a need that never seemed to burn out. It was becoming a lot harder to keep reminding herself that this was temporary. When he was better, Jake would go back to his own life, and she'd go back to hers.

Her problem, as she lay in bed most nights in his arms, was that she wasn't so sure anymore she wanted to go back to what she thought of as her "real" life. Her emotions were in a whirl where Jake Russell was concerned. She'd discovered she enjoyed being with him, spending time with him. They laughed at the same places in the movies they watched and yelled at the same scenes of conflict. They liked to eat mostly the same things and even wanted to travel to a lot of the same places. And learning more and more about the real Jake Russell turned her ironclad image of football jocks on its ear. Oh, she wasn't foolish enough to think they were all like him, but he was real, he was respectful, he was a decent guy who'd been dealt a really bad blow.

That was a fact that still shocked her. Bit by bit her negative expectations of him were crumbling away. She might even—

Nope. Forget it. Not going there.

But at least her changing view of him made life between the two of them much easier and more pleasant. Enjoyable.

Jake continued to insist on holing up in the house, but Erin did manage one small victory. At the moment, Joe Reilly was in San Antonio with his wife, visiting her brother, and they wanted to have dinner with Jake. They extended the invitation to her also, but probably because she'd be his transportation. Getting Jake to this dinner tonight had taken a combination of threats and bribery, but she'd finally convinced him to accept. He was doing a lot better with the crutches, though, and she worried that if he just stayed in the house refusing to see anyone he'd sink into a deep depression. Plus, the big SUV gave him plenty of room to stretch out his leg if she pushed the seat all the way back.

She'd made reservations at a place known for good food but way out of the mainstream, where Jake would not likely run into people he didn't want to see.

"I hope you don't mind doing this at such an out of the way restaurant," Jake said after he crutched his way to the table where Shay and Joe were waiting.

"Not at all," Shay told him. "It's kind of nice for us, too. It's a change to be somewhere that everyone doesn't immediately recognize Joe."

"Of course it is," Erin agreed.

Without making an obvious fuss about it, she inched Jake's chair away from the table, quietly took his crutches, and stood by while he eased himself into the seat. Erin leaned the crutches against the wall near them, seated herself, and smiled at everyone.

"Joe, it's nice to see you again. And Shay, it's a pleasure to meet you." She held out a hand. "Erin Bass."

"Pleasure here too," the other woman said.

They ordered drinks and set aside the menus while they chatted. Erin found the Reillys extremely comfortable to be with. She'd looked Joe up on Google after his first visit to the house and was somewhat stunned at what she found. He'd been a typical jock as far as she was concerned, no less than she'd expected. A playboy. A skirt chaser. He took full advantage of all the non-financial benefits his position as a star quarterback presented him with. But apparently when an injury had forced him to retire, he'd cleaned up his act, gotten a plum job with Fox Sports, and spent his free time raising money for scholarships and conducting clinics for coaches on teaching responsibility to athletes.

He'd gotten married last year to Shay Beckham, sister of the man who'd been his best friend since childhood and who had also been on the championship Coyotes team. Erin was pretty sure that was an interesting story.

She was glad to see Jake relax over dinner, enjoy a drink, indulge in some chitchat with Joe. Except for the interview at the house and the visits by DiMarco and Manchin, this was the first time he'd spent with anyone in any way related to football. She watched him carefully to make sure he wasn't getting upset or irritated by something, but he seemed to be having a good time.

"Have you been together long?" Shay asked in a low voice.

"What?" Erin's hand jerked and spilled some of the water she was holding. "Oh, no, that's…I mean, we aren't… That is, you've got this all wrong."

Shay's mouth curved in a small grin. "If you say so, but the signs are pretty clear. He's definitely got a thing for you."

Oh, yes. Sure. A sexual thing, but that was about it.

"We're just, um, what I mean to say is this is just a business arrangement."

"Uh-huh. None of my clients ever looked at me that way." She chuckled. "Which is a good thing, because Joe would take their head off."

"You've been married a year, right?" Erin sipped at her water.

Shay nodded. "That's right. But I've known Joe practically all my life. In the beginning that was a drawback but we got past it." She smiled. "We got past a lot of things."

Erin studied her. "Your brother is a football player as is Joe, so you've probably been around jocks all your life. Don't you worry about their ability to stick to one woman?"

Shay lifted an eyebrow. "I'm going to assume there's a specific reason for that question, and I won't ask what it is. Unless, of course, you want to tell me." When Erin shook her head, Shay leaned back in her chair. "Well, then, what I can tell you is there are a lot of players in professional sports. Not just football. They come out of high school thinking they are God's gift to women, the pro teams pay them a ton of money, and no one has taught them a sense of responsibility."

Erin gave an unladylike snort. "No kidding."

"But then there are guys like my brother, who's an engineer, and Jake, whose mother made sure he was completely grounded." She gave a soft laugh. "Joe had a few lessons to learn, but when he had to retire he was a quick study."

"You guys look really happy."

Shay looked at her husband, her gaze softening. "We sure are but enough of that. I'm sure Joe told you guys about the Facebook page I designed for the Coyotes, didn't he?" Shay asked.

"He did." She leaned closer to the other woman. "Don't let on I told you, but Jake has actually visited it a few times."

Shay's eyes widened. "Really? Because Joe had the distinct impression Jake wanted nothing to do with it."

"Maybe at first. But his curiosity got the better of him and he's logged on a few times."

"How do you know that? Did he say something?"

Erin laughed. "Lord, no. He has me doing his e-mails because, you know, he's Mr. Antisocial right now. So when I'm on his laptop I always check his browser history." She grinned. "Sneaky, huh?"

"I knew I liked you."

"I figure it's the best way to find out what he's into, what gets his attention. He's sure not too forthcoming."

Shay winked. "Your secret is safe with me."

All in all Erin considered the evening a success. The socializing seemed to do Jake some good. At least it got him out of the house and talking to someone besides her. She hoped she could urge him to do more of it. The two men told stories about the golden years in Granite Falls, and for a short while Jake seemed to forget about his injury and his uncertain future. Jake and Joe made plans for one more meeting before the big night in Granite Falls. The men shook hands.

Shay gave Erin a hug, then pulled a business card out of her purse and wrote something on the back of it. Then she handed it to Erin. "Here. The number on the front is my business cell, the one on the back is my personal one. You can always reach me at one of them."

"Thank you, but I wouldn't dream of bothering you," Erin protested.

"No bother." She leaned closer to Erin and lowered her voice. "I was in a—situation once with Joe. I wished then I'd had someone to talk to. Please feel free to call me any time."

Shay's words gave her a warm feeling. "Thank you."

Jake was unusually quiet on the drive home so Erin turned on the radio, found some easy listening music, and adjusted the volume fairly low. They were close to the house when Jake finally broke his silence.

"You and Shay seemed to be getting along well."

"Yes, we did. She's very nice. I like her."

"And Joe?" he asked. "What about him?"

"I met Joe before," she reminded him.

"So you've had more than one chance to form an opinion. Right?"

Erin frowned. "Joe is a nice guy. Is that what you wanted to hear? I enjoyed dinner with them. So did you. Don't deny it."

"I'm not."

"What's this all about?"

"Just trying to make you see that here's a guy who was a football jock, as you call them, who's a really nice person. Married to a woman who obviously loves him and who he treats very well."

Okay. She saw where this was going. And she actually had to admit he was right. That was a shocker.

"If I agree that not all jocks are assholes, is that good enough for you?" she asked.

He gave a soft laugh. "Did that hurt very much?"

"No, but what's the point you're trying to make? If I say you're not so bad, will that satisfy you?"

Jake shook his head. "You're a hard nut to crack, Erin Bass."

"Oh, so I'm a nut now?" she teased.

"You know what I mean." His voice was dead serious. "We're not all serious trash. And I hope you're getting to know me well enough that you realize who and what I am."

She was definitely not ready for this conversation. Maybe she'd never be.

"I have come to the conclusion maybe you're not so bad after all. But if you're trying to convince me you're good for the long haul, can we keep in mind that this situation has an end date? And just enjoy it the way we are right now?"

Another long silence filled the car. Erin waited uncomfortably for Jake to say something, but they were already at the house before he spoke again.

"Enjoy it. Right." He touched her arm. "But we won't shut out any possibilities, right?"

"Right." She glanced over at him. "But we'll just take it as it goes, okay?"

He chuckled. "You're a sly one, but watch out. I'm a sly one, too."

"Have you looked at the Facebook page yet?" She hoped he'd admit it so she could talk to him about it.

"Yeah." The word came out grudgingly.

"Then you should have complimented Shay on it."

"She'd want to know if I'd post something on it. Give her a picture and info she could put on there. All that crap."

"You should think about it." *Don't push. Baby steps here.*

She pulled into the garage, and the next few minutes were taken up with getting Jake out of the car and into the house.

"I'll be glad when I get to finally trash these damn crutches," he complained. "They're nothing but a fucking pain in the ass."

"Bitch, bitch, bitch," she teased. "At least you're moving around so much better. And you had a great time tonight, right?"

"Yeah." His voice was edged with reluctance. It was obvious he was still full of self-pity. "It wasn't so bad."

"Come on. I saw you enjoying yourself."

They were in his bedroom now. Erin followed him to the bed and watched as he eased himself down and leaned the crutches against the nightstand. He was moving so much better. Every day she kept her fingers crossed that the next doctor's appointment would give positive results. So far, each time they'd gone and his leg was x-rayed through the cast, Dr. Moline had just studied the graphs, nodded his head, and said the leg was coming along. But Erin knew "coming along" meant different things to the doctor and to Jake.

"Ivy called today to ask when your next doctor's appointment is." She took the shirt Jake had stripped off and handed to her.

"I don't want her to come." His tone of voice left no wiggle room.

"She's your sister," Erin protested. "She's concerned for you."

"So concerned she tricked me into this arrangement we have—you and me—and then avoided us until she was sure we weren't going to kill each other or her."

"Is that why you won't let her come to see you now? We're past all that crappy stuff. And you keep telling me you two have only each other."

He lifted his good leg, bent it, and pulled off his shoe. "Maybe I just don't want to see pity in her eyes."

"Damn it." She fisted her hands on her hips. "Nobody pities you. Least of all Ivy. Or me."

"You say that now, but wait until we get the final prognosis. My sister knows exactly how important football is to my life. If I get bad news, I want time to process it before I have to face her."

Jake undid his trousers and boosted himself up on his hands so Erin could slide them off his body.

"I think you're getting too used to this," she teased.

"To having you undress me? You bet." He gave a low chuckle. "Think I could hire you to do it permanently?"

She was kneeling between his legs, but she looked up at him, frowning. "Don't joke. You know this is temporary. The minute you've got both legs back I'm gone."

He cupped her chin and looked at her with eyes now darker than espresso. Again she had the impression he wanted to say something but held back. "One of these days, if I'm ever whole again, we're going to discuss that subject at length. Not now." He held up his hand when she opened her mouth to protest. "But after."

"After what?"

"After I decide whether or not I can be any good to anyone again." His mouth curved in a slow smile. "Meanwhile, let's discuss more pleasant subjects. Like how fast you can get your clothes and my boxers off."

Erin deliberately pushed errant thoughts aside and bent to the task at hand, eyes focused on the swollen bulge of Jake's thick cock.

Chapter 14

The next weeks passed without incident. To Erin it hardly seemed possible that more than two months had passed. They'd come a long way from those early days when they circled each other like fighters in a cage. In fact, life at the house was actually and unexpectedly pleasant.

Jake required less personal assistance, physically, although he often yelled for her through the intercom, just to watch her annoyed frown when she came to find him chuckling. With the installation of the security system on steroids, they'd had no more visits from Eye Candy Mandys, although sometimes when Erin looked out the window she could see a couple of them hanging out at the gate, trying to look in.

Jake did his exercises for his wrist every day, and she continued to work his toes the way the physical therapist had shown her. Funny, she felt closer to him doing something that simple than she did when they were in bed together. As she came to understand who he really was, the walls around her heart began to slowly crumble despite her efforts to shore them up.

She kept telling herself she'd soon be gone and this would be over. But each day she found herself falling for him more and more.

She continued to take care of both his snail mail and his e-mail, writing letters and posts as he dictated them. There wasn't that much, really. Scott Manchin handled everything that related to his endorsements and personal appearances, usually e-mailing Jake to keep him up to date, calling when he needed an immediate answer.

"Scott says the networks are still all over him about doing an interview with you." Erin read from the latest e-mail she opened. "He said they'll even send a crew to your house. Make it very easy for you."

"No." Just the one word, but it cut the air like a knife. "I told him over and over. No interviews until I know whether I even have a career anymore."

Erin huffed a sigh and leaned back in her chair. This was an ongoing argument between them, and she was getting very frustrated.

"I wish you would tell me the reason you believe football is the only thing defining you. You have a media presence that you could use to do a lot of good."

He looked up from a letter he was reading. "So you're telling me that people already adore me so much, admire me, that whether or not I play they'll fall all over me?"

She wrinkled her forehead, irritated at his phrasing. "Well, yes. Sort of. I mean—"

"Then why is it so hard for you to see that I'm different from all those guys you refer to as waste case jocks?"

He had her there. She really didn't want to tell him about her poor judgment where Trace McKay was concerned, or how she'd discovered everything in a very public venue.

"Moving right along," she said instead. "I'll e-mail Scott back and tell him we're tabling it for the moment."

"Good idea. You want my secrets? Then you have to share yours. Otherwise we're status quo where all that stuff is concerned."

One of these days, maybe the last day she was here in this house, she might tell him her story. Or maybe not. But she'd definitely be gone. Because one way or another, she didn't trust a future with him. Not that he'd really brought it up. Instead they ignored all the elephants in the room and life progressed.

She constantly battled her conflicted feelings about him. She didn't want to care, because old habits died hard. She continued to have the feeling he wanted to say something to her, but maybe he was waiting for some kind of sign? After all, she was the one who set the rules to begin with. She just wasn't sure what this was she felt, and she didn't want to get burned again. What if, for example, he was a really nice guy but he didn't want any more from her than what they had right now? And she had no idea what that actually was.

Drive yourself crazy much?

"Scott answered back," she told him. "He said he'll be here for the doctor's appointment next week."

"No." Jake slammed his hand on the table. Erin gave thanks it wasn't the one still healing.

"Jake, he's your agent. He has a vested interest in what happens to you."

"I don't want him there."

"Too bad. He says he's coming no matter what. You're being completely unreasonable."

"You think so? Wait until the doc tells me I'm done. You'll see how fast Scott flies out the door to his other clients."

"What is with you about people leaving you when you can't play anymore? How many times do I have to tell you football doesn't define you? Only a part of you."

"And how many times do I have to tell *you* that you are completely wrong."

She looked up from the laptop to see him glaring at her, muscle twitching in his cheek.

"Bull. Look at Joe Reilly," she reminded him. "Scott didn't drop him when he had to retire. He got him a great job with Fox Sports and helps him with his philanthropy. And he still does a ton of endorsements."

"Fine, fine, fine. Whatever."

She heaved a sigh. "Just—please. Do us all a favor and don't make a scene in the doctor's office."

As the day of the appointment approached, Jake became more tense and withdrawn and Erin worried constantly. If the news was bad, she had no idea how he'd react. Maybe if she took the first step, told him how she felt about him, she could convince him she'd be there for him no matter what.

"He's as tight as a high wire," she told Ivy one evening on the phone. "He's got so much anger and pressure building up inside him I'm afraid he'll explode and self destruct."

"I can imagine. This is a huge deal for him."

"Can you tell me why he's so insistent that if he can't play, his whole life will change?" She bit her lip. "Other players get hurt and have to retire and they move on to other things." She nibbled a fingernail. "I know this will shock you, but you were right. Jake really is one of the good ones. He's not a horndog or any of the stuff I thought all football players were. So why—"

"I'm so glad to hear you say that," Ivy interrupted. "If nothing else comes out of this, at least you've come to realize that."

"Nothing else?" Erin frowned. "What *else* did you have in mind? What was going on in that devious little mind of yours?"

"Just trying to get my two favorite people to like each other," she said nonchalantly.

"Oh, right. Uh-huh. And you still didn't answer my question. What is it that drives him like this?"

There was a long pause, silence humming across the connection.

"I think Jake needs to explain that to you himself," Ivy said at last.

"But he won't tell me." She wanted to stamp her foot in frustration. "How can I help him if I don't know what I'm up against?"

Another pause.

"Let's get through the doctor's visit and the x-rays first. Then we'll take it one step at a time. If he self-destructs, I will help you with this."

"Why do we have to wait for disaster?" she demanded. "Does that even make sense?"

"Please trust me on this," Ivy pleaded. "If his leg is good to go, all this will go away."

But Erin wasn't all that convinced.

Even when they made love he seemed to be in a distant place. It broke Erin's heart to think the wrong verdict might destroy his life. Could she find something to give him hope for the future?

* * * *

The day of the appointment, he was up early. Although Erin had slept with him most nights, sometimes she knew when to give him space, and last night had been one of those times. He'd tossed and turned all night and finally ended up sprawled on the bed, covers in disarray. Still, even before he buzzed the intercom, she had fixed two mugs of coffee and carried them into the room. It was obvious her night hadn't been any more restful than his.

"Hot java for you." She seemed to be trying to put as much cheer in her voice as possible.

"I think I might need a shot of bourbon in it," he told her. "Just to get through this."

She set both mugs on the nightstand and sat beside him on the bed.

"How about this? If you are a very good boy and behave yourself, tonight I will have a real treat for you."

"Yeah?" He lifted an eyebrow. "What kind of treat?"

"That's for me to know and you to find out. So do you promise to behave?"

"We'll see."

She wrapped his leg so he could shower, then left him alone to shave and brush his teeth. When he crutched his way back into the bedroom, she had clothes laid out for him on the bed, black cargo shorts and a blue sports shirt. No slacks until the cast came off, hopefully today.

"Is this okay?" For the first time in days, she looked nervous.

"Yeah. Fine. It's good." His lack of enthusiasm was more than evident.

He looked at the clothes set out for him. "You gonna help me dress?" he asked.

"Of course."

He could do the shirt okay, but anything below the waist was still a problem for him. Anyway, he liked the thought of her touching his body, even if that might not last much longer.

He tried to control the tension vibrating through him, but it was impossible. Today was too important. Whatever happened in the next couple of hours would determine what happened to the rest of his life. It had been a long time since he'd felt such total despair, already anticipating bad news.

He wanted to put his arms around Erin and hold her tight to his body. Tell her how he really felt. Know that she would be there for him.

And wasn't that a damn fantasy.

Because it all came down to the fucking leg. He'd just been fooling himself these past weeks, thinking he and Erin could have something together. If he was out of the game for good, he would be nothing. Nobody. Worthless, just as he'd had drummed into him all those years ago. His sense of self-worth would be gone, and he would have nothing to give to a relationship.

He crutched outside to the driveway where he waited while she backed the SUV out of the garage. While she hurried back inside to set the alarm on the inside door, he climbed clumsily into the vehicle. As they drove through the gate and turned onto the street, his stomach knotted in unpleasant anticipation of what lay ahead.

Neither of them spoke a word on the drive to the office building. They'd had silences before, most of them comfortable, but not this one. Today his nerves were all over the place and his desperation filled the vehicle like a living thing. So many years he'd worked to become someone, to gain respect. To be viewed as a person with value. It made him sick to realize yet again that in a few hours it could all be gone, and with it any chance with Erin. Who would want a worthless has been?

The silence grew when they pulled into the underground parking garage and on the ride up in the elevator. When they walked into Dr. Moline's waiting room, Scott was waiting for them and Jake clenched his fists. For Erin's sake he wouldn't make a scene. Instead he just nodded at Scott, tightlipped, and found a chair to sit in. Erin and Scott found seats in the corner, respecting his silent request for separation. He stretched out his bad leg in front of him, leaned back, and closed his eyes.

The memory of his early years in Granite Falls swept over him. He and Ivy had moved with their mother when he was fourteen and Ivy was nine. Life had taken a big jump forward when that happened. Their mother got a good job working at one of the banks, and they became part of the community. Then he tried out for the high school football team and Coach Fenelli became a huge influence in his life. He'd busted his balls to excel for that man.

A small school like Granite Falls High wasn't a recruiting target for the major colleges. The Big Five, so to speak. But Ray Fenelli was a man apart from a lot of other coaches. He'd made a video of each of the players on that state championship team and sent them out to dozens of universities. Jake still remembered the explosion of excitement when scouts saw those disks. They'd gone nuts. Every starter on that team had been heavily recruited and was offered at least three scholarships.

Jake looked across at Scott through slitted eyelids. The man had come to see him the summer before his final college season. The NCAA didn't allow contact before then. Although other agents approached him, he'd connected with Scott right away. They'd had a good ride together, but Jake just knew it was all ending today.

"Jacob Russell?"

He levered himself out of the chair and onto his crutches. He was sick with trepidation as he followed the woman who had called for him to an examination room. He knew Erin and Scott were right behind him, but he tried to blank them from his mind. He really wished to hell they'd stayed in the waiting room. He didn't need them to be there for the final nail in his coffin.

They were no sooner settled when a man in scrubs came to fetch Jake for his x-rays. Erin started to say something to him, but he just scowled at her as he clumped out of the room. Again, he tried to blank his mind as they x-rayed the leg, hoping for the best, expecting the worst. But when he was back in the examining room, lowering himself into a chair, he couldn't help praying just a little bit. If the x-rays showed complete recovery, the cast would come off today and he could begin his rehab.

He avoided looking at or talking to Scott and Erin, who seemed to be taking their cues from him. Once, Scott opened his mouth to say something, but Jake glared at him so he just shook his head. The tension in the room was thicker than pea soup by the time Dr. Moline entered, patient file in his hand. He shook hands with everyone and asked Jake how he was feeling.

"You tell me." Jake was in no mood for small talk. "I think that depends on what you have to say about the x-rays."

"Okay, let's talk about that, shall we?" He sat down in front of a computer screen, danced his fingers over the keyboard, and in seconds four x-rays appeared. Using his pen, he pointed to the images. "Jake, I know you're aware how complicated the break was. As I explained in the hospital, it's what we call a comminuted fracture. That's where the bone is broken in several places. Here, here, and here." Moline indicated them as he spoke. "We had to use rods and screws to stabilize the leg."

Jake clenched his hands into fists. He just wished the doctor would get to the results. He didn't need all the details if the axe was about to fall. The apprehension was already making him nauseous.

"The good news," the doctor went on, "is I'm pleased with the healing process, enough that the cast can come off today. We'll fit you with a soft boot, a hard plastic shell that immobilizes, protects, and supports the lower leg. You can toss the crutches and I'm going to write orders for your physical therapy. We have to start strengthening those muscles again."

"And?" Jake prompted.

"In a perfect world I'd tell you the leg is good as new and that after therapy you can get right back on the field."

"But this isn't a perfect world, right, Doc?" Sweat trickled down his spine. He could already hear the death knell sounding for his career and for Jake Russell.

"No, it isn't. I'm sorry, Jake. The breaks were just too complex. I hate having to tell you, but I can't clear you to play again. Even if you had the ability, one more injury and you could lose that leg."

"So what you're saying is, I'm done."

He sat there, staring at the x-rays as if he could somehow make them change. He felt dizzy and disoriented, knocked off balance. When an assistant came to take him to the casting room, he pushed himself up, grabbed his crutches, and wordlessly followed the man out the door.

He stoically endured the removal of the cast, thankful that the tech was not a talkative person. Or maybe he got the silent signal from Jake that he should just shut up. He barely absorbed what the guy was saying about adjusting to the absence of the cast and caring for the leg, now exposed to light.

As the tech was finishing with him, the nurse popped in with a sheet of instructions for him.

"In addition to the therapy," she said, "you'll need to be sure to massage that leg every day to stimulate the circulation. Or have someone do it for you."

"Just give it to one of my babysitters," he griped. "Can I get out of here now?"

The nurse nodded. "I'll get your friends, and they can meet you by the back door."

Thank God for that, he thought. At least she'd gotten the hint he didn't want to parade before a roomful of patients. When the tech was finished fitting him with the soft boot, he made Jake walk a few steps for him, so he could see how he managed.

"Better than I expected," he told Jake. "You can pass those crutches on to somebody else."

"You can burn the damn things for all I care," Jake snarled.

He made his limping way to the rear entrance of the offices. Erin and Scott were already there, waiting for him.

"Not a word. Not. One. Word." Each word sounded as if it was an effort for him to speak.

They made slow progress to the elevator, Jake walking awkwardly as he adjusted to the absence of the cast and the new appliance. He refused to let anyone help him, so by the time they rode downstairs to the garage and Erin got him to the car, he was covered with sweat.

When they reached the garage level, Scott turned to Erin. "Give us a minute, will you?"

She looked from him to Jake and back again. "Of course."

"We don't need a minute," Jake said at the same time. "Not even a second."

"Well, we're going to get it whether you want it or not," Scott snapped. "Listen Jake. We've been together a long time and had great success. Do I wish this hadn't happened? Certainly. But life as Jake Russell is *not* over yet."

"Easy for you to say." Jake practically bit off the words. Okay, maybe he was being rude, but he didn't feel like being polite right now. Maybe never again. He just wished the man would shut the fuck up and go away so he could crawl into a corner and shut out the world.

"You have a life beyond the playing field," Scott said, "if you aren't too dumb to realize it. And you are so lucky to have Erin supporting you through this." He paused. "You know she's in love with you, right?"

Jake snorted. "Her bad luck."

"To the contrary. I think she sees it as good luck. You're the one who is lucky, and you need to stop and appreciate it. Don't kick her to the curb, which is what I figure you're planning to do."

"She needs someone who is worth something. That's not me. Leave it alone, Scott."

"You think you have nothing to give her anymore? You're dead wrong. You have a lot to give. Everything, as a matter of fact. I'll give you twenty-four hours to get your shit together, and then we're going to put together a new plan for your future. And you can plan on Erin being part of it."

Didn't the man realize he didn't have any fucking future? Without football he was just that kid who'd been told over and over he was worthless. Useless. Less than garbage.

He turned his back on the agent and climbed somewhat clumsily into the SUV.

Scott walked around to the driver's side and tapped on the window for Erin to roll it down. He handed her a business card.

"I know Jake has all my info," he told her, "but there are two cell numbers on the back. If the first doesn't answer, you can always get me at the second one. It's my emergency cell. I never turn it off."

"Thank you, Scott. I'll call you later."

"Do that. You can give me a status report."

Oh, great. They were going to discuss him to death. He waited for her to make some kind of comment, but she just concentrated on her driving.

"When we get back to my house," he told her, "you can pack your stuff."

"Are you throwing me out?" He heard the surprise in her voice.

"Whatever you want to call it. There's just no need for you anymore. You have a life to get back to, remember?"

"What if I changed my mind?" she asked. "What if I want to stick around?"

"For what?" He closed his eyes and leaned back against the seat, wishing this would turn out to be nothing more than a bad nightmare. "There's no Jake Russell any more, Erin. Go find yourself a whole man who's worth something. That's not me."

Her hands tightened on the steering wheel. "Maybe I think it is. Maybe—" She flipped her hand in the air. "I'm not a quitter, Jake, whatever the situation. You have to have figured that out by now, since I didn't run screaming from your house. Not even on your worse days. That means I stick around for the bad as well as the good."

"There's plenty of bad to go around here." Anguish surged through him.

"But there's also plenty of good," she insisted. "I know the future looks pretty miserable right now, but—"

"Miserable?" He went rigid with hostility. "You can't begin to know what miserable is."

She tried to help him when he had some difficulty getting out of the SUV, but he brushed her aside.

"Leave me alone." He was weak and sweating and nauseous, and it wasn't all from discomfort. "I don't want your help. I'll manage. Somehow. Go away."

He ignored the flash of hurt on her face. Better for her to feel it now than later. How fucking long would it take for her to realize he was back to being worse than nothing?

Using the walls as support, he walked slowly and with difficulty down the hall to his bedroom. Thank God, she didn't try to help him again. When he got to his bedroom, he limped inside and slammed the door in Erin's face. Then he threw himself on the bed, and for the first time in years had an uncontrollable urge to cry.

* * * *

Erin tried to follow him into the bedroom, figuring she could at least help him get comfortable. Or maybe even just be there for him. If he wanted to yell, she'd let him yell at her. But getting the door slammed in her face was a message she heard loud and clear.

Letting out a breath, she headed into the kitchen to make a cup of coffee. She sat at the kitchen table with it for a long time, trying to figure out what to do.

She knew she should call Ivy. Jake had forbidden his sister from coming to the doctor, but the woman would be on pins and needles waiting for the final prognosis. Maybe Ivy could tell her what on earth had happened to Jake that he thought without football he was nothing and nobody. That wasn't just his ego talking. She'd heard real pain in his voice and seen it on his face.

She also had to make plans for herself. It would be impossible for her to stay here, yet she also knew there was no way she could leave. Waiting for Jake to get his cast off, she had tried to get the answer from Scott, only he was as clueless as she was. But he'd said one thing she couldn't get out of her head.

"Whatever happened in your life to make you hate football players so much you need to forget it, because Jake is a totally different breed of

animal. He's smart and decent. Pay attention to that, Erin. You know he's in love with you, right?"

In love with her?

Before all this, she would never have believed that possible. Or that she would feel the same way about him. Now everything she had believed about football players was in the wind and her opinion of him had done a one-eighty. Apparently she had been stupid enough to let one immature man and a few assholes color her opinion of an entire profession. So if he was in love with her and she felt the same way, where did they go from here?

She finished her coffee, fixed another mug, and took out her cell. She'd put it on silent at the doctor's office and forgotten to turn it on. Plus, she'd been so distracted she hadn't even noticed it vibrated. There were a dozen messages from Ivy, the last one saying,

Call me right now. At once. I'm going nuts.

Sighing, she punched in the speed dial.

"It's about time. Damn, I've been going crazy here. What did the doctor say?"

Methodically, doing her best to remember everything Dr. Moline had said, she gave Ivy the bad news. Although she wanted to say, *He's alive and has the use of his leg. Isn't that the best news out of all this?*

"He has to be destroyed." Ivy sounded so sad. So distressed. "Without football, I don't know what he'll do."

Erin was finally losing patience with this whole "football is my entire life" thing. "Damn it. He still has his whole life ahead of him, he can still walk on two feet, he has a brain if he'd ever get around to using it, and more money than he knows what to do with. Pardon my language but what's the big fucking deal?"

She waited for Ivy to answer her. When her friend said nothing, she prodded, "Ivy?"

A heavy sigh swooshed over the connection. "Jake should tell you this himself. Let's give him until tomorrow. If he hasn't opened up by then, I'll open up the family skeleton closet for you. But let's wait, okay?"

"I don't know what on earth is so terrible but okay. But if tomorrow comes and no info, you'll owe me an explanation."

"Call me later and let me know how he is, will you?"

"Why don't you come over and see for yourself?"

"Because he won't want me to see him like this. Jake has always been very good about locking his feelings away. He'll just shut me out."

Locking his feelings away? Was that why he always had a certain reluctance to express himself except when they were having wild sex?

"All right. I have to figure out how we go forward from here."

"You're not leaving, are you?" Ivy's voice was laced with panic. "He needs you now more than ever."

"Let's get through tonight and maybe tomorrow," Erin suggested. "He'll have settled down enough so you can come over."

"Good idea. Call me first thing in the morning. No, call me later or even text me, just to let me know how he's doing."

"I will."

Erin disconnected the call, rinsed her mug, and put it in the dishwasher. She was suddenly so tired, the lack of sleep catching up with her. Jake was still barricaded in his bedroom, so she headed for her own room, intending to lie down for just a moment. But she was so tired from last night and exhausted from today's tension that without realizing it she dozed off.

She came awake with a start, sensing something was wrong but not sure what. She glanced at the little clock beside her bed and nearly screeched. Four o'clock. How could she have slept so long? Her intercom hadn't yelled at her, so maybe Jake was asleep, too. Or lying on his bed in a comatose state. Or—

She pushed herself to her feet and hurried down the hall to his room. The door was still closed. She opened it gently and stuck her head into the room.

"Jake? Are you—?"

She nearly passed out. Jake was not on the bed. Nor was he any place else. She searched the bathroom, the patio, every room in the house. She worried he'd fallen down and hurt himself, but by the time she finished her search she'd almost have been grateful for an unconscious body. Having looked everywhere else, she opened the door to the garage and nearly had another heart attack. The SUV was gone. She still had the keys she'd used, but obviously Jake had more than one set. If she was grateful for anything, it was that his left leg was the one injured. At least he'd be able to drive.

Where could he have gone? Crap, crap, crap.

Dreading what she was about to do, she pulled out her phone again and speed-dialed Ivy.

"You'd better come over here," she said as soon as there was an answer.

"Why? What's wrong? I have to finish this project, but I can be there in a couple hours."

"No. Now. Come right now."

"What's going on? You're scaring me."

After taking a deep breath and blowing it out, she said, "I dozed off. I guess I was more tired than I thought. Jake's gone."

Chapter 15

While she waited for Ivy, Erin called Scott. She just hoped he wasn't tied up in something he couldn't break away from.

He answered on the second ring. "What's up, Erin? How's it going? Any better?"

"Not really. Um, I'm not sure how to tell you this but Jake's gone."

"Gone?" She could hear the stunned surprise in his voice. "Where could he go? He isn't in great shape and he hasn't driven for three months."

"I know, I know, I know." She raked her hands through her hair. "It's my fault."

But when she told him what happened, he said, "Not your fault at all. People have to sleep, and frankly, this morning, you looked exhausted. Don't beat yourself up over it."

"But he's not really capable of getting around."

"One thing I've learned about Jake is if he wants to do something, he'll find a way to do it. Listen, fix yourself a drink so you don't fall apart. I'm on my way."

A drink was the last thing she wanted but probably the first thing she needed. Her hands were shaking so much it took her three attempts to shove her phone back in her pocket. When she'd seen Jake's empty bedroom and discovered the SUV missing, two things had slammed into her brain: She was terrified he'd end up in an accident, and she'd never get to tell him she loved him. Scott had certainly seen it. She'd been so busy protecting her heart that she'd actually lost it when she wasn't looking. So did that mean he was right that Jake had fallen in love with her, too?

Now she wished she'd had the courage to tell him how she felt, even if he wasn't ready to hear it yet. So where did they go from here? Right now, she just knew she wanted to find him safe and sound and bring him home.

She had no idea where Jake kept his liquor. In the three months she'd been here they'd only had wine or beer. She tried all the cupboards in the kitchen and the big credenza in the great room without finding anything. Finally she decided to look in the den.

Other than when she'd ushered Lynne Corday and Joe Reilly in to their meetings with Jake and took care of the refreshments, she hadn't set foot in this room. Jake always closed the door when he left it. It was a typical male inner sanctum. Bookshelves lined the walls, some of them holding awards and trophies going all the way back to high school. A massive polished oak desk faced a bay window that gave a great view of the yard, the extension holding a computer and printer. Two framed pictures sat on the desk. One was the championship Granite Falls football team holding the state trophy. The other was of Jake and Ivy and a woman she realized must be their mother. Erin picked it up and studied it. The resemblance between her and Ivy was very clear.

But where was his father? Why were there no pictures of him? Jake never mentioned him. Ever. Had he died a long time ago? But then wouldn't there be at least one picture of him?

After setting the picture back on the desk, she continued her search for alcohol. A cabinet mounted on the wall beside the desk looked promising. It opened smoothly at her touch, and she gave thanks Jake wasn't one of those people who kept his liquor locked up. Of course when you never had company, you didn't have to worry about hiding anything.

Bingo! A small array of bottles containing gin, scotch, and bourbon. She grabbed the bottle of Jack Daniel's Black and was about to close the cupboard up again when she noticed a manila folder. It was shoved between the bottles and the wood, almost as if it had been stuck there and forgotten. Curiosity getting the better of her, she pulled it out, set the bottle of liquor down on the desk, and flipped the folder open.

And caught her breath.

There were three pictures in there, of a woman and two children that appeared to have been taken a long time ago. She recognized a younger version of Jake's mother, which meant the children were Jake and Ivy. What shocked her was their condition. All three of them were covered with bruises and Ivy's left arm was in a cast. From the expression on their faces, they looked as if they had been through hell. She also realized these were not the usual type of photos but ones that had been taken for a specific purpose.

What the hell?

Who had done this to them and how long ago had it happened? Was this why Jake never talked about his past?

Suddenly consumed by guilt for prying into Jake's private life, even accidentally, she closed the folder, replaced it, and carried the bourbon into the kitchen. Now she really needed a drink. After taking down a glass, she filled it with ice and poured the liquor to the halfway mark. Without hesitating, she lifted the glass and took a healthy swallow. She coughed a little and her eyes watered, but as the alcohol coursed through her bloodstream, it steadied her and took the edge off her nerves.

Too nervous to sit still, she carried the glass with her as she went to the foyer to wait for Ivy and Scott. As she sipped it more slowly, she tried to think where Jake might have gone. To a bar? To Lisa and Lucy or a replica of them? She still had his cell phone with all his contacts, but she had no intention of calling everyone in there and alerting them that there was a problem. When Scott arrived, he could pick out the ones to reach out to and maybe do it himself. Yes, it would be a lot better coming from him.

Just as she took another sip of her drink, Scott buzzed her from the gate, and she pressed the button to open it. Ivy had the codes so she'd let herself in when she arrived. She had the door open and was waiting for him when he pulled up in front of the house, leaped out of the car, and jogged into the foyer.

"I have a feeling a lot of this is my fault," she said at once. "If Jake thought he could talk to me, tell me what he was feeling, maybe he wouldn't have taken off on his own. I probably should have anticipated something like this."

"I think you're heaping too much blame on yourself. If anyone should have expected this, it should have been me. Let's stop beating ourselves up, sit down, and figure out what's what here."

She dumped the rest of her drink and fixed two mugs of coffee for them. They had just seated themselves at the kitchen table when the front door opened and Ivy rushed in.

"Did you hear anything yet?" she asked Erin. "Did he even call you? What happened?"

"Easy, easy." Scott rose from his chair, gave her a friendly hug, then eased her down next to Erin. "Let's take this one thing at a time. Erin? How about telling us again what happened."

"We need to start looking for him," she insisted, a slightly hysterical edge to her voice. "Right now."

"We will," Scott promised her, "but first we need to know what happened here."

Ivy accepted the coffee Erin handed her and took a sip from it. "Thanks. I needed this. Erin, what's the deal?"

She told them everything she could, from the time she and Jake arrived home to the moment she woke up and found him gone.

"I left him alone in his room," she told them, "because I knew he didn't want anyone around just yet. He didn't say anything, but it was obvious he was distraught over the news from Dr. Moline." She looked at Scott. "You were there. What do you think?"

"I agree he was upset. Jake doesn't rant and rave, he just gets deathly quiet, but it was obvious from the look on his face and the fact he didn't speak to either of us. Okay, so we're going to assume he's out trying to blunt the shock with either alcohol or—" He paused and looked at Erin.

"It's okay," she told him. "Go ahead and say it. He could be with another woman." She shrugged. "Maybe even many women, right now the important thing is finding him and getting him home and through all this."

Ivy nodded. "We can kick his ass later." She pulled her cell phone from her purse. "I don't think he'd go out and get drunk. That's not how he rolls. But we can't overlook anything. Jake isn't a big one for bar hopping, like I said, but he has a few he likes to go to when the urge hits him. I dictated what I remember into my phone on the way over here."

"Would he go there this early? It's barely five o'clock."

"No. Maybe." Ivy threw up her hands. "Of course not, but we have to start somewhere. He hasn't reached out to anyone else while he's been going through this, so I have no idea what he's liable to do." She looked from one to the other. "Scott, I'm sure you're aware he hasn't really formed any close friendships with his teammates. He's certainly withdrawn from all of them while he's been going through this."

"You're right," Scott agreed. "He's very social and sociable, but inside I think he's pretty much isolated himself. I always thought that was why he never formed a relationship with a woman."

"Out of the public eye he's very private," Ivy agreed. "Even when he goes to parties he circulates, chats, and then leaves. But maybe today he thought alcohol would be the answer."

"Let's have the names of the places," Scott told her. "We can get the numbers and split up the calls."

There were ten places on Ivy's list, and they called all of them but with zero results.

"I knew this would be a bust," Ivy said, "but at least we tried."

"Now what?" Erin asked. She drummed her fingers on the table, but when she realized what she was doing, she clutched her hands together to stop herself.

"I'm going to call a couple of the guys on the team I know well enough. Most of them are also my clients."

"I just don't want to start the rumor mill," Ivy told him. "Even if Jake can't play again, we still want to protect his name as much as possible."

"I don't care about that," Erin blurted. "I just want to find him and bring him home safe."

Scott put one of his large hands over both of hers. "I agree. But let's do it sensibly."

It was hard for her, though, to sit quietly while Scott made his calls, his tone of voice casual, the conversation almost offhand. But in the end he still had nothing.

"Maybe he *is* with one of his Eye Candy Mandys," Erin said bitterly, even as she realized she knew better.

"That's never been his style," Scott answered. "I'd think you'd know that by now."

"People do weird things when they get dealt a life-changing blow like this."

"Scott's right," Ivy protested. "Anyway, I wouldn't know where to start to find out, if that's what he's done."

"What about one of his former lady friends," Scott interjected. "If you can give me their names, I can get their numbers."

Ivy sighed. "You'd be surprised at how few of those there have been, none of them what you'd call really serious."

Erin nibbled on a fingernail. She wanted so badly to believe Ivy, but she had such a painful history that stood in her way. She'd often wondered, since what she called the Trace disaster, if a man could be satisfied with just her. If he could be faithful, or maybe her flaw was just picking the wrong men. Or man.

"You mean his first reaction wouldn't be to find some female to hook up with? Or go somewhere to get drunk? I thought that's what football players did."

"As much as you've been around Jake these past couple of months, are you saying you haven't gotten a different picture, at least of him?" Ivy frowned at her. "I haven't said much about this, but I'd really like to know why you have such a low opinion of football players. Especially Jake, who in no way fits the image you've got."

"Me, too," Scott put in. "We need to get past this so we can concentrate on Jake."

Erin sighed, picked up her mug, and took a sip of her coffee. At the moment, she wished they hadn't ditched the bourbon. Then she looked from one to the other.

"You know—or know of—Trace McKay, right?"

Scott frowned. "Not one of mine, that's for sure. How do you know Trace?"

God, this was so painful. "Seven years ago when I was working at a resort and spa in Houston I met Trace. A friend introduced us. I usually didn't give the teams the time of day. Mostly their behavior turned me off. They were loud, arrogant, and obnoxious."

"Welcome to my world," Scott muttered. "Or at least part of it."

"I guess my hormones overrode my common sense. How trite is it to say he swept me off my feet?"

"Excuse me," Scott interrupted, "but I wouldn't think he's quite your style."

Erin snorted. "I should have had you advising me then. But what did I know? I was young, impressionable, and excited that a big star like Trace even wanted to date me." She raked a hand through her hair. "We were hot and heavy for most of the season. It was hard carving time out, what with his playing schedule and my work schedule. We worked it out, though. I managed a lot of Sundays off so I could see him play and then we'd have until Tuesday together."

"Building a relationship during the season is difficult," Scott agreed.

"Anyway, moving right along. We agreed to be exclusive, and he gave me every indication that after the season we'd be taking a big step. I assumed he was going to ask me to marry him, idiot that I was."

"So what happened?" Ivy wanted to know.

"I wasn't able to get to Dallas for the game they were playing that weekend, but I figured I'd get there that night and surprise him. It was the middle of the evening before I got to the hotel and checked in. By that time the team was back at the hotel and celebrating their win."

Ivy frowned. "I think I'm not liking where this is going."

"I was standing at the front desk finishing my registration, just in time to see Trace walk out of the hotel bar with two very busty, scantily clad blondes, one under each arm. Before I could move or even say anything, the reservations clerk helping me laughed. 'There he goes again,' she said. 'We call him Trace Twofer.'"

Erin curled her fingers into her palms. "Want to know why? Because he was known for always celebrating with two women, not just one. Even breaking team curfew when he could get away with it. So while I was dreaming of wedding bells, he was busy with sexual gymnastics."

"Oh, Erin." Ivy reached across the table to touch her arm. "I am so very, very sorry. That must have been so painful."

"Yeah, well, the breakup is legendary. After I got past the pain, they heard me screaming at him all over the hotel." She looked from one to the other. "So you can see why I'm allergic to football players."

"They aren't all like that," Scott told her. "Jake is the total opposite, as a matter of fact. A lot of my clients are, and I say that with pride."

"And maybe I'm learning that. In the meantime, enough with the weepy stories. What do we do next? I worry that if we're not actively looking, he's out there doing himself some damage."

"Well, running around looking in every bar in Austin won't be very productive," Scott pointed out. "We need to figure out another option."

"Ivy, while we're playing true confessions," Erin said, "can you tell me why Jake is so obsessed with football being the only thing that identifies him? Validates him? That without it he's nothing?"

For a long moment, no one said anything. Then Ivy cleared her throat.

"Only if you promise not to let Jake know I told you." She waited while they both nodded their agreement. "Jake and I grew up with a very abusive father, and I mean completely vicious and sadistic."

The pictures.

"Jake stood up for my mother and me all the time. He took the brunt of everything. Our father denigrated him all the time, told him he was useless and worthless. Beat him into the ground physically and verbally. Made him feel he was nothing."

Lines of anger deepened in Scott's face. "How did you get away from him?"

"One night things got so bad my mother actually took Jake and me and fled from the house. A friend took us to a shelter and they helped us relocate. Got our mom some counseling and relocated us to Granite Falls with a job for her." She closed her eyes for a moment, then opened them again. "When Jake tried out for the football team, that became who he was. He was admired and respected, and Coach Fenelli became a real father to him."

"Which is why football defines him," Erin said. "It brought him relationships and respect and an identity in the community. It's why he thinks without it he's nothing."

"What about his father?" Scott asked. "Didn't he try to find you?"

"The shelter where we were taken took pictures of us," Ivy answered. "They called the police who took my statement and that of our neighbors. They talked to the people at the shelter, too. Then they arrested our dad." She looked down at the table. "He couldn't make bail, and while he was awaiting trial he got into a fight in prison and was killed. I-I don't think I can talk about this anymore. Jake and I have both buried it pretty deep."

"That's why he's so focused on Jake Russell, running back," Scott explained. "It's a self-esteem issue. It blots out everything that was bad in his life and makes him feel valued."

"And why he finances the Good Shepard House," Erin guessed.

Ivy nodded. "And a lot of other things no one knows about."

Erin wanted to cry. "But he is a person of value. Football is only part of it. He's bright and funny, and smart and sharp and—"

Ivy actually gave a small laugh. "Spoken like a woman in love."

Erin blinked back tears. "You're right. I fought it for so long. Now he might not ever want to hear it from me."

"Why?" Ivy asked. "If I know my brother, I'd say he's in love with you."

Scott gave her a little smile. "You heard it here first."

"But I don't—we haven't…"

"We can discuss that later." Ivy drained her coffee mug. "Right now none of this helps us find Jake."

Love. Exactly what happened when she wasn't looking. Maybe if she'd had the courage to tell him, she could have provided the emotional support he needed with this devastating news and he wouldn't have run off God knows where on his own.

Scott opened his mouth to say something when the landline rang, startling all three of them.

Erin jumped up from the table and grabbed the receiver. "Jake Russell's house." Maybe, maybe, maybe this would be someone who had some news of Jake.

"Is this Erin Bass?" a woman asked.

"It is." Please, please, please let this be some information.

"This is Lynne Corday. With the Good Shepard House? We met when I came to see Jake."

"Yes, yes, I remember you. If you're looking, he's, ah, not here at the moment."

"I know that. That's why I'm calling. Jake is here with me, at Good Shepard. He has been for the past couple of hours."

"He is? He's safe?" Erin felt as if a ton of bricks had been lifted from her. "Can I speak to him?"

"Actually, he asked me to call you to pick him up."

"Oh, thank God." Tears ran down her cheeks as an enormous feeling of relief coursed through her. He was okay. More importantly, he had asked for her. Just her.

"I believe he's ready to go home, but I'm not sure he should be driving."

A thread of fear wiggled through her. "Is he drunk?" She asked in a hesitant tone of voice.

"Not at all," Lynne assured her. "He's just emotionally wrung out and physically exhausted."

"Tell him I'm on my way. We'll worry about his car tomorrow." She turned to face the others. "He's okay. He's at Good Shepard and he wants to come home."

"He went to the environment where he felt safest," Scott commented. "Where he felt worthwhile."

"Lynne Corday is a wonderful woman," Ivy told them. "If anyone can help Jake get his head on straight, it's her." She stood up. "I'm going with you."

Erin shook her head. "I know you want to but he asked for me. Only me. This is my chance to show him I care. Let me do this."

"Okay, but I'm going to wait here." Ivy looked from one to the other. "Just so I can see for myself that he's okay. Then I'll take off."

Scott pushed away from the table. "I'm going back to the hotel. Erin, please let me know that he's okay, will you?"

"Of course. But right now I really need to get going."

* * * *

When Erin walked into Lynne Corday's office, she was so relieved to see Jake sitting in a chair in one piece that she drew a breath for the first time in hours. He appeared slightly the worse for wear, but he managed a smile for her. And then he shocked her by pushing himself to his feet and then wrapping his arms around her in a tight hug.

"I'm sorry," he told her. "I'm so sorry."

"Nothing to be sorry for." She rubbed her hands up and down his back, feeling his tension. "I'm just glad you're in one piece."

"I just—"

"Shhh. It's okay. Let's just get you home."

With her arm around his waist, she turned to Lynne and thanked her profusely.

"I'm just glad he felt he could come here. Before you take him home I want to clue you in on something." She looked at Jake. "You don't mind if I borrow Erin for a few minutes, do you?"

"Giving away all my secrets, are you?" He gave them a tired grin.

"Only a few," Lynne said kindly.

He looked at Erin. "I never say no to her. I'll wait in the other room."

When he was gone, Lynne gave Erin a searching look. "He'll need a lot of healing, my dear. A lot. He's lived with one image of himself for so long it won't be easy for him to change."

Erin nodded. "I know that. Ivy told me his story and now I understand."

"He was the buffer between his brute of a father and his mother and sister. He often took the brunt of the punishment, both verbal and physical. Someone needs to make him understand his value as a human being."

"Not to worry." Erin squeezed the other woman's hand. "I believe I'm up to the job."

"He's in love with you, you know."

Erin's laugh had a slight hysterical edge to it. "You're the third person to tell me that today. I think I might actually begin to believe it if I could hear it from him."

"You will. I have every confidence."

"The other big shock is I'm in love with him."

Lynne smiled at her. "Then I'm convinced everything will work itself out. He's in good hands. We'll take care of getting his car back to him tomorrow. He gave me his keys." She gave Erin a quick hug. "Now go on and get him home. He's ready."

Neither Erin nor Jake said much on the ride to the house. Erin was determined not to pepper him with questions or criticize him for leaving the way he did. That wasn't what he needed now. She'd let him tell her whatever he had to say in his own time. The one thing she was sure of was how badly she'd misjudged him in the beginning. And yes, she was in love with him. The admission still stunned her. When she'd discovered him gone, her heart had stopped and a fear greater than she'd ever known gripped her body. How had she never seen that he and Trace McKay were polar opposites?

Because she'd been an idiot.

Ivy was waiting in the foyer for them when they walked into the house.

"I'm not staying," she said before they could get a word out. "I just had to make sure you were okay, Jakie."

He gave a strangled laugh. "Didn't I tell you not to call me that?"

"I'll call you anything I want as long as I know you're safe and sound."

They said good-bye to Ivy and reset all the alarms. Then Jake took her hand and led her to his bedroom. He wanted sex? Well, okay, whatever made him feel better.

But when they got to the bedroom he just stretched out on the bed and pulled her down next to him. He wrapped his arm around her, tucking her head into the crook of his neck.

"I just want to hold you," he told her. "Feel you next to me. You're better than any medicine."

"Whatever you need," she promised.

"I'm sorry I ran off the way I did. I just—"

"Shhh, shhh, shhh." She touched her fingertips to his lips. "It's okay. You had a bad shock and that was your first reaction." She smoothed her hand on his chest. "I'm just glad I'm the one you wanted to come get you."

"I'll always want you. You're my safety net, don't you know that?"

They lay that way for a long time. The sun had set and fading light eased its way into the room, casting them in shadow. Finally Jake cleared his throat.

"I'm going to guess Ivy told you our story."

"She did, but we don't have to discuss it." She stroked his cheek. "It helps me understand you better, though." She turned slightly. "The one thing I just want to help you understand is that you are so much more than football. You're a credit to Ivy and the team and the community. They all respect you enormously. And you?" she asked, lightly stoking his arm. "How do you feel?"

"As if a weight has been lifted from my head. Lynne Corday is a wonder. She made me take a good hard look at things."

"I'm glad you went there, to the place you felt safest."

"Now you know why that place is so important to me." He swallowed. "And always will be."

"And I love you for it." There. She'd said it. She was amazed at how easily the words fell out of her mouth.

"Love?" His arm tightened around her. "That's a strong word for you to be tossing around."

She pushed herself up so she had full eye contact with him. Was that hope flickering in there? "And I don't just toss that around. You should know that."

"What happened to your thing that all football players are lower than scum?" He asked the question lightly but his face was dead serious.

"Yeah, well, about that. I have a story to tell you." She cuddled her body to his and closed her eyes while she told him the Trace McKay story. "So you can see where I was coming from."

"Aw, honey." He stroked her hair. "I wish you'd told me about this a long time ago. He really is an asshole, and has a rep throughout the NFL. I'm sorry you had to be one of his casualties."

Erin smoothed her hand over his chest. "I know. Or if I didn't, I do now."

He was silent for a long moment before he spoke again. "You know, I think I actually fell in love with you that one night we spent together. I knew it was fast, but that's probably why it hurt so much when you tossed me out."

"I'm sorry." She continued to rub her hand in soothing circles over his very masculine chest. "Maybe I knew it at the time, too, but I wasn't ready for it. Especially with…"

"A football player?" he joked.

Lord, she was glad he could find some humor in this whole thing. "Only with this football player," she teased.

"I guess it's all a learning curve." Jake blew out a breath. "I've been focused for so long on the belief that without football I was nothing, that it's going to take some time for me to change."

She reached up a hand to caress his cheek, loving the feel of his sexy late-day scruff. "I'll be here with you every step of the way. Count on it. Physical therapy, rehab, and planning what you want to do as you move into the next phase of your life."

"Next phase of my life. I like the way that sounds." He turned his head and adjusted the way he was holding her so he could look directly at her face. "This won't be easy. I have a long road ahead of me until my leg works acceptably again. And I don't mean for the football field, in case that's what you were going to say. Plus, I'm going to have to readjust a lot of my thinking."

"And make new plans," she reminded him. "It's okay. Not to worry. Like I said, I'm not going anywhere."

He pressed a soft kiss to her forehead. "What about your hot career? I thought you were looking for a new job."

"Hmm. Well, funny thing about that. It turns out I have a better job here, taking care of you."

He actually managed to grin. "I suppose you want me to keep paying you that exorbitant salary."

"Exorbitant?" She smacked his chest. "I earned every dime of that money, mister."

"Actually I might have an idea, but we'll discuss it later." He rolled her onto her back. "Right now I have something better in mind."

"And what would that be?"

"How about this?"

The kiss started out soft and gentle, a brush of lips, a flick of the tongue. But he pressed harder and she opened for him, welcoming the sweep of his tongue and the absolute male taste of him. She slid her fingers into the thick cap of his hair, holding him to her as they explored each other's mouths, tongues dancing and teasing. When he broke the kiss, they were both panting. He placed a soft kiss at the hollow of her throat, then moved his mouth back up to trace the shell of her ear with his lips. He nibbled his way down to the soft flesh of her lobe, the graze of his teeth sending shivers through her body and igniting the pulse in her sex. Her pussy clenched in anticipation of things to come.

Erin pressed her body up against his, trying to convey the sudden urgency of her need. But Jake seemed determined to take his time, to tease and arouse her. Even through the layers of their clothes she could feel the hard ridge of his cock pressing against her. She wanted to touch it and hold it and then feel it inside her, filling all the empty spaces.

"We have too many clothes on," she managed as she tipped her head back and arched her neck to his mouth.

His laugh was low and rough. "We do, and guess what?"

"Hmm?"

"Today I can undress both of us." He shifted one hand to slide it up between them and cupped a breast through her blouse and her bra.

"Prove it," she teased, wanting desperately to be naked with him.

But it appeared Jake had other ideas. He took forever to undo the buttons on her blouse, tracing the upper swell of her breasts with the tip of his tongue when he parted the fabric, then sucking hard on each nipple through the satin of her bra.

"I love your breasts." He blew gently on the damp material "And your nipples. Better than candy."

"Can we get on with the undressing, please?" She had a desperate need now to be naked with him, skin to skin, nothing between them and no cast to be careful of.

"Don't rush me. I'm enjoying myself."

When he divested her of the blouse, the cool air of the room made her wet nipples harden and peak even more. Jake grazed his teeth over them, her body jerking in response to the touch she loved so much.

"You have to take your clothes off, too," she reminded him.

He braced himself on one arm while he yanked his shirt over his head and tossed it to the floor. Then he came down on her again, the muscular wall of his chest hard against her breasts and the soft curls of hair covering it tickling her skin. He went back to work on her breasts, her nipples, then her mouth again until her pussy was so wet she had soaked her panties and her pulse beat an accelerated tattoo.

It seemed forever before he finally slid her slacks and panties from her body and kicked his shorts and boxers away. Then he went to work on her pussy, opening the lips gently with his fingers, blowing a soft stream of air on her overheated skin and licking every surface with slow, tantalizing strokes. She writhed on the bed, little moans rippling from her mouth, her body begging for more.

"I want to touch you," she pleaded.

"Touch me where?" he asked, a knowing sound in his voice.

"You know." She hitched her hips upward, but that just brought her into greater contact with his mouth.

"If you don't tell me, I won't know what you want."

She wet her lips. "I want to touch you *there*."

"Uh-huh. And exactly where is that? You have to tell me, sugar, or I won't know."

Damn!

"I want to touch your, uh, your cock."

His low laugh rumbled through both of them. "There you go. Now I can grant your wish."

He pulled himself up until he was lying next to her, his shaft rising proud and thick from his body.

Erin licked her lips at the sight of it and slowly wrapped her fingers. It was hot and hard in her hand, a welcoming thickness. She stroked it slowly up and down, feeling it swell under her touch. With each movement of her hand his cock became even more engorged, a tiny bead of fluid slipping out to sit right on the slit on the velvety head. With a gentle swipe of her tongue, she scooped it up and swallowed it, licking her lips at the taste.

Slipping one hand between his thighs, she cupped the sac with his balls, caressing and stroking, drawing a series of low moans from him. When she bent and slipped her mouth over him, his entire body tautened.

"Oh, Jesus. That's so damn fucking good."

"Mm-hmm," she hummed against him as she worked him with her fingers and her mouth.

Abruptly he lifted her head from his body and moved her to the side. She looked at him, wide-eyed.

"What's wrong?"

"Not a damn thing except you stretch my control past the brink. I can't wait any more. I have to have you. Right now."

Before she could stop and figure what he was doing, he had turned her over and arranged her on her hands and knees, bracing pillows beneath her. He trailed kisses over both cheeks of her ass, then drew little lines with his tongue while his fingers teased her clit. Again he abruptly moved away from her.

"Are you trying to drive me crazy?" she asked.

"Uh-huh." His chuckle was low and erotic. "Hold on."

She heard the drawer in his nightstand open and close, then he was back behind her, stroking her buttocks and sliding his fingers through the hot crevice. She was so hot for him she was sure she'd climax by herself if he didn't hurry. Then she felt something cool at her anus, cool and creamy. Lube. She shivered at the thought of what he was about to do.

He stopped for a moment. "You okay with this?"

"Yes, I am. But please hurry."

"Your wish is my command."

He slipped a well-coated finger into her tight passage, working the lube into her hot tissues. Then he added another finger, scissoring them to stretch her even more. And finally a third. All the time the walls of her pussy contracted and pulsed and her cream flooded her tissues.

The pressure of his cock against her opening almost triggered her release right then and there.

"Breathe," he told her. "In and out. Easy does it. I'll take it real slow."

That was exactly what he did, pressing very slowly into her tight channel, pulling back a little, then thrusting forward again. In and out, backward and forward, steadily moving in deeper until he was fully seated inside her.

Oh, God!

"Ready, babe?" Jake's voice was raw.

"Yes. Now."

The ride was beyond anything. Heat raced through her body as he surged into her again and again, over and over until she couldn't hold on much longer.

Then they exploded, held in the powerful grip of an orgasm unlike anything she'd ever experienced. Their bodies shook together, spasms rocketing through both of them as if they were one person. Over and over, until she splintered into a million pieces, taking him with her.

Long after—she had no idea how long—he eased himself from her body, laced soft kisses on her buttock, and climbed slowly from the bed.

"Be right back," he told her.

When he returned, she realized it was his turn to tend to her, with a warm cloth that eased her pussy and her ass. When he was satisfied, he dropped it on the carpet, turned her over, and pulled her into his arms.

"Mine," he said, stroking her hair. "All mine."

The words sent an unaccustomed warmth through her and settled the last of her nerves.

"All yours," she agreed.

"I love you, Erin, and I want you. I've never said that to another woman."

She snuggled against him. "I will always be here for you."

"But more than that I need you, to ground me and to help me realize my value."

"And I need you, too. You're very valuable to me," she told him. "And you always will be. I love you, too, Jake Russell."

"I'll never get tired of hearing you say that."

"Good, because I'm going to be saying it for a lot of years to come."

Epilogue

It was a typical night in central Texas, the air just a little brisk, the stars like crystal in a black velvet sky. Every seat in the stands at Granite Falls High School was filled, and the sidelines were jammed with people with VIP tags hanging around their necks. The local San Antonio television channels had sent reporters and cameramen to cover this as did the major networks. Jake Russell was a big name in football, more so because the story of his injury and subsequent retirement had fed the media all week since the announcement was made.

Jake stood on the sidelines with Joe Reilly and Coach Fenelli, Erin close to his side. Joe had done the majority of the interview earlier in the high school, his cameraman capturing footage of the trophies in the showcases and the banners on the walls. Joe had talked to Fenelli and some of the other players from that team who were here for the big night. They, too, had VIP passes and were excited for this event.

Big night.

Jake grinned to himself. Tonight the Coyotes were retiring his number, and apparently, even though he was now out of the game, it was still a big deal to everyone. He looked around at all the people who were here to meet him, and Erin's words, her mantra that she repeated daily, flooded his brain.

"You are so important to these people," she'd told him over and over. "Jake Russell, the person. That's who they want to know and who they admire."

He was even beginning to believe it, although it had been a long hard row to hoe.

The week had been productive in many other ways. He told Erin he wanted to put the money he'd earned to work doing something important, and she'd been on board with that. They kicked around a lot of ideas and came up with two. One was to set up a permanent trust for Good Shepard

House and the other was to set up a foundation that would entertain grants for shelters and programs for abused women and children. Erin was going to be the foundation director and Jake would spend a lot of his time lecturing on the subject of domestic violence and helping communities form groups and programs to deal with it.

"Mom would have loved this," Ivy told him. "I'm so proud of you."

Ivy had taken on the pro bono job of developing a public relations plan for the foundation, which would be named for their mother, and she was already tossing ideas at him.

Everything had been taken care of except the one thing that to him was the most important. Tonight he planned to take care of that.

Now they were waiting for everything to begin. Jake had requested they have the ceremony before the game in order to not take anything away from the players at halftime. Everyone had agreed, and now he was just waiting for the signal to start. The players, the fans, everyone else was excited about the ceremony. Jake was, too, but he had something else planned, something that was even more important to him. He slid his hand into his jacket pocket to make sure what he needed was still there.

Okay. Good to go.

Now they needed the band to stop playing. But when they did, they did not march off the field the way they usually did. They played the Granite Falls fight song, and when they finished their marching formation, he saw that on the field they spelled out *Jake* and his high school number, *thirty-one.*

"Ohmigod, Jake." Erin was jumping up and down. "I hope Ivy is getting all this on camera because I'm too excited to take pictures."

Holy shit!

Joe nudged his arm. "We're ready." He had his own camera crew standing by.

Jake walked out to midfield with Coach Fenelli, Principal Andrew Reinsdorf, and the team co-captains.

Reinsdorf took the mic.

"Good evening," he boomed.

"Good evening," everyone shouted back.

"You all know why we're here today, to honor one of the finest young men ever to come out of Granite Falls High School. Jake Russell!"

The crowd chanted, "Jake! Jake! Jake!"

He could see Erin beaming on the sidelines.

"I'm going to turn the microphone over to Coach Fenelli, since he is far more acquainted with Jake than I am. Coach?"

Fenelli stepped up and took the mic. "When Jake Russell moved to Granite Falls with his mother and sister, I saw a young man who desperately needed goals in life and a place to belong. He found it in football, in the discipline required to excel. And excel he did, in academics and in football, here as well as in college and finally in the NFL, where he set the standard for behavior very high. He continues to make us proud."

He spoke of Jake's injury, his forced retirement, and finally the establishment of the Valerie Russell Foundation.

"He is an icon that I hope every young man who passes through these walls will strive to copy. It gives me great pleasure to retire with honor jersey number thirty-one." He held out his hand and Reinsdorf handed him the box he'd been holding. Fenelli took out the jersey and held it up for everyone to see, turning so both sides of the stadium got a view. "Let's hear it for Jake Russell."

Again there were thunderous chants of, "Jake! Jake! Jake!"

Fenelli held out the mic to Jake who stepped forward and took it from him. He held up his hand for silence.

"I will never be able to thank the town of Granite Falls and Coach Fenelli in particular for giving me the opportunity for the life I now have, and for the way it embraced me, my mother, and my sister. You helped us in more ways than you will ever know and as a small thank you, the Valerie Russell Foundation is setting up a permanent trust for athletic scholarships for deserving graduating seniors."

The noise now was thunderous, as in addition to shouting his name the crowd stomped in rhythm on the bleachers. Finally he held up his hand again.

"I have one more thing that's not exactly on the agenda, but it's special to me and I want to share it with a very special community. I'd like you to meet Erin Bass, an extraordinary woman who saved me from despair and helped me get my life back on track. Erin, will you come out here, honey?"

He could see, even at this distance, she was blushing furiously, but unwilling to embarrass him, she walked slowly out to center field. He saw Joe motion to his cameraman who moved into position. Apparently this was also going to end up on Fox Sports.

"I'm going to kill you," she mouthed to him, but she pasted on a big grin.

"My sister, Ivy, who knew how pigheaded I was, concocted a scheme that threw Erin and me together, and for that I will always be grateful."

"I won't let you forget that," Ivy yelled from the sidelines.

Shifting the mic to his left hand, he reached into his pocket, flipped open the little box, and took out its contents. Then he went down on one knee and held out the ring that he'd managed to sneak away to buy.

"Erin Bass, you are the sunshine of my life, the beat of my heart, and the woman who helps me make it through each day. I love you more than life itself. Will you do me the very great honor of becoming my wife?"

She was grinning broadly even as fat tears rolled down her cheeks.

"Yes, yes, Jake Russell, I will marry you."

He slipped the ring on her finger, handed off the mic, and pulled her into his arms for a kiss.

Fenelli took the mic back.

"Well, I'd say the center has snapped the ball and it's time to cross the line of scrimmage. I know you all join me in wishing Jake and Erin the very best life has to offer. And now I think it's time to play some football!"

Meet the Author

Referred to by USA Today as the Nora Roberts of erotic romance, Desiree Holt is the world's oldest living published erotic romance author. A graduate of the University of Michigan with double majors in English and History, her earlier careers include agent and manager in the music industry, public television, associate vice president of university advancement, public relations, and economic development. She is three times a finalist for an EPIC E-Book Award (and a winner in 2014), a nominee for a Romantic Times Reviewers Choice Award, winner of the first 5 Heart Sweetheart of the Year Award at The Romance Studio, as well as twice a CAPA Award winner for best BDSM book of the year, and winner of the Holt Medallion for Excellence in Romance Literature.

She has been featured on CBS Sunday Morning and in The Village Voice, The Daily Beast, USA Today, The (London) Daily Mail, The New Delhi Times, The Huffington Post and numerous other national and international publications. She is also the Authors After Dark 2014 Author of the Year. Readers can visit her at www.desiremeonly.com.

In case you missed it, keep reading for a sample of the first book in the Game On series by Desiree Holt:

FORWARD PASS

Get Ready to Play Rough

Shay Beckham grew up idolizing her brother's best friend, star quarterback Joe Reilly. There was no one in their Texas town who had the moves to match Joe on or off the field. Years later, he's still a player who has what it takes to drive any hot-blooded woman wild. But Shay isn't a kid with a bad case of hero-worship anymore. She's grown-up and independent, with her feet on the ground and a serious head on her shoulders. If she could just say the same for Joe.

It's been fifteen years, but Joe Reilly hasn't forgotten the skinny little kid who used to follow him around like a shadow. What he can't get over is that the skinny shadow has grown into one hell of an incredible woman. One any man in his right mind would kill to get his hands on. And one who seems to be completely immune to him. He knows he and Shay could have something special together. If he could only convince her he's about more than just the game.

A Lyrical e-book on sale now.

Learn more about Desiree at
http://www.kensingtonbooks.com/author.aspx/31606

Chapter 1

"Damn it, Hank. Why don't you answer?"

Shay Beckham pressed End on her cell phone yet again and sighed. She and her brother had been playing telephone tag for two days. When he called, she was in meetings. When she called, he was out of signal range. The only voices talking to each other were their voice mails. How godforsaken could it be in Wyoming, anyway? It was still in the United States, right?

And why was he trying so hard to reach her? They exchanged texts now and then, but they were both so busy they only called each other in case of emergency. The places he went, cell reception was spotty at best and talking to him was like playing leapfrog. Wait! Was he okay? Her heart stopped for a moment at the thought he might be hurt, but then she relaxed. If something had happened to him, his boss would have reached out to her. So what was on his mind that had generated this flurry of aborted phone calls? Obviously, he wanted something because he was the one who'd initiated this current game of phone tag.

She leaned back in the taxi as it turned from the airport access road onto the interstate. Less than half an hour and she'd be home, thank God, and she could get out of her sweatshirt and jeans that wore the remnants of her diet cola from the plane.

With the way her luck was running, maybe she shouldn't have accepted her complimentary beverage. On the flight out to New York a week before, a little turbulence had been responsible for her arriving with a huge coffee stain on her favorite yellow sweater. Maybe she should carry a bib with her. Or a large tarpaulin.

On today's flight, she had just set up her iPad and lifted her glass gingerly to take a sip when the plane hit an air pocket and everything bounced. Her iPad. The purse beneath the seat. Worst of all, her drink.

Her hand flew up, with it her diet soda and, most importantly, the ice cubes. Up in the air. Over the back of her seat. Into the seat behind her.

She could still hear the man behind her growling. "Shit!"

Then, "Damn it anyway."

She'd used the miniscule courtesy napkin to blot up what she could from her sweatshirt and jeans. Shay had cringed as the man behind her continued to mutter under his breath.

"Hey, you in front. Didn't you ever learn to pay attention on a plane? You got your damn drink all over me."

He hadn't seemed impressed with her mumbled apology so she'd just slid down even farther and buried her nose in her iPad again. And been damn glad to get to the end of the flight without further incident. When it was time to deplane, she'd avoided even looking back at the man, hustling up the Jetway into the terminal as fast as she could. Getting home was all she could think of.

Sighing, she brushed a few wisps of hair away from her cheeks and tugged on the brim of her red ball cap. A lean cougar prowled across the red background, a new graphic she'd created for Dazzling Designs. The company she worked for produced merchandise for college and professional sports teams. This prototype had been waiting for her when she flew in for four days at the main office and she'd decided to wear it on her trip home.

She was worn out from the long, intense days of discussions and brainstorming. This was her third round trip to New York since she'd made the move back to Texas. After five months, she was piling up plenty of frequent-flyer miles, which she hoped to use one of these days.

She realized with a start the taxi, which had slowed a moment ago, had come to a standstill. The driver's two-way radio crackled in the front seat, but she ignored its staticky sound as she checked her phone again. Still no answer from Hank. She leaned forward, seeing rows of vehicles stopped in every lane of the interstate as far ahead as she could see. Shit.

"Is there an accident ahead of us?"

"Yes, miss." The driver was nothing if not polite. "Dispatch radioed me a moment ago. Sorry, miss."

Well, crap. Just what she didn't need. She wanted a hot bath, a glass of wine, and pizza delivery.

She checked her watch again. Was it really only two minutes since she'd tried calling Hank? Maybe a text would reach him. Sometimes she had better success with that.

"In cab on way home from airport. What's up? Try a tin can for reception."

She hit Send and waited to see if he answered. In less than two minutes, her phone chimed.

"Good trip?"

"Yes. What's up with you? What's with all the phone calls?"

"Just wanted 2 let you know Laura had 2 vacate condo for repairs for 2 days. Told her she could stay at house. She knows where extra key is."

That was what was so important?

Shay snorted and wrote, *"I'll bet."*

"She'll be gone sometime 2day. Just a heads up." Shay ground her teeth. Damn it. Why couldn't the damn woman have gone to a hotel? And what was with giving out the location of the key? She loved her big brother and was grateful to him for sharing his house with her but she definitely needed to find a place of her own. She didn't need his females driving her crazy when he wasn't there.

"She'd better be out of there when I get home. Want peace and quiet."

"I'll text her now. Just wanted to get yr flight info."

"On my way home from airport now."

"Thx. I'll tell her. How was NY?"

"Same old same old. U home soon?"

"Maybe. Don't know. Take care."

"You, too."

Traffic was still not moving. Shay bit down on her frustration, sighed again, and unzipped the front pocket of her carry-on. She'd grabbed a sports magazine in the airport, planning to check the ads her company was running, but hadn't bothered to read it on the plane. Maybe she could use it to pass the time now.

Flipping it open, the first thing she saw was Joe Reilly's face smiling at her in full living color. Crap. Joe Reilly. Her childhood hero, her teenage crush, and the star of her adult erotic fantasies. The same Joe Reilly who'd called her squirt and pest when she tagged after him and Hank. The football idol who had been a babe magnet since his voice changed.

The man she'd been secretly in love with all these years, a love that stilted every other relationship she'd had. When was she ever going to admit that it was an impossibility? That she needed to stomp on it, bury it, and move forward?

In Texas, where football was the number one religion, high school stars wrote their own tickets. As the star quarterback for the Granite Falls High School Coyotes, Joe had had women hanging over him like so much drapery. During his outstanding career in college and then in the NFL, it seemed every time she turned on the television or checked sports online she saw his picture with one female or another. She was sure he had a black book that rivaled an encyclopedia in size. She might as well have been chopped liver for as much attention as he ever paid to her.

She'd wasted so much of her time studying football, until she could diagram games almost as well as Joe could. She could even point out the percentage of success for each play. Joe had always grinned and winked at her. Only in hindsight had she realized he'd tolerated her because she was Hank's baby sister, with the emphasis on baby, even as she stupidly wanted him to wait for her to grow up.

She needed to find a way to get Joe Reilly out of her head. For good. Certainly her obsession with him wasn't helping her love life. She needed to stop looking for Joe Reilly substitutes. The men she tried to build relationships with may not have been athletes, but they were ardent sports fans and that was what attracted her.

And look how far that had gotten her. One cheated on her with a coworker, one out and out lied about who and what he was, another wanted to move in with her and have her pay the rent. Thank God she'd never said *I love you* to any of them, probably because, in retrospect, she hadn't. All those experiences left her with a strong distrust of the male sex, Joe Reilly being no exception.

Yeah, she was the champion of stupid. What was with her, anyway? She was smart, savvy, successful at her work. She'd braved the Big Apple and found herself a dream job she loved, which paid her extremely well. People would be lining up to be her if she let them. Now she needed to find a way to get rid of this restless, unfulfilled feeling she hadn't been able to shake in years.

For weeks she'd been telling herself tomorrow she'd take the first step to build a new life here in San Antonio, back in Texas where her roots were. Reach out to old friends. Meet new people. Rebuild her life and shake the ghosts of the past. Stop burying herself in the house with her work and marathon sessions with old movies and popcorn. How pathetic was that?

What she needed was the right guy, one who understood emotion and who respected her. One who wasn't a Joe Reilly substitute. It wouldn't hurt if he was really hot and could make every one of her erotic fantasies come to life. And also didn't lie or cheat. Time to finally put the vestiges of her crush, her childish daydreams, where they belonged—in the mental Dumpster. She was through lusting after Joe Reilly.

Enough already.

If she was going to hero worship someone she should have stuck to Joe Montana. He'd be a lot safer. And better. Yes, way better.

She closed the magazine, putting Joe Reilly where he belonged. In her carryon.

Time to get on with life.

* * * *

Joe Reilly wheeled his rental car out of the parking lot toward San Antonio. Checking his cell phone for traffic alerts, he discovered an accident on Interstate 10 that had traffic at a standstill. He programmed the GPS for an alternate route and headed out.

He could still smell the traces of a soft drink on his slacks. He'd done his best to wipe away the stains but the rental clerk had given him the fisheye, probably thinking he was a real slob. It wasn't his fault some idiot who couldn't walk and chew gum, or manage to hold onto her drink on the plane, had dumped its contents over the back of her seat and onto him. Just another indication of how crummy his day was going.

He'd seen this trip as a chance to spend some quality time with Hank Beckham, who, despite geographical differences, was still his best friend. He didn't get to see as much of him as he'd like to these days. The last time had been three years ago.

Their schedules just hadn't allowed for any time together since then. Hank was an engineer who was always being sent to some assignment for his company while Joe ran around the country for Fox Sports One and for the Coaches Conference business he'd started. The latter was an important project for him, workshops for high school coaches on how to lead as well as coach. How to teach players personal values as well as diagrams and game plans. He'd seen too many kids come out of high school without understanding that playing was only half the deal. Personal responsibility was a big part of it. His programs were geared to help coaches pass that along.

Unfortunately Hank had texted that morning he was still in Wyoming working on plans to build a bridge, but Joe should make himself at home in the house.

"I'll try and catch a quick couple of days while you're there, buddy," Hank had assured him. "But if not, just make yourself at home."

He'd also hoped to spend some time with his parents, of course, who were happy in their new adults-only community, except they were away on a trip. Bad timing, but it couldn't be helped.

So he'd be alone in the house.

Joe shifted in his seat, trying to stretch out his left leg. The ache served as a constant reminder the glory days had come to an abrupt end.

His cell phone rang, interrupting his thoughts. He looked at the readout and swore. Lisa Margolin. No doubt calling for his help with Gina again. God. How had he gotten himself in this pickle anyway? Because his parents raised him to take care of people who couldn't take care of themselves. That was how. He let the call go to voice mail, not in a mood to deal with it right now.

He was aware the most recent company Gina worked for had gone out of business a few weeks ago. Employees had received a one-month severance package and Joe knew Gina was coming to the end of hers. She didn't deal well with uncertainty. Her dysfunctional family had set off her battle with the bottle to begin with and he knew the thread of sobriety was always very shaky.

Ten minutes later the ringtone chimed again and he knew without looking who it was. She was nothing if not persistent. Setting his jaw, he pressed Accept.

"What is it this time, Lisa?"

"You know I wouldn't call you unless it was important, Joe. Really." She always began the calls that way.

Except it was always important. "Yeah, okay. Just tell me what's up now."

"I hope you aren't mad."

She was as good at sounding tearful as Gina always had been.

"Lisa, I'm kind of busy. What's the deal?"

"Well, um…" She paused.

"Look." He chuffed with impatience. "Just spit it out. How much?" It was always money. Of course.

"She's got a few job interviews coming up and she could use a couple new outfits."

Joe squeezed the phone so hard he was amazed he didn't crush it. "What happened to the money I just sent her?"

Pause. "She got sick." Lisa's voice was very quiet. "I mean, really sick. She needed medicine."

He could only imagine. Medicine that came in bottles of cheap booze.

"She really wants to make a good impression at these interviews," Lisa added.

A headache began to burrow its way into his temples.

"Fine. Give me an hour and I'll transfer some money into your account."

"Can't you just meet me with a check?" she whined.

"No. I'm busy. It's the transfer or nothing."

"Whatever." Her heavy sigh was clear across the connection. "Sorry. I just want this to happen for her."

"We're coming to the end of the road here, Lisa. It's time Gina took responsibility for her own life."

"But you're all she has," Lisa protested, a familiar refrain. "You can't let go of her now. I-I'll make sure she stays clean. Gets a job. Goes to work."

"Do that. I'll check back with you to see what's going on." He disconnected the call in the middle of her thanks, grinding his teeth.

Gina Rivera. High school bombshell. Wild child who'd captured his virtue. He hadn't seen her, had even forgotten about her, until his third year in the NFL. She'd shown up at a game, waiting for him at the player's gate, all masses of blond hair and tight clothes. He'd been high enough on the excitement of the win to succumb to her sexiness and spend the night with her.

He hadn't thought much of it, not even when she showed up twice more. Then he'd discovered her secret, answered her one plea for help and after that he was trapped, just because he was basically a good guy. Occasional contact turned into regular contact. And when he'd stopped taking her calls, she'd had Lisa contact him with a sob story that plucked at his conscience.

How long was he expected to offer aid to a raging alcoholic who didn't help herself? He should have told Scott Manchin, his agent, about it from the beginning. By now so much time had passed if word got out, the media wouldn't look at him as doing something kind for a friend. They'd want to know why he'd kept her hidden all this time. Did they have a child together? All that shit. He'd seen it happen to others and hadn't been smart enough to protect himself. It would be gossip fodder for weeks and kill all the work he'd done to clean up his act. He really had to cut the cord here.

Okay, enough of that.

Following the GPS directions, he pulled off the interstate and into an attractive neighborhood of larger homes and mature trees. A little farther on and the GPS directed him to turn left into the long driveway of a two-story colonial. *Nice digs, Hank,* he thought. But the guy was making big bucks. He deserved a good place to come home to.

He parked in front of the garage door. Maybe when he got inside he could grab the opener from Hank's car and use it while he was here. The key was right where Hank had said it would be. He opened the front door, pulled his suitcase inside, and headed toward the room Hank had said was his to use. On the way he passed a room that looked far too feminine to be Hank's. He wondered briefly whose room it was. Hank hadn't mentioned anything about sharing the house with someone.

Too much for him to think about right now. He wanted a shower, and then he'd see about ordering some dinner. Less than five minutes later he was under hot, steaming water, washing away the grime of the day.

* * * *

The taxi moved forward with a jerk and Shay's eyes popped open. She leaned forward and tapped the driver on the shoulder.

"Did they clear away the wreck? We're finally moving, right?"

"Yes, miss." He shrugged. "But slowly."

She rotated her neck, trying to work out some of the kinks. She'd been sitting in uncomfortable seats since she got in the shuttle to the airport and every muscle in her body ached. The hot shower was looking better and better. Or maybe she'd fire up the hot tub Hank had installed on the rear deck.

Hopefully, with all this delay caused by the wreck, by the time she got to the house Laura would be packed and gone. They pulled off the interstate and she mentally crossed her fingers and silently chanted, *Let her be gone*. But bad luck was still with her. When they turned onto her street and she spotted the car parked in the driveway, she swore under her breath. Laura Whoever was still here. Well, she'd better be getting ready to leave. Shay was in no mood to put up with bullshit. Sighing, she hauled her suitcase into the house, closed the door, and headed through the living room to her bedroom.

And stopped.

A hissing sound came from the shower in the bathroom connected to her bedroom and the guest room. Damn it! The least Hank could do was tell his little friends to use the master bath and leave hers alone. He had, after all, promised her that she'd have complete privacy.

"I travel a lot," he'd told her. Then grinned. "And I'll keep the sleepovers to those times you're in New York."

Yeah, yeah, yeah.

So how come this female hadn't gotten the message she was supposed to be gone?

Crap! The door wasn't even closed. Clouds of steam billowed in the bathroom and obscured the figure in the frosted-glass shower enclosure. Okay, enough was enough.

Shay stepped into the bathroom and banged her hand on the glass.

"This is my bathroom," she ground out. "I've had a tough day and you don't want to mess with me. Next time use Hank's bathroom. This one is off-limits. Get your ass out of here in five seconds, or I won't be responsible for my actions."

She turned away, not the least bit interested in a glimpse of Laura Whoever's nudity. She just wanted her out of the house.

The water stopped and the door slid open.

"Okay. I don't want to cause you any more stress. But Hank said I should use this one."

The deep voice shocked her and she turned around before she even thought about it. And nearly swallowed her tongue. A very wet, very naked Joe Reilly stood in her shower stall, grinning at her.

Just when she'd finally made up her mind to stop thinking about him and obsessing over him.

At that exact moment her cell phone chimed. A message from Hank.

"BTW, Joe's in town. Take good care of him."